Home Sweet Home

Home Sweet Home

FERN MICHAELS
DONNA KAUFFMAN
MELISSA STORM

ZEBRA BOOKS
KENSINGTON PUBLISHING CORP.

www.kensingtonbooks.com

ZEBRA BOOKS are published by

Kensington Publishing Corp.
119 West 40th Street
New York, NY 10018

All Kensington titles, imprints, and distributed lines are available at special quantity discounts for bulk purchases for sales promotion, premiums, fund-raising, educational, or institutional use.

Special book excerpts or customized printings can also be created to fit specific needs. For details, write or phone the office of the Kensington Sales Manager: Attn.: Sales Department. Kensington Publishing Corp., 119 West 40th Street, New York, NY 10018. Phone: 1-800-221-2647.

Zebra and the Z logo Reg. U.S. Pat. & TM Off.

First Printing: March 2020
ISBN-13: 978-1-4201-4609-7
ISBN-10: 1-4201-4609-2

ISBN-13: 978-1-4201-4612-7 (eBook)
ISBN-10: 1-4201-4612-2 (eBook)

10 9 8 7 6 5 4 3 2 1

Printed in the United States of America

Contents

Three's a Crowd

FERN MICHAELS

Prologue

Miami, Florida

Samantha Stewart swallowed, her throat as dry as the dust that had gathered on her dressing table. Being promoted to senior international correspondent at WNN, World Network News, would send her to countries that she'd call home for an indefinite length of time. Though she had wanted this job for as long as she could remember, now that she'd actually achieved the goal she'd worked for so hard, she wasn't sure if accepting the new position with WNN was the right decision. For the first few months, she would be embedded with the military, which branch still undetermined. It didn't really matter; she would be doing an excellent service for her country just by reporting on the never-ending conflicts that continued to make headlines.

Samantha was thirty years old, and with no serious relationship to keep her stateside, she was prepared to take the assignment as soon as the network wanted her to start. Her roommate, Maria Salvatore, head meteorologist at Miami's affiliate station, MWNN, knew she'd been waiting for this opportunity, and both were prepared for her absence. She'd sublet her share of the apartment as agreed upon, and when she returned to the States, she would find a new place. Sam knew she'd never find another roommate like Maria, but at thirty years old, she secretly hoped her next roommate would be a partner, preferably a husband. Not that she was actively looking, but her biological clock was ticking. While she was a long way from being too old to have children, as an only child, she had always wanted a family and at least three children. Maybe more. Her parents were the best, and though they'd already been in their early forties when she was born, she'd always longed for a brother or a sister. Growing up in Naples, Florida, she'd been surrounded by aunts and uncles, and a dozen cousins, but at the end of the day, she was still an only child. Someday, she wanted a big family of her own. Samantha never told her parents she had these thoughts though they'd always been in the back of her mind.

Now, having achieved her lifelong career ambition, Samantha knew that her dreams of a family and happily-ever-after would have to be put on hold, and right now she was okay with that. In her line of work, she'd had to learn to adjust to whatever circumstances she found herself in, which hardly ever involved establishing a normal daily routine. One day, she'd be reporting in Miami, and the next day she would be chief White House correspondent, working out of Washington but ready, on a moment's notice, to travel wherever the political news of the moment took her. It was an exciting life, and knowing that her political reporting days were numbered, Samantha felt a shimmer of excitement at what lay ahead. What with a new beginning in a foreign country, she knew this assignment would be the riskiest of her career, even life-altering, but she'd dreamed of this for so long that she was able to put aside the normal fears of embarking on such an assignment. Tonight, she would make a trip to Naples to deliver the news to her parents. It was too important to tell them about it over the phone. Knowing that her parents would be against her taking this assignment, which carried no little risk, she would do her best to assure them of her safety and convince them that she would stay in touch as much as the situation allowed. This would do very little to ease her mother's anxiety, but it was the best she could offer.

Though she was the wife of a retired police officer and thereby accustomed to fearing for her husband's safety, her mother was cursed with an overactive imagination. Add to that the addiction to mystery novels she had developed as a librarian, her mother was a worrier. To provide her parents with some extra assurance, Samantha would teach them how to use FaceTime on the new phones she'd given them for Christmas. Just the knowledge that her mother could actually *see* her would probably do much to alleviate the anxiety of having her only daughter in danger.

Samantha had a zillion things to take care of before her trip across Alligator Alley this evening. Life was about to change, and she was so over the moon, it was all she could do to contain herself. Smiling, she set about finishing her final day as chief White House correspondent.

Chapter 1

Three years later

On the plane, Samantha took a small powder compact case out of her bag, snapped it open, and glanced at her image. Almost that of a funhouse freak, she thought as she closed the mirror. She'd aged more in the past three years than most women did in ten. Her once-lustrous blond hair, now lackluster, hung limply to her shoulders. Dark blue eyes that normally shimmered like sapphires were dull and flat. *There's plenty of reason for the way I look,* she observed, tossing the case back in her bag. She had only spent a few weeks as an embedded reporter when the Powers That Be gave her the new title of chief senior international correspondent. Spending most of her time watching the war and reporting the often-devastating news left little time for a social life, but in spite of the war-torn area she'd temporarily called home, love had found its way to her when she'd least expected it, slamming into her heart and soul with as much force as the bombs that fell around her, so much so that they almost became white noise.

Almost.

And that's what had aged her. The days spent with the

soldiers, her sources, the fixers, her driver and interpreter, searching for the latest stories fit for the evening news, then hurriedly wiping her face with wet wipes, tugging her hair in a ponytail, and swiping on some lipstick to ensure she'd look halfway decent on camera. She would spend about five minutes reporting, then slip into her flak jacket, dust off her Blundstone boots, and prepare for a special report if called on. She'd been embedded with the army for only six weeks when she learned of her new assignment. Part of her felt relief, but another part of her was sad to leave the men and women she'd grown close to in such a short period of time. It was just another aspect of her job, one she didn't like too much, but it is what it is, she'd told herself.

Now, here she was on a plane headed back to the States, back to Florida, to spend Mother's Day with her mom for the first time in three years. As planned, she'd kept in close contact with her family through e-mails, an occasional letter, and FaceTime chats. She'd missed her parents more than she would admit and hoped they would slip into the familiar ease they'd always shared. More mature than when she'd left three years ago, Samantha had witnessed so much violence and sometimes death that it had hardened her. The soft edges of her former self were nothing more than a sweet memory. She smiled, recalling her arrival in Afghanistan. Despite the culture shock, she'd quickly learned the ropes and jumped into her new position as though she'd been doing it her entire life. But it was now time to look to the future as she had enormous, completely life-changing responsibilities.

"Ma'am, you'll need to buckle your seat belt, we're ready to taxi," a pretty young flight attendant instructed her.

Samantha had been so caught up in her thoughts that she hadn't paid attention to what was going on around her.

She fastened her seat belt, then adjusted the belt securing the infant seat next to her. Caroline was sound asleep.

Her daughter, almost eight months old, was used to travel. Samantha marveled at how adept she'd become in her short life. They'd been on the move two weeks after she'd given birth in Italy, and travel was just a part of their routine. She'd taken a leave of absence from the network when she was six months pregnant, telling her parents that her on-air assignment had changed. She still FaceTimed them, but she was always careful not to show anything more than her face. Her mother had mentioned a few times that she had a glow about her, and Samantha told her it was a new face cream she was using. She hated to deceive her mother, but she would learn the truth soon enough; there was no way around it.

The network had been supportive of her choice and sent a new—and much younger—reporter to take her place. Samantha had taken an assignment as a staff reporter of sorts for the Associated Press, e-mailing her articles to them daily. It wasn't a perfect solution, but it would keep her out of the States for a few months.

She'd reluctantly given her flak jacket to the new girl. The young reporter knew what it was and how hard they were to come by. She had been in tears when she placed her arms through the holes and fastened the closures that kept the life-saving armored vest close to her torso.

Samantha knew that returning to Florida would have its ups and downs, but she hoped for more ups than downs. She'd been very secretive about her life for the past few years, and she would have a lot of explaining to do when she arrived home.

First and foremost, Caroline's existence would need an explanation. Samantha had arranged to stay at a bed-and-breakfast in Naples for a few days before she went to her parents' home. She needed time to prepare her story, adjust to life in the States again, and continue her search, which she would not go into details about should the topic come up. It was too personal, and she was not ready to talk about that aspect of her life.

The flight had been uneventful– Caroline slept the entire time—and when they landed in Orlando, Samantha wheeled her daughter into the nearest ladies' room, changed and fed her, then headed for the car rental agency's booth. She decided to drive to Naples rather than catch a connecting flight because she wanted to think; she needed time to decide how she was going to explain Caroline. Nine months of pregnancy, then nearly eight months of having Caroline all to herself without telling her parents was not going to be easy to explain. And her child's father? That was a matter for another time; it was a subject she would not discuss with either parent no matter how much they insisted. And she knew they would because that's just how they were.

She knew the drive from Orlando to Naples took roughly four hours, having made the drive more than once. Samantha prepared to make several stops as she couldn't feed and change her daughter and drive at the same time, but she would also need the break. The traffic on I-4 was horrendous, and it made her a bit nervous since she hadn't driven much in the past three years. Forty-five minutes later, she was through the worst of the traffic, noting that even though it was May—not the normal tourist season—Orlando was already packed with tourists wearing their Disney gear, Mickey Mouse ears, and all that went with the whole Disney experience. She would take Caroline as soon as she was old enough to appreciate it, but that was still years away. As she drove out of Orlando, she passed all the theme park billboards, hotels offering family discounts, and restaurants enticing customers by advertising that children could eat free. Samantha smiled. Not much had changed about the tourist traps, but that was Florida. With no real industry to speak of, tourism was it. There was a great deal of competition, and businesses had to do all they could to grab the attention of potential customers. That would never change.

When she reached Tampa, she stopped at a McDonald's. Caroline perked up as soon as Samantha turned off the engine. Baby jabbering and a toothless smile met Samantha as she took Caroline from her car seat. "You are a cutie, little lady," Samantha said to her daughter, grabbing the diaper bag and her large tote. Once inside the restaurant, the smell of greasy burgers and fries hit her. She'd craved Mickey D's cheeseburgers when she was pregnant, and though she'd had a few in her travels as a reporter, none were as tasty as those in America.

She ordered two cheeseburgers, a large fries, and a vanilla milkshake. "We'll bring it to your table," the teenage cashier said. This was new, she thought, as she took a metal stand with a number and placed it on her table. Definitely needed, though, as she only had two hands. Another worker pulled a high chair over to her table. Samantha couldn't remember a fast-food place ever being so accommodating. Times were changing. These were all good changes, too, she thought.

Once she had Caroline in the high chair, she sat in the booth relaxing for a few minutes while she waited for her food. As soon as they brought the tray to her table, Caroline's little hands waved through the air, knowing it was time to eat. Samantha took a couple fries from the red-and-yellow box and set them aside to cool. With Caroline almost eight months old, Samantha had stopped nursing when the baby reached six months, and had begun to introduce her to real food this last month. She knew fast food wasn't the healthiest, but figured as a special treat it couldn't hurt every once in a while.

She opened the yellow wrapper and took a bite of the cheeseburger, rolling her eyes as though digging into a gourmet meal. She ate a few fries, then took a disposable plastic table mat from the diaper bag, stuck it to the table, and placed the fries on it. Caroline grabbed the fries, her tiny hand making a fist as she crammed them into her mouth. Her dark blue eyes, an exact match of Samantha's, widened at the unexpected taste and texture. Samantha laughed out loud. "I take it you like french fries, little lady," she said. She broke a few more fries into pieces and waited until Caroline swallowed the mouthful, then placed a few more on the placemat.

Samantha finished off her food, then took a jar of carrots from the diaper bag and fed Caroline the entire contents. "Good girl," she said as she wiped the bright orange carrot off her daughter's face. A face that reminded her so much of the man who had changed her life. Stop. *Stop*, she told herself. It wouldn't do her any good to go there.

Not now.

She made quick work of cleaning up the table as much as she could, then packed up the bags and took Caroline out of the chair. She slid the contents of the brown tray into the garbage while also holding her child and two bags—a delicate balancing act. Motherhood had taught her a whole new set of skills.

Once she was on I-75, she relaxed a bit as the traffic eased up. Caroline was fast asleep, as she always fell asleep in the car. During the first few weeks after she was born, Samantha had to get Felipe to drive them around during the wee hours of the morning when Caroline had gone through a few colicky nights. This, Samantha knew, was the beginning of her baby's love of sleeping in a car. Poor Felipe, she thought. He and his wife, Angelica, had been such good friends to her after the baby was born. Hired as her driver in Italy when she'd returned to cover a devastating earthquake, he and Angelica became her anchors on those nights when poor Caroline was a newborn. Having fathered eight children himself, he'd offered so many helpful tips that she wished he and Angelica lived in the States in case she ever needed help with the baby even though she would have her own family nearby.

Once her mom and dad got over the shock of learning they were grandparents, she knew they'd be awesome with Caroline. She'd seen them with her cousins, and they were naturals, just as they'd always been with her. Revealing the secret she'd kept for so long surely wouldn't be as frightening as she imagined. Or at least that's what she hoped.

After driving for three and a half hours, Samantha was ready for a break. She pulled into a service station. Though she was able to fill the tank while Caroline slept, Samantha had to wake her since she needed to be changed and was probably ready for a bottle. Although she was almost eight months old and could hold her own bottle, Samantha didn't feel comfortable letting her do so in the car seat while the car was moving, so she found a small seating area in the back of the station and spent the next twenty minutes feeding her. She grabbed a coffee to go on her way out. She needed a caffeine boost if she planned to make it to Naples without stopping for the night.

Though she was tempted just to stop and spend the night at one of the many hotels just off the interstate, she'd arranged to spend tonight at the bed-and-breakfast, so the owners were expecting her. Also, she'd sent Maria an e-mail telling her where she was staying. She'd made her swear she wouldn't tell anyone she was in town and promised to have lunch with her at her new house the next day. They'd kept in touch throughout her time in Afghanistan and Europe. Maria was the only person back home who had known that Samantha was pregnant. Since Samantha had left the States, Maria had married and now had a son, Ian, who was just four months old. Samantha was looking forward to seeing her former roommate and meeting her new family. She knew Maria would have plenty of questions for her about the baby and her plans for the future. Samantha would tell her friend as much as she could without giving away too much.

Once she'd settled Caroline back in the car seat, Samantha headed south, counting the minutes until she saw the sign WELCOME TO NAPLES at she entered Collier County.

Forty minutes later, she found the Orange Tree Bed-and-Breakfast and pulled into the driveway. The timing couldn't have been better. It was six fifteen, which would give her time to get Caroline settled in for the night, then call Maria to let her know she'd arrived safely, just as she'd promised to do in their last e-mail exchange.

Once again, life as she knew it was about to change.

Chapter 2

"You look fantastic," Samantha said as she gave Maria a hug. "If I didn't know you'd given birth four months ago, I'd never know you just had a baby," she observed. Maria, with her dark hair styled in a sleek bob, her makeup as perfect as it'd been when they'd lived together, hadn't changed a bit.

Samantha stepped inside the airy foyer and hugged her friend as best she could with a baby in one hand and a diaper bag in the other.

"Or you," Maria added, pulling her in and grabbing the diaper bag. "Hard to believe we're both moms now."

"I know," Samantha agreed.

They were having lunch at Maria's house. It would give them time to talk, and easily take care of their babies' needs. "I'll take this little beauty off your hands," Maria said, relieving Samantha of her daughter. "I don't have time to go to the gym anymore. A trip out with Ian is enough of a workout for me these days."

"Never thought of it that way, but it makes sense," Samantha said, laughing. "I've developed arm muscles since Caroline's birth."

"Let me have a look at this little gal," Maria said,

holding Caroline away from her. "She's beautiful! Has your eyes. Her olive coloring is definitely not from you—you're still as pale as a ghost."

"Still queen of sunscreen, nothing new there. Of course, I knew you'd say that, so before you ask any more questions, her father's Italian. That's all I'm saying," Caroline announced to head off any more discussion of the subject. Her daughter's thick black hair and olive complexion were a complete contrast to her own. Then there were the dark blue eyes. *Those are definitely from me,* she thought as she remembered a set of deep brown eyes, so dark they looked black at times. Eyes that she'd loved. *Still love. Don't go there, Sam. Not today.*

"You okay?" Maria asked.

"I am. Now, you haven't introduced me to Ian, and I'm dying to meet the little guy. Who knows, maybe these two will end up being best friends like us," she added, hoping to direct the conversation away from Caroline's father.

"As soon as he wakes up from his nap, if that's okay?" Maria replied. "He wasn't a good sleeper last night."

"Colicky?"

"I think he was just awake and wanted to check out the world. I set up Ian's Pack 'n Play for Caroline if you want to put her down for a bit," Maria added.

"Grand idea. She's about due for her midmorning nap."

Maria returned Caroline to her mother. "I'll get us a glass of tea; the Pack 'n Play is in the dining room right around the corner."

Samantha made fast work of settling her daughter into the portable Pack 'n Play. "I need one of these," she said under her breath.

After settling Caroline in, she found Maria in the kitchen, where yummy scents filled the room. The kitchen was modern, with marble counters, white cupboards with black-and-white subway tiles on the wall space behind the countertops. The dishes were bright yellow, and Samantha noticed many accent pieces in the same shade.

"You cook now?" Caroline asked incredulously. "I didn't know you knew how to cook, unless it was a frozen microwave meal."

Maria gestured for her to sit at a small table in a corner of the large kitchen.

"When I was pregnant, I had a few issues with sugar and salt, so I decided I'd learn to cook. Found I loved tinkering around in the kitchen, and well, here I am. I hope you still like shrimp," she said as she removed a bright yellow bowl from the refrigerator.

"Of course I still love shrimp," Samantha answered. "Just because I've been away for three years doesn't mean I've changed my eating habits. What's in the oven? It smells scrumptious!"

They both laughed. Caroline thought that of all the other changes she'd experienced since leaving America, her eating habits had to be the one she'd given the least thought to during her time away.

"Your favorite," Maria said. "With all these new baking skills, I had to give it a try."

"Real red devil's food cake that doesn't come from a box?" Samantha teased.

"The real deal, and you are in for the treat of a lifetime," Maria said, grabbing potholders from a drawer next to the double ovens and removing three round cake pans and placing them on a cooling rack. "It's not your mother's recipe, but I'm hoping it's close enough."

"I had McDonald's yesterday afternoon, and just a piece of toast this morning. I'm dying for some decent food. Though I have to admit, Mickey D's isn't bad when you're hungry. I found myself craving their cheeseburgers when I was pregnant with Caroline. The ones at McDonald's in Europe aren't the same as ours."

Maria made fast work of dishing out the shrimp salad with slices of chilled mango and kiwi placed decoratively around the plate.

"Go on, we have to eat fast before the babies wake up. I've learned to appreciate every free minute these days," Maria said.

Samantha took a bite of the cool shrimp salad and felt like she'd died and gone to heaven. "Oh my gosh, you weren't kidding when you said you'd learned to cook. This is divine."

For the next ten minutes, they ate, neither speaking much until their plates were scraped completely clean. Samantha leaned back in her chair, closing her eyes for a moment. Florida seafood was the best.

"So, tell me about Mark."

Maria took their plates and placed them on the center island. "It was love at first sight. He took over as the six o'clock news anchor not too long after you left, and I should say the rest is history, which it is, but we wanted to make sure we took things slowly. Then, when we realized we were meant for each other"—Maria held out a hand— "yes, I know that's cliché, but it's the way we are. To make a long story short, we married a year and a half ago, now we have Ian, and I never dreamed I'd ever be this happy."

Samantha could see that her friend was in seventh heaven. Her face glowed, her dark eyes sparkled, and her smile was genuine. If only things had turned out the same for her.

She reached for her friend's hand. "I'm happy for you. Truly. So, when do I get to meet this dream guy?" She didn't want to talk about herself because she knew Maria would ask questions.

"We'll have dinner soon. On a weekend, if you can. I'll make something, that way you can bring Caroline, and we won't be rushed. Restaurants want you in and out now. The days of lingering over coffee and dessert are long gone, especially when you have a baby."

Samantha knew they were keeping the conversation light, but she felt the small talk was about to run out. "Listen, I know I told you I didn't want to talk about . . . Caroline's dad, but I just want you to know, it's not what you think."

"So, you're thinking that I'm thinking, *what*?" Maria asked.

She raked a hand through her still-damp hair. "Sorry. It's not that I don't want to tell you, it's just . . . I can't."

"Okayyy," Maria said, dragging out the word. "But?"

"There is no but. It's just that I can't talk about him. I know that sounds insane, but it's the way it has to be." She knew she sounded like a high schooler, what with all the intrigue surrounding her "mystery man," but there were reasons why she couldn't talk about her daughter's father.

"Then we won't talk about him. Just tell me this—why haven't you told Helena and Charles? They're going to be hurt, you realize this?"

She nodded. "Of course I do, and I'll be forever sorry, but there are reasons."

A high-pitched cry came out of nowhere.

"That's Ian. I'll be right back."

Samantha rinsed their dishes and put them in the dishwasher, then made them each a cup of coffee. Yellow-and-black mugs were sitting beside a black Keurig coffee machine, their favorite dark brew pods neatly arranged next to it. She hoped Maria still drank her coffee after lunch as she had in the past. She took both mugs and put them on the table.

Maria entered, carrying a tiny little bundle cocooned in a swaddle blanket.

"Let me see," Samantha said, walking over to where Maria was standing.

"Can I?" She held her arms out.

"Sure." Maria placed her son in Samantha's arms, and Sam held him close to her chest, breathing in his soft baby scent.

"Nothing like it, is there?"

Samantha knew exactly what she referred to. "Nope. Nothing in the world is sweeter. He's perfect." A tiny fist found its way out of the swaddle blanket to a rosebud mouth. "I think this little guy is hungry."

"Starving." Maria took her son and prepared to feed him. As soon as she had him settled to her breast, she spied the coffee and smiled. "You remembered."

"No, *you* remembered. I wasn't sure if you could have the caffeine." She nodded at Ian.

"I shouldn't, but I allow myself a couple of cups a day. Our mothers drank and smoked when they were pregnant, can you believe that?" Maria asked.

"Mom didn't smoke, but I know she was addicted to caffeine when she was pregnant with me. In her day, or this is what she used to tell me, doctors didn't offer too much advice other than eat healthy and make sure you showed up for your next appointment." Samantha was about to take another sip of her coffee when she heard Caroline stirring in the next room. "Hold that thought," she said.

Caroline was all smiles, her blue eyes scanning the unfamiliar room. "This little girl needs changing. I hope you can direct me to a room that's dirty-diaper friendly"— Samantha laughed—"'cause this kid is a mess."

Maria laughed. "Follow me," she said, the now-content Ian sound asleep in her arms.

They walked down a short hall, then to a room at the end. "This is the changing room. His nursery is upstairs; I'll give you a tour before you leave," Maria said. "I can't be bothered running up and down the stairs all day, so I use this room." She gestured toward a beautiful changing table surrounded by shelves that held diapers and all the supplies one needed for diaper duties.

Samantha placed Caroline on the table, grabbed a diaper from the diaper bag hanging from her shoulder, and used the wipes that were provided in a nifty wipe warmer. "This is fancy," she said, disposing the diaper in the pail next to the table.

Maria smiled. "A gift from my mother-in-law. It's certainly convenient. I'll turn this room into a playroom when he's older, but for now, it's practical."

"It's nice," Samantha said, suddenly reminded of all Caroline hadn't experienced, such as a room like this of her own. A changing table. Not good. Children needed to feel a sense of permanency and security no matter their age.

"Want to have another coffee and catch up? Really?" Maria asked, her tone serious.

Sighing, Sam nodded and followed Maria. The den faced an Olympic-sized swimming pool. Lounge chairs with bright blue-and-white-striped cushions were placed at one end of the pool, an outdoor kitchen on the opposite end. Caroline whistled. "You are definitely living in better conditions than you were three years ago," she teased.

"The pictures you e-mailed aren't nearly as awesome as the real deal."

The den was comfortable, with plush off-white chairs, yellow cushions casually tossed about, and a large off-white sofa, all facing the floor-to-ceiling windows with the spectacular view. A closed-off triangular area held a stuffed pig, a giant plush rabbit, and a few other toys she couldn't put a name to. The floor was covered in thick cream carpet.

"I use the space for tummy time," Maria said when she saw the look on Samantha's face. "I know the white and creams will need to be changed, but this works for the moment."

"I like the idea," Samantha said, as she opened a gate to the playpen and placed Caroline inside. She slobbered and made funny noises when she saw the stuffed animals and the brightly colored toys. Maria placed Ian on his belly on a brightly colored mat, roughly the size of a child's sleeping bag, except one end had small developmental infant toys attached.

"Supposedly a few minutes a day will ensure your child develops properly and learns to crawl sooner," Maria explained. "I put Ian in here most days. He seems to like it."

"I see that." Samantha watched as tiny Ian's large eyes opened wide the way babies do when they see certain objects. His little hand tried to reach a ring with three brightly colored keys that were about six inches from his fingers. "So, when he reaches the keys, time's up?"

"Something like that. You keep an eye on these two for a minute, and I'll bring the coffee. We can have the cake if you want, minus the frosting?"

"Sounds perfect." Samantha stood next to what she thought of as a cross between a giant playpen and a miniature jail cell, ensuring Caroline wouldn't grab one of the hard plastic toys and toss it in Ian's direction. Her new skill, throwing things. Briefly, she wondered if experts also listed that as a skill to be reached by a certain age.

"You can close the gate; they'll be fine," Maria said. She carried a tray holding two fresh mugs of coffee and small cake plates with flatware, placing them on the table between the two plush chairs, which gave them a bird's-eye view of the babies.

"Caroline's new skill is throwing whatever she can get her hands on." She picked up a few of the plastic toys, placing them outside of her daughter's reach. "Looks like Ian is in the line of fire."

They both laughed.

She sat down, taking a sip of coffee, then a giant bite of the cake. She closed her eyes. "This is divine. Oh. My. Gosh. You are a real baker!"

"Told you."

Samantha finished the cake in three giant bites. "Best I've had in years." And it was. However, her mother's red devil's food cake, with the sickly sweet white frosting, was still her favorite.

"Thanks," Maria said, finishing off her slice. "I love days like this. Eat and gab."

Samantha laughed, then asked, "How long before you go back to the station?"

Maria took a deep breath, exhaling slowly. "I'm not."

"Really? No more tracking hurricanes? I find that hard to believe."

"I do, too, at times. I gave my notice three weeks ago. We have six months of maternity leave, which is awesome, but mine is almost over, so Mark and I decided I'd stay home with Ian, do all the soccer mom things, at least when he's old enough, then I'll decide if I want to go back to work. Not that having him isn't enough work. I don't know,

I guess I'm just tired of the whole news-weather scene. I haven't stopped and smelled the roses since high school, and this is precisely what I want at this stage in my life."

"I'm happy for you," Samantha said, wishing she had such a plan, *any* future plans for her and Caroline. She'd existed from day to day for so long, she wasn't sure she even knew how to plan for the future. One day at a time, she thought, because that's how it had to be for now.

"Are *you* happy?" Maria asked. "You seem, I don't know . . . a little lost."

How to answer? she thought. "That's a tough one." She paused, trying to find the words to convey how she felt. She took a drink of coffee. "I'm not unhappy, that much I'm sure of. I have her"—she looked at her daughter, who was engrossed in chewing the ear on the giant rabbit—"so how could I *not* be happy. It's a state of mind, don't you think? Something we choose to be, regardless of circumstances. I can't allow . . . I want to be the best I can be for Caroline at this stage of my life, and *that* I'm good with. Happy as in 'love-life' happy? I can't answer that. I've spent three years delivering bad news, and that doesn't always put one in a happy place, but it was my job, and I liked delivering the news." She stopped. There was so much more to say, but she couldn't.

"*Was* your job?" Maria asked, her voice up an octave or two.

Samantha wasn't surprised that she picked up on the past tense.

"Was. Yes. I can't raise Caroline in that environment. It's too much. She needs stability, a mother who isn't placing herself in life-and-death situations every time she leaves for work. Though I did back off a bit in the latter months of my pregnancy, I did all my reporting by writing for the AP. I didn't want Caroline to grow up in a foreign country even though she is also Italian by birth. I knew I had to return to Florida because I wanted her to grow up around family."

She could see that Maria was taking in her words.

"So why wait this long? Why didn't you return right after she was born? How did you manage?"

Samantha glanced at the babies. They were still occupied though Ian had rolled onto his back. "Look at that," she said, gesturing.

Maria turned her gaze to Ian. "Yes, he's been turning himself over for weeks. I have to be extra careful when I lay him on my bed now. He's a gift." She stared at her son. Samantha knew exactly how she felt, as there was no other love like that of a mother for her child. "You're avoiding my question. I know you well, remember?"

Samantha smiled. "That you do. Suffice it to say I put much thought into my decision. There are legitimate reasons that kept me out of the States. Most were professional, a few are personal and remain so. I know that's not what you want to hear, but that's all I can give. I'm sorry."

"Don't be sorry. Good grief, I sound like an interrogator, don't I?"

She grinned. "A little bit, but I'll forgive you. Listen, it's probably best that I go. I need to make a couple of stops on my way back to the B&B."

"You know you can stay here? I've plenty of room. And you'd get to meet Mark. He'd like that; I've talked him to death about you, plus he's seen you on the national news. He's impressed. And you're missing the house tour I promised."

"Thanks, Maria, but I need these few days to come to terms with my choice, figure out how I'm going to tell Mom and Dad about Caroline. Plus I want to spend this time with her, because from now on, well, you know my family, once they get wind there's a baby, they'll descend on Mom's house like vultures. Not that it's a bad thing—she'll be well loved—but I just need the alone time. TMI, right?" she asked.

"I think I understand, but you're always welcome, just so you know."

They chatted for another fifteen minutes, then Sam packed up Caroline and headed for their temporary home.

Chapter 3

The Saturday before Mother's Day, Samantha called her mom, careful to make sure Caroline was asleep in her car seat. They'd just checked out of the B&B an hour ago.

"Oh, Sam, it's so good to hear your voice," her mother gushed. "Hold on a minute." A few seconds later, her mother spoke. "Had to tell your father you're here. You sound so close."

Samantha—Sam to her family—laughed. "It's not like we haven't spoken on the phone," she reminded her mother.

"It was so crackly at times, and now you sound as clear as a bell. Do you still have the Uber lined up? We can zip over to Fort Myers in half an hour if not. Oh, sweetie, I can't wait to wrap my arms around you."

Samantha felt like crap for deceiving her family. "Uh." Should she keep the rental car? Yes, she decided. "Actually, I rented a car." At least that much was true.

"The traffic is horrendous, even in May, can you believe that? I hope you can make it in time for dinner. I've made all your favorites, and your cake, too."

She laughed. If she continued eating sweets like this, she'd get back to her pregnancy weight in no time. "That's great, Mom. I'm looking forward to it. No one makes the cake like you." That was true, too. She couldn't tell her about Maria's cake because then she'd have to explain that she'd already been in Florida for a few days, and she knew she would have enough explaining to do once she arrived.

"I've scheduled us a detox bath at the spa. Hopefully, it will get rid of all the junk we consume. Oh, Sam, I am so excited. Now, let me hang up so you can get on the road. Your dad is beside himself. He painted your old room last week. I thought that pastel blue might be a bit much for you now. He's hanging new shades. Get this, they have a remote control! Who would've thought? I told your dad the world is too fast for us, and you know him, he just rolled his eyes. Here I am, keeping you from getting on the road. Just be careful, there are all kinds of crazies out there. Drive safely, dear. See you soon."

She didn't have a chance to reply. Her mother could talk endlessly. She said bye to a dial tone, and glanced at Caroline in the car seat. She was only a couple of miles from her parents' house. If she arrived too soon, they might not . . . *what?*

Have dinner ready? Who was she kidding? *She* wasn't ready.

With that thought in mind she drove to the Coastland Mall, figuring she could kill an hour or so, plus she needed to get a few things. She didn't have a stroller for Caroline, so as soon as she went inside, she located a children's shop and bought the latest model of UPPAbaby stroller, along with a new car seat. The owner of the shop helped her assemble it right then and there. "Thank you so much," she said. Before venturing out into the mall again, she promised herself that she would donate Caroline's old car seat to a local secondhand children's store.

Caro cooed and jabbered at the bright neon lights. She smacked her hands together when she saw a giant stuffed giraffe in the center of the mall, with several other jungle animals grouped together to entice the little ones.

"Not now, baby, that'll have to wait until we have a place of our own."

She hurried through several shops, picking up shorts and shirts for herself and a few summery dresses for Caroline. She didn't have a lot of Florida-style clothing, as most of hers had been purchased for durability and practicality. It would be nice to wear shorts and flip-flops again. She wanted a decent haircut, too. Spying a salon with a sign that said WALK-INS WELCOME, she did just that.

An hour and a half later, Samantha sported a shoulder-length bob, similar to Maria's. The staff talked her into a manicure and a pedicure, and she gave in. These luxuries hadn't made sense before. Now, however, she felt she needed to treat herself. While they pampered and polished her, Caroline slept in her new stroller, which virtually turned into a mini crib. All were amazed that she'd slept through the buzzing of nail drills, blow-dryers, and loud conversation. She didn't tell them that Caroline had been conditioned to far worse noise as an infant. Remembering the small apartment they'd had in Italy made her cringe. The neighbors had been true Italians. Lots of talk and plenty of company.

She looked at the giant clock in the center of the mall. Usually, her parents had dinner around six, so that gave her a decent amount of time to drive to their house without arousing suspicion if she arrived too early.

"Okay, little one, you are about to meet two of the most

spectacular people you'll ever meet," she said as she maneuvered the new stroller out of the mall to the parking lot. More jibber-jabbering. This brought a grin. Her daughter sounded as though she were trying to respond in an unknown language.

Samantha removed the car seat she'd picked up in a shop in Italy and secured the newer one in its place. Once Caroline was strapped in, she put the old seat in the trunk. She removed all the clothes from their bags and stuffed them inside her luggage. Apparently, she was trying to hide her trip to the mall, her way of killing time, but none of that would matter once she told her parents the truth. She stuffed the shopping bags in the trunk, figuring she might as well go all the way with her pretense.

Checking once more to make sure the new car seat was secure, she hit the engine button on the key fob and headed to her parents' house on Lilac Lane, her childhood home.

She could've asked Maria to watch Caroline while she explained her situation to her parents, but she'd best face them head-on. Knowing they would have many more questions about Caroline's father than Maria had, she prepared to tell them as much of the truth as possible. *I've deceived them enough*, she decided.

As soon as she pulled in the driveway, her mom and dad came bursting out the front door. She jumped out of the car, leaving her door open, and held her arms out to them.

"Oh, oh, I think I'm going to cry," her mother said, wrapping her in her arms. Still tiny, tanned, and blond, made up to perfection, Samantha thought. Her mother was beautiful and unchanged.

"Sammy," her dad said as he embraced her. "Good to have you home. Real good." Tears filled his eyes, and he hugged her again. "A sight to see," he said, stepping aside so her mother could hug her again. Her dad was generally an unemotional man, a retired police officer who'd been trained to keep his feelings in check. When she saw the tears streaming down his face, her own eyes filled. She sniffed, grinning at her dad, a bear of a man, tall, muscular, with a full head of sandy-brown hair, and the same dark blue eyes as hers. She suddenly realized just how much she'd missed her parents.

He knuckled his eyes, and her mother kept an arm around her as if she were afraid to let go. "I've made all your favorites, at least I hope they're still your favorites. It's been too long, sweet girl, much too long. Now, let your father get your things, and you can settle in before dinner," her mother said, trying to guide her to the front door.

"Mom, Dad, wait."

Knowing there wasn't any other way to do this, she closed the driver's door, hurried around, and opened the passenger door on the opposite side. Caroline was quiet, as though she knew now was not the time to gurgle, jabber, or cry. Without hesitation, Samantha took her daughter from her car seat and walked to the front of the car.

Both her mom and dad were silent for a few seconds, the shock preventing them from speaking. Before they could say a word, she said, "Mom, Dad, I'd like you to meet my daughter, Caroline Helena."

Chapter 4

Samantha could see from their expressions that her parents were stunned, but both recovered quickly.

"Well, I'm sure you've got one hell of an explanation," her father said. "I'll get your luggage. You do have luggage?" he asked. She tossed him the keys.

"Sam, what . . . how? Why?" her mother asked, though she couldn't take her eyes off Caroline. "Here, let me take her."

"Soon, Mom. She's a little overwhelmed. Once she's settled in, then she'll warm up to you."

"Good gravy almighty, Samantha! Warm up to me?" Her mother was angry, and she couldn't blame her.

"Let's go inside, out of the sun," Sam said. "Please."

By this time, her father had her small suitcase in one hand and Caroline's diaper bag in the other. "We need to talk," was all he said.

As soon as she entered the house, the scents of her favorite dishes greeted her. Lobster mac and cheese, and she could smell the tanginess of the anchovies her mother put in her famous Caesar dressing. Homemade rolls, too. She could smell the garlic she knew her mother had chopped and sautéed in Irish butter. Her mouth actually watered, but dinner would have to wait.

When they were inside, had it not been for the hum of the refrigerator, one could've heard the proverbial pin drop.

At that moment, Caroline decided it was too quiet, and she burst out in tears. "Oh, baby, it's okay." Sam cuddled her daughter close to her and searched for her diaper bag. "She needs to be changed; it's about the only time she cries."

Her father took the diaper bag from the foyer. "I'll take this to your room."

"Mom?" she asked.

"I need to check the cheese sauce," her mother said, turning her back on Sam and going to the kitchen.

This was *not* the homecoming she'd imagined or expected. She hurried upstairs to her old room. Tears were now streaming down her face. "What have I done?" she whispered, locating the changing mat in the diaper bag. Like an automaton, she went through the motions of diaper changing, looked for a bin to dispose the messy diaper, and since there was none, she left the soiled diaper on the mat.

What had you expected when they had no clue you'd be returning with an eight-month-old baby in tow? This is my own fault!

She wanted to shout *his* name, along with a few chosen words, but refrained because it would scare her daughter and wouldn't solve anything. Remembering Maria's invitation, she decided then and there to take her up on her offer. She couldn't stay here with all the tension, which was only bound to get worse. So she placed Caroline in the center of her old bed and dug through her tote bag for her cell phone. She scrolled through the numbers, and hit CALL. Then she hit END.

She couldn't run away from this. She'd been running

for almost three years, and it had to stop. This was the real world, the world where her daughter would grow up. Where she'd learn to walk, talk, and love the two people who meant so much to her, and would to her daughter soon enough.

Her parents had every right to be angry. She'd knowingly deceived them, deprived them of their grandchild, all for reasons that would make no sense to them, but she wasn't going to run away without telling her story. She changed into a pair of new navy shorts and pulled a navy-and-white tank top over her head. Caroline was fine in the pink onesie she had on. Besides, she wouldn't let her wear new clothes without washing them first.

She took a clean bottle and the can of powdered formula from the diaper bag and headed downstairs. They would have to talk, but first she needed to feed her child.

Both of her parents were in the kitchen. Her mother was busy stirring something in a pot. "Mom, do you have bottled water? I need it for Caroline's formula."

Without uttering a word, her mother went to the large pantry, removed a jug of distilled water, and placed it on the counter.

"Thank you," she said as she tried to scoop out the powdered formula while adjusting Caroline on her hip.

"Here, let me," her father said. "I've done this a time or two. How many ounces?"

Samantha raised her brows. "Uh, six."

He poured the water into the bottle, shook it up until the powder dissolved. "Need heating?"

"No."

Her mother whirled around. "What do you mean? Of course her milk, uh, formula needs to be heated. Cold milk will give her colic."

"I don't heat it, Mom. Really. It doesn't bother her."

Maybe this was her olive branch. Whatever, she would go with it. "I nursed her for six months. My milk was . . . uh, room temperature. She seems to do just fine now with the formula, as long as the water isn't too cold." Actually, she loved her formula cool when it was hot outside, but she didn't need to go into detail right now.

"How times have changed," her mother said, her voice softening a bit.

Her father stood by the sink. "Yes, I agree with your mother. Times certainly have changed. Why don't we sit down and talk about her?"

"She is my *daughter,* Dad. I agree we need to talk but I'm going to feed her first." She emphasized *daughter,* letting her parents know her child was her number one priority.

"Of course, I didn't mean to imply that you shouldn't. Why don't we go to the front room? Mom's rocker is in there now."

"You still have that old thing?" she asked without thinking. It used to be in her parents' bedroom when she lived at home.

Her mother smiled. "That old thing belonged to my grandmother, so to answer your question, yes."

In the living room, her father and mother both sat expectantly on the edge of a new sofa that was a soft beige color that matched the new blinds. The rocker sat catty-corner, opposite the sofa. Samantha sat down, arranging her daughter in a reclining position where she hungrily took her bottle. A minute or so passed, and she realized they were waiting for her to explain.

"I don't know where to start," she said, suddenly unsure of herself.

"The beginning," her father suggested. "That's what we used to tell witnesses."

She couldn't help but laugh. "It never goes away, does it?"

"What?" her dad asked.

"The cop talk," she answered.

He relaxed into the sofa, the cushions receiving the brunt of his bulk. "You're right; it doesn't. I didn't mean to imply you're a witness, but the beginning is usually a good place to start."

"Of course," she agreed as she rhythmically rocked back and forth, seeing that Caroline was drifting. She removed the bottle from her mouth and placed it on the floor beside the chair.

"The beginning," She took a deep breath. It seemed so long ago, but it wasn't. "You know that I was in Afghanistan, embedded with an army unit for several weeks. It wasn't too long after I was promoted when I found I'd come across some information that I'm not at liberty to tell you, and I never will be, so don't ask me to explain. Just know it has to be this way. Not too long after I discovered this material I . . . uh, I had to meet with people whose job it was to . . . work with what I'd uncovered." She stopped. Was she telling too much? No, she assured herself, she was being as generic as possible. They undoubtedly thought she'd lost it, but that didn't matter in the scheme of things.

"Top-secret stuff?" her mother asked.

"Lena"—her dad had always shortened her mother's name as he did hers—"Sam said she couldn't tell. Just listen to what she has to say."

"I spent a lot of time with people, lots of people. I became close to"—she didn't dare say his name—"a guy, no one important, but we became friends, then, our friendship turned into more." She'd never had trouble talking about boys when she was a teenager, and now she was thirty-three years old and found it difficult to discuss a mature relationship with a man. "Actually, that's not true. He was very important to me." Pausing, she remembered his smile, those dark, sexy eyes, and could almost imagine him as he'd stared at her, sending chills up and down her spine, even in desert conditions. She'd told him that once; later, they both laughed about it.

"So, is he her father?" her mother asked, never one for subtleties.

"Let her tell the story, Lena. You're too impatient for your own good."

Samantha smiled. "It's okay, Dad. Yes, he's Caroline's father."

She gave them a minute to let that bit of information sink in. *What next?* she thought, without revealing any more than she had to.

"Why didn't you tell us you were having a baby? I could have sent care packages."

"Lena," her dad said, but Samantha heard the humor in his voice.

She laughed out loud, startling the baby. "Mom, you're a prize, and I love your spontaneity, but let me tell my story, at least as much as I can. I would've appreciated your care packages, too. The food in Afghanistan, at least what I had, wasn't the best. I had to continue my work, but not in the same way as before."

"Were you a spy?"

Samantha's heart raced. She swallowed, hoping neither parent saw her reaction. "Of course not. I'm a reporter. You know that. I . . . well, once I found out I was pregnant, I needed a job more suitable to my condition, out of harm's way, so when the Associated Press offered me a job as staff reporter, I decided, as did the network, that it was the perfect solution." She was bungling the story, but it was the best she could do.

"Wasn't that a step down for you?" her father asked.

Leave it to him to start questioning. Always a cop. So, she did what was suggested to her back then. Stick as close to the truth as possible.

"It was, but not financially. I'd just learned I was going to be a mother. I had to think of my child and our financial future. Yes, I was no longer headlining the evening news and special reports, but my salary increased by quite a bit."

Caroline shifted in her lap. "Is there a blanket we can put down? She needs to stretch out a bit."

"I'm sorry, sweetie. I'm not thinking. Charles, get that quilt out of the coat closet."

Samantha always thought of it as an umbrella closet. One didn't really need coats in Florida.

Her dad went for the quilt, then folded it into fourths, placing it on the floor next to the rocking chair.

"Thanks, Dad. She likes to stretch out, just like"—she almost said, "her father," but she didn't want that image in her head or her parents'—"me."

"You don't sleep in the fetal position anymore? Why not? You always slept that way when you were growing up. Looked terribly confining to me, but you always seemed so comfortable."

"I guess the adult me decided it wasn't comfortable. Mom, can we eat now while she's sleeping? I'm starving. I can finish my story later." Anything to get her mother focused elsewhere, even if it were only for a little while. And she was hungry.

Helena, all four-foot-ten of her, stood and smoothed out the salmon-colored capris she wore. "I'm almost ashamed of myself for not putting dinner on the table. I have to put the rolls in the oven, but the Caesar salad is ready. We can start with that if you two don't mind?"

Samantha almost rolled her eyes. "I've been craving your Caesar dressing lately."

Her mother stopped dead in her tracks, whirling around to face her. "You're not pregnant again, are you?"

Samantha put a finger to her mouth, the other pointing to Caroline still sleeping on the quilt. Her father placed his arm at her mother's waist, guiding her to the kitchen. "Lena," he said, his voice almost stern.

The kitchen had been changed since she'd left. They'd changed everything in color, but the style was similar. The appliances were sleek and new, and the countertops a soft white granite, the cabinets a soft gray. "I like the new kitchen, it's modern like Maria's new house."

Crud! Massive slip of the tongue.

"She sent me a picture in an e-mail." Of the outside of her house, so at least that much was true, she consoled herself as she sat down, positioning herself so she could keep an eye on Caroline from where she sat.

"I heard she got married and had a baby," her mother said as she slid the rolls into the oven.

"I know, Mom. I told you, remember?" Samantha said. "She's married to the six o'clock anchor. Mark Mason."

"Oh yes, I remember now. He's a handsome young man, all dark and mysterious-looking. His teeth are too white though. I wonder if they're real? Seems like most newspeople have really white teeth."

They all laughed, and Samantha felt like the ice had finally cracked. They were on their way back to their old ways: relaxed, comfortable, at ease with one another. She really had dealt them a blow, showing up after three years with a baby. And on Mother's Day weekend, which she'd just now remembered.

"Mom, about the spa weekend, I'll have to cancel. With the baby and all," she said.

"You'll do no such thing. I'm quite capable of baby-sitting my . . . granddaughter. You two can go as planned," her father insisted.

She raised her brows and smiled at him. "Thanks, Dad. It's wonderful to hear you acknowledge your grand-daughter."

"Hey, she's *my* granddaughter, too. Just because I've just learned I'm a grandmother doesn't mean I don't want to acknowledge her, and besides, Evelyn and Stella both have grandsons but wanted granddaughters, so I'll have one up on them now. Bryan is married, by the way. This is such a good one-up, too. Don't get me wrong, their grandsons are cute as bugs, but they're wishing for more grandchildren, specifically granddaughters, so we shall see."

Leave it to her mother to get her two best friends involved. They'd been friends for as long as Samantha could remember. She'd once had a crush on Stella's oldest son, Bryan. As soon as he'd left for college, she'd forgotten all about him. She'd met Michael, and he'd been her main guy during her freshman and sophomore years, then that had fizzled out, then there was Will, whose family moved away not long after they became an item. And on it went. She always had a boyfriend in high school. She'd had a semi-serious relationship in college, but like all the others, it, too, fizzled out. It was then that she decided she'd devote herself to her career.

Until *him*.

"They must be around Caroline's age?" Samantha probed.

Her mom and dad looked at her.

"You never told us. How old is she?" Her mother stopped stirring whatever concoction was on the stovetop to stare at her.

"I'm sorry, I didn't even think to tell you. She's almost eight months old. She was born this past September. The twenty-seventh."

Her father smiled. "Just missed my birthday by a day, huh?"

"She did. I tried to hold out to the twenty-eighth, but she was having no part of that. She was ready to meet . . ." She paused, wanting to say her father, but instead she said, "Me."

Samantha knew the more she said, the more questions her parents would ask. She didn't blame them, either, as she would feel the same if she were in their position. For now, this was how it had to be.

"It's close enough. We can celebrate together this year. I hope," her father suggested.

"Yes, of course we will," Samantha said, hoping there would be one more person to help celebrate her daughter's first birthday.

"I can't wait to take her to Heaven to Seven," her mother said as she placed bowls of chilled romaine on the table.

"That's still open? I'd forgotten all about that place." Heaven to Seven was a children's shop on the beach; it had been around forever. "Maybe we could go? Together?" Samantha said, knowing this would please her mother.

"I'd love that, Sam. I just can't believe I have a grandchild. I do hope she gets used to being around us, given the circumstances."

"Of course, she will; she's just a baby. We'll do our best to make up for lost time," Sam's father remarked.

"If you don't mind, I'd love a dollop of that Caesar dressing you made."

"Me too," Sam added, her mouth watering just thinking of the briny, salty taste. No one made Caesar dressing like her mom.

"Yes, of course." Helena removed the pot from the burner, placed it aside, then took a small bowl out of the refrigerator. She spooned the creamy dressing on top of the three bowls of romaine. "The rolls should be ready anytime, so please, eat up."

For the second time that day, Sam's mouth watered at the tastes she'd longed for while she was gone. Though she had to admit, the food she'd had in Italy was awesome, it wasn't her mother's food. It seemed she'd been a bit obsessed with her mom's cooking while she was away. She'd learned to appreciate it.

Peering around the table, she saw that Caroline was still sound asleep. She'd been uprooted for days now, and still, she was a dream baby. She was lucky to have such a precious child, and she would never take that for granted.

Using her fork, pointing it at her salad, she announced, "I've dreamed of this, Mom. I can't tell you how"—her eyes filled with tears—"I've missed you two so much. I'm sorry I didn't tell you about the baby, but I couldn't." Tears streamed down her face. She used the pretty gray-and-pink cloth napkin to wipe them away. "Sorry," she said, then proceeded to blow her nose on the fancy napkin. Both parents watched her, and she began to giggle. She couldn't help herself. She was happier than she'd been in months. Here she was with her family and her child. She just knew everything was going to turn out fine.

Her mom began laughing, then her father joined in. They giggled like a bunch of kids, just the way they used to.

Her mother took her fancy napkin, dabbed at her eyes, her mascara running down her face like two muddy streams.

Samantha shook her head. "I take it your mascara isn't waterproof?"

This sent them into another fit of laugher.

"No, I can't get the stuff off, gave up on it," her mother said, a wide grin on her face. "Maybe it's time to give it another go."

"You should get lash extensions—I hear they're all the rage now," Samantha said, grinning.

"Now you're being silly. I'm too old for that sort of thing," her mother replied.

"Says who?" Sam asked. Her mom had always worn makeup, and never left the house without it. "You should give them a try. It'll save you time when you're doing your makeup." She took another bite of salad.

A noise from the living room sent Samantha running. Caroline was sitting on her quilt, scoping out her surroundings. "There's my sweet girl," she said. "I'll bet you're hungry again."

Samantha returned to the kitchen. "Have you mixed the lobster in with the macaroni yet?"

"I was about to, why?" her mother asked.

"Leave a bit out for her. I think it's time she tried grandma's food."

"You sure?" her father asked. "She's just a baby."

Samantha sat down with the baby in her lap. Caroline tried to grab Sam's fork, then the empty salad bowl. "I think she's ready for a bit of mac and cheese. I'll mash it up."

"I'll do it," her mother said. "When she's older, we'll

make sure to tell her that Grammy Lena made her very first meal."

"Grammy Lena?" Samantha said. "I like it. What about you, Dad? Do you want to be called Grandpa or Poppa Chuck?"

"I think Grandpa will be just fine."

Her mother made fast work of mashing a bit of macaroni with her homemade cheese sauce into a small plastic bowl. "I don't have baby spoons, but I do have some little dessert spoons somewhere. At least I think that's what they're for." She rummaged through a drawer. "Here."

"That'll work, Mom, thanks. I'll need to get a few essentials for her later." She hadn't planned well, she thought. She'd have to make a trip to Target or Walmart.

As soon as the macaroni cooled, she gave Caroline a small bite. She gobbled it down, opening her mouth for a second bite. "I think your macaroni's a success. A bit too soon for her to try lobster, but we'll get there eventually."

Caroline ate every bite and whimpered when Sam moved the dish aside. "I'll give you some carrots, baby, okay? Dad, can you hold her while I run upstairs? I have her food in the diaper bag."

He stood up, reached across the table, and took Caroline from Sam. His eyes lit up like sparklers. "She has my eyes," he said, gazing at his grandchild in amazement.

"Yes, she does. I'll be right back." She hurried out of the kitchen, went to her old room, and grabbed four jars of carrots from the bag. She'd need to make a food run soon.

Caroline was giggling when Sam returned to the kitchen. "She likes me," her dad said.

"I can see that," Sam said as she reached for the baby.

"I've got her, Sam. Enjoy your meal."

"If you're sure," she said. "She can be a wiggle worm."

"Just like you," her mother chimed in. "Give me a few minutes to heat this, then you two can dig in. I'm off my game today," her mother said.

"We all are, so let's just get through this meal, and take it one day at a time."

"Good idea, Dad. I took you both off guard, and I'm sorry." That was all she could say. And she was sorry, but she wouldn't keep apologizing. They would be fantastic grandparents; she just had to let them get used to the idea.

Finally, the lobster mac and cheese and hot garlic rolls were served. Samantha loaded her plate, taking two of the steaming-hot rolls. "Mom, this is a dream meal. I know it's crazy, but it's true. Lots of nights we—the crew and I—would have stale crackers and peanut butter for dinner. I don't think I'll ever take another bite of peanut butter again, but it was convenient at the time."

For the next half hour, Samantha ate and talked to her parents. They discussed things she would need for the baby, steering clear of any mention of Caroline's father. She knew they wanted details, but that was impossible.

For now, she had to focus on getting Caroline settled in, whether it be here, an apartment, or maybe a house. Her daughter deserved a stable life, and that was all that mattered at the moment.

Chapter 5

After dinner, Samantha helped her mother clean the kitchen while her dad played with Caroline in the front room.

"It feels good to be back home," she said as she put the floral arrangement back in the center of the table.

"I'll be able to sleep through the night for the first time since you left," her mother said. "That's always the worst time for me. When the day is over, and you have nothing but your thoughts, it was a struggle for me. I imagined all sorts of terrible scenarios and prayed that you'd come home safely. That prayer has been answered. I'm going to sleep like a baby tonight, knowing you and Caroline are safe."

It wasn't like her mom to get too serious, so when she did, Samantha listened. "I had no idea. Why didn't you tell me?"

"Now, why would I want to burden you with my problems? You needed to stay focused on your job. I managed. It comes with the territory. You'll understand in time."

"If you're talking about worrying about your child, I get that. I can't begin to imagine how my choices affected you and Dad."

"It's all part of being a parent, Sam. There's good times and the occasional bad time. It's just what it is. The best thing about being a parent is the love. There is just nothing comparable to loving a child."

"What about Dad? I mean, loving him. How is that in comparison?" she asked.

"It's a completely different type of love, no less intense, just different. I'm sure you understand." Her mother's face lit up. After all these years, she knew her parents were still very much in love.

"I suppose." She couldn't say more. "On a different subject, I need to make a trip to Target, or Walmart, whichever is closest. Caro, I call her that sometimes, needs a few things. I was thinking maybe you'd like to come shopping with me? Dad seems to be glorying in playing on the floor right now. It's just after seven, not too late."

"I don't care if it's midnight, you and I are going shopping. We can take the baby and your dad if you want."

"That's perfect. It'll be your first outing as grandparents. Let me clean her up and change her clothes, and you're on." Her heart felt light at such a simple pleasure. Going shopping with Mom and Dad as an adult woman was just about as awesome as she could get, at least at this point in her life. Recently, Maria had asked if she was happy, and she'd answered honestly. But she hadn't really given the question as much thought as she should have. Even though there was someone missing in her life, she wanted to breathe in this moment, this feeling of total contentment that absorbed her. Today was the best day she'd had in a very long time. If *he* were here, life would be complete.

Thirty minutes later, they were in the rental car, Dad at the wheel and her mother in the back seat entertaining Caroline, who seemed to be enjoying Grammy Lena's undivided attention. They drove south on Tamiami Trail, and Samantha was shocked at the changes since she had left. Big-box stores, specialty stores, and so many restaurants for fine dining, it would take months to visit all of them. Naples was definitely a ritzy area now. When she had grown up here, it hadn't seemed so upscale, yet it was now.

As they made the turn onto Pine Ridge Road to their local Target, again there were more shops than she remembered, and the traffic was horrendous. "Lots of changes in the time I've been away," she observed. "Traffic is just as you said." She hadn't told them about her drive from Orlando four days ago, or that she'd spent the afternoon with Maria, but that didn't matter. What mattered was the here and now. Her parents seemed thrilled to be grandparents, and Caroline was healthy and happy. What more could a mother ask for?

They parked in a lot that was packed, what with its being the Saturday before Mother's Day. She took Caroline out of the car seat, and her father insisted on carrying her. Her little legs kicked, and she waved her arms in the air. "She's excited."

"Typical little girl, excited to shop," her dad joked.

Inside, Samantha took a shopping cart and headed for the baby section. "If you two want to take her to the toy aisle, you can."

"We'd love to," her mother said. "Are you sure?"

"Of course. Get to know her. She loves Sophie the Giraffe. It's a teether, and she lost hers. If you could find one, I would be forever thankful. She has a couple teeth ready to pop through. Any chew toy would be nice, but Sophie's long neck is especially tasty."

Her parents nodded. "So we are to look for a giraffe with a chewable neck?"

"Yep, you got it," she said.

"Times have changed is all I'm going to say," her mother said. "We'll find you when we're finished."

"Thanks, Mom."

She pushed the cart to the baby department. She'd left all of Caro's furniture, what little she'd had, in Italy. A crib was out of the question tonight, as she wanted to get something special, so she went on the hunt for that Pack 'n Play Maria had introduced her to. Up and down a few aisles, she spied a Fisher-Price Pack 'n Play. She grabbed it, crammed it beneath her cart, then continued to peruse the aisles. She bought diapers, another pack of bottles, wipes, Children's Tylenol, which she knew she would need soon as Caroline's teeth were bound to give her some discomfort. She found spoons, baby dishes, and squeezable tubes of baby food. *This is new,* she thought. She hadn't seen this in Italy, so she grabbed carrots, beets, peaches, and bananas. Spying boxes of teething biscuits, she grabbed two, just in case. Little rice puffs for ages six months and up in strawberry, banana, and apple would be good on the days she couldn't get her to eat. Two packs of onesies, and three light blankets should be enough to get her through the next few days. Formula, how could she forget that? She was used to nursing, so that was understandable. She placed three cans of the powdered formula in the cart, along with two gallons of distilled water. The label said "nursery water." Hopefully, no one took it for water to use on their houseplants.

She grabbed some diaper cream just in case, and baby body wash. Babies were high-maintenance, she thought, but worth every bit and more. She saw a couple of age-appropriate toys and placed them on top of her tote, as there was no room left in her shopping cart. She'd be lucky if she were able to get all of this in the trunk of the car.

"I didn't know you were planning on buying out the store," her dad said when they met up. They, too, had a cart full of toys and who knew what else. Caroline giggled in the shopping cart seat. Another first for her.

Her father must've seen the surprised look on her face. "You're okay with her sitting in the seat? It's probably okay. Mom had some antibacterial wipes, gave it the once-over."

She laughed. "It's fine. It's just her first time sitting in a shopping cart. I'm not too much of a germaphobe." Some of the places she'd been with her daughter were filthy, so she'd learned not to wig out about conditions. Actually, she believed it had boosted Caroline's immune system because she had never been sick, other than a slight runny nose a time or two, and that had only lasted for a day.

"Good, I was never too fussy with you, either," her mom explained. "There were a few limits, such as the time you tried to eat a tube of red lipstick. You thought it was candy, but thankfully, you didn't have a chance to eat the lipstick though you did manage to smear it all over your face. You were about a year and a half old."

"So, is this a warning to hide my lipstick?" Samantha asked, as they strolled through the aisles toward the checkout.

"It's a suggestion," her mom said.

"I'll file it away for future reference."

It took twenty minutes for the cashier to check out their items, then another ten for her dad to load the car. There wasn't an inch to spare.

"We couldn't get another bag in that trunk if we had to. I think next time we'll take your father's SUV."

"Good idea. So, Dad, are you still volunteering your services tomorrow? If not, it's fine. I just need to write down a few instructions for you if you decide you're still game. She can be a little squirmy at times. She's trying to crawl, so it's a race to keep up with her."

"I managed to keep up with you. And you were squirmy most of the time, too," he replied. "You wore your poor mother out."

"I'm sure you both can give me some parenting tips. I read dozens of baby books when I was pregnant, but they don't really prepare you for the real thing," she said to her father.

"There isn't a book around that can prepare you for children. I read a few during my pregnancy, too. I wasn't worried too much about caring for you, as we'd both wanted children for so long. Mostly, I was concerned with carrying you the entire nine months. I wasn't a spring chicken," her mother reminded her.

Samantha rolled her eyes. "Women are giving birth at all ages now, and many are way older than you were. I met a lady in Italy, she was fifty-three, pregnant with her eleventh child." She watched the expressions on their faces.

"She must be a saint," her mother said, wide-eyed with surprise.

Her dad laughed. "Or crazy." He paused. "Maybe a little of both."

"Dad! Shame on you," Sam teased back. "She was a . . . passionate woman."

"Sounds like it," he joshed. "I guess it's all a matter of perspective, I suppose."

Caroline chimed in, too, with all sorts of new jibber-jabbering sounds.

"She also has an opinion on the subject," Helena said.

"And we're not exactly sure what it is, either," Sam tossed over her shoulder, laughing.

Half an hour later, her father had unpacked the car, she'd bathed Caroline, and her mother was slicing her famous red devil's food cake.

Today was the beginning, again, of a new way of life.

Chapter 6

The next morning, Samantha had just finished feeding Caroline her breakfast when she heard a car pull into the drive. Peering out the kitchen window, she spotted a sleek white limousine taking up enough space for at least two decent-sized vehicles.

"Mother!" she hollered as loud as she could without scaring the baby.

"Yes, dear?"

Her mother stood at the bottom of the stairs. *Without her makeup, she looks exactly like me*, Sam thought. *And much younger.* She was wearing a mauve sundress with camel-colored sandals. "Mom, you want to explain that?" She nodded toward the drive.

"Samantha, there is nothing to explain. And Happy Mother's Day to you, too," her mom said sweetly.

Shoot, how could she have forgotten? She hadn't slept well; Caro had tossed and turned most of the night in her new Pack 'n Play. All she'd thought about this morning when she came downstairs was coffee and feeding her daughter.

"Mom, I'm such a poop! Come here," she said. She

placed her one free arm around her mother's shoulders. "Happy Mother's Day. I didn't mean to blow the wind out of your sails. I was just feeding her, and then I heard a car pulling into the drive. I thought Stella and Evelyn were here. Not a limo. Mom, exactly *why* is there a limousine parked in the drive?"

"It's part of your surprise. Spa day, remember? This is your first Mother's Day. Last night your father called in a favor, and now we're traveling to the spa in style. Isn't that exciting?"

Smiling, Samantha thought this sounded just like something he would do. Always that little extra. When she was growing up, he'd always said nothing was too good for his girls. Having received a small inheritance from his father, he never dipped into it except for special occasions. He'd said his salary as a police officer and her mother's income from the library was plenty for a family of three to live on comfortably, but Samantha knew there was no mortgage on the house and that her father bought new cars every three years and always paid in cash. Money was never an issue growing up, and apparently, that hadn't changed. Not that the cost of hiring a limo was earth-shattering, but it meant a lot that he'd taken the time at the last minute to ensure that her first Mother's Day was special, memorable.

Taking a deep breath, Samantha said, "It's very exciting. Where is he anyway?"

"He's in the garage putting a little walker together for the baby. Thought we could use it as a temporary high chair, and she'd have the added benefit of learning to push it around with those precious little legs."

Why hadn't she thought of that when they were at Target last night? "A great idea, Mom. I didn't even think

about a high chair. I always hold her when I feed her."
She felt silly and inexperienced.

"Your lifestyle was different, Sam. And this is your first
baby. You'll get the hang of these things soon enough.
He wanted to get her a regular high chair since she sits up
so well but thought you might want to pick one out for her
yourself."

"That's sweet of him. We'll all pick one out together,"
she said. "Would you mind watching this little lady while
I run upstairs for a quick change?"

"Of course. Now pass that little beauty to Grammy,"
she said, and Samantha placed Caroline in her grandmother's outstretched arms.

"I'll be down in five minutes, tops."

"No hurry, they're not expecting us at the spa until ten."

Samantha raced upstairs, turned the shower on, soaped
off in record time, then dressed in a pair of yellow shorts
with a matching flowery blouse. She found a pair of her
sandals from high school still in the closet. They looked
brand-new, she thought. Then she remembered that she
hadn't really cared for them too much at the time, but now
they were all the rage. Proof that styles repeat themselves.
She found the list she'd made for her father last night,
checked to make sure all the necessary supplies were laid
out, then hurried back downstairs, where her daughter
was inside this new walker from Grandpa and Grammy.
She laughed. "Look at Mommy's big girl. Standing up
already." She leaned down and planted a kiss on the top
of her dark curls.

"Thanks, Dad. I didn't even think of this . . . or that."
She motioned toward the driveway. "A limo. A bit fancy,
but I'm ready for my first Mother's Day. Are you sure you
don't mind staying with her? I've a list in my room with

her nap routine, rather her sort of nap routine, and her food and formula are in the kitchen."

"Sweetie, I think I'm going to enjoy today as much as I enjoyed spending time with you when you were this age. I've got this covered, Sam. I may be an old tough cop, but I know how to care for little girls. Look how perfect you turned out."

Her eyes filled with tears. "Dad, you're awesome, did I ever tell you that? And Mom, too." She hugged him, kissed her daughter's pudgy little cheeks, then looked at her mom. "Are you ready?"

Grammy gave Caro a dozen kisses, then said, "More than you can imagine. I've been planning this day all year."

"I bet you didn't factor in I'd be a mom, too, when you were making these plans," she joked as they headed out to the limo.

"I didn't, but it's even better. I have two special girls now. I just wish I had known. I would've helped out in whatever way I could. We still have our passports; we would've traveled to Italy, but that's hindsight. Now, I want to enjoy you and Caro every minute possible."

The driver, a man who appeared to be in his early sixties, with white hair combed back from his forehead and a neatly trimmed matching goatee, was the personification of a classy limo driver. He opened the door, stepping aside as he waited for them to enter. "Ladies," he said, and gave a slight bow.

Inside the luxurious vehicle there were wraparound white-leather seats, plush white carpeting, and soft music that played from hidden speakers.

After they were seated, their driver directed them to a chilled bottle of Cristal, next to two elegant Waterford crystal champagne flutes. A silver plate with fresh strawberries invited one to enjoy the offered amenities.

"It's your father's way of telling you how much he loves us. He's a special man," her mother said, all dreamy-eyed.

"I know, and I'll never take either of you for granted again. I promise." She wanted to tell her she'd never keep them in the dark again, either, but she wasn't sure that was a promise she could keep.

"Let's try this fancy champagne, or is it too early for you?" her mother asked.

"For champagne? Never!"

"Shall I?" her mother asked.

"Yes, you shall, Mother dear," Samantha said in a fake British accent.

They both laughed.

"We're quite the sophisticates, aren't we?" her mom asked.

"We are today, and so far, I'm loving it."

After her mother expertly uncorked the champagne, she filled their flutes, then placed the Cristal back into the ice bucket. "I think we should propose a toast, don't you?"

"I do," Sam answered.

"To family, together forever," Helena said, and they carefully clinked their fancy flutes together.

"To family," Samantha singsonged.

"So, tell me about this spa we're going to. Is it as fancy as this limo ride?"

"Sam, it's the hottest spa in town. I booked this last summer, that's how fancy it is. I heard that Angelina Jolie was here right before Christmas."

"Wow, that's impressive. I like her movies."

"And she has six children, too. Can you imagine? And still has her figure," her mother added. Samantha didn't want to remind her that she'd only been pregnant twice. One daughter and a set of twins, and the other three were adopted.

"She's a beautiful woman."

"It would be something if we were to bump into a celebrity," her mom gushed. "Stella and Evelyn would have a hissy fit."

"I'm sure they would, but I want this day to ourselves, don't you? I can tell Caroline all about it when she's older."

"Of course, you're right. You know how I am with all the celebrity stuff. I think all those years working at the library seeing *People* magazine every week did something to me. Your father says I'm starstruck, and I admit I am, but I know that's not their real world. It's just something fun."

"Mom, you can be starstruck; that doesn't make you a bad person. If it's what you like, go for it. It isn't like you're going to become one of those stalkers that you hear about on the news. At least I hope not."

"Samantha Renee! I would never do something like that, and shame on you for even suggesting it."

They both laughed because they knew they were simply teasing each other. This was the type of relationship she had with her mom. There'd rarely been drama of any kind in her life. Of course, that was before she'd traveled to Afghanistan. But she was not going to spoil the day thinking about her past.

"Ladies," the driver's voice came through the hidden speakers. "We have arrived at your destination."

"So much for knocking back this bottle of Cristal," Sam said.

"We're taking it," her mother said, removing the bottle, and wiping it off with a tissue.

"Are you sure? This place might not allow alcohol inside."

"They serve alcohol," her mother informed her.

"Then let's not waste a drop," Samantha agreed.

They thanked their limo driver as he escorted them to the door of the Serenity Spa. The minute they stepped inside, Samantha discovered what "relaxing" smelled like. A light rose scent and maybe cucumber? She couldn't identify the exact smell other than it was spa-like and luxurious . . . *relaxing*.

"Mrs. Stewart?" a woman inquired as soon as they were inside.

"Mrs. and Ms. Stewart," her mother said. "This is my daughter, Samantha."

The woman was around Sam's age, taller than her with long black hair. Her features were plain, but her makeup was pure artistry. She'd learned a few tricks herself when she'd worked as a TV newsperson but hadn't used them in a very long time.

"Happy Mother's Day," the woman said, then looked at her scheduling sheet. "It looks like you're both here for the entire day. The elite package, I see." She glanced at the bottle of champagne her mother had a death grip on. "Looks like you'll be needing a couple of flutes, as well."

Her mom mouthed, "Told you." And it was all she could do to keep from laughing out loud.

"If you two will follow me, you can enjoy your champagne in our lounge."

They followed the dark-haired woman to a room filled with the sounds of a small waterfall and a light tinkling of music. "Make yourselves comfortable. I'm Layne. I apologize for not introducing myself before." She stood there, waiting for a reply.

"No worries," was all Samantha could say, as the champagne's influence was beginning to ease its way through her, making her feel warm and fuzzy. "We'll be just fine, Layne."

"I'll return in a bit, then you all may begin your spa experience." She smiled, then left them to finish off their champagne.

"Isn't she a doll? I bet she gets facials every day. Did you see how perfect her skin was? I bet she gets Botox, which I'll admit, I do myself, but I think she's too young—"

"Mom! You're talking too fast," Sam told her, knowing it was the champagne. They had best stop while they were ahead, or they'd pass out before their spa experience even began. "Did I hear you say you'd had Botox?" she asked.

"That's exactly what you heard," Helena replied. "Are you going to preach me a sermon like your father does? He thinks it's vain of me."

"Mom, of course not. I might try it myself someday. I've got plenty of wrinkles. Dad doesn't approve?" she said, then wished she'd worded it another way. Her dad was not the kind of guy who had to approve what her mother did or didn't do. Actually, he was quite mellow.

"He doesn't care, really. He likes to tease me, tells me I'm beautiful without it, but it's just that little something extra I like to do. Does that make me a vain woman?"

"Not at all," she said, then swallowed the last bit of champagne. "I don't think I'll have another glass. This is the first time I've had alcohol since Caroline's birth." And it was hitting her full force. She felt lightheaded.

"I don't want any either. I want to enjoy this experience with you. I'm so happy you're home, Sam. By the way, I slept like a newborn baby last night."

"You woke up every four hours?" She couldn't help herself.

"You know what I mean; I slept through the night. I didn't even get up once to go to the bathroom."

"Mom, you do realize the more you talk, the more it sounds like you're either a baby or ready for a nursing home." Sam was loving jousting with her mother. This was their relationship for the most part, but when she needed her mother to act motherly, she'd never failed her in thirty-three years. She was just a funny woman. Maybe she'd missed her calling? A stint on a comedy show would've suited her sense of humor. Hard to see her as the quiet library lady.

"Stop, you're going to critique my every word. This is not the news, dear, or the library. I loved my work there, but I didn't like the hush-hush atmosphere. I studied music . . . maybe I should've been a teacher? I'll never know, but Caroline will reap the benefit of what knowledge I have. I can't wait to take her to the library. She's going to love story time."

"We're ready for you, ladies, that is, if you're ready," Layne said, interrupting her mother's constant flow of words.

"Yes, we're more than ready," Sam told her.

"Excellent. Now, I have your day sheets, and I'll need you both to look them over, fill out the form with your emergency contact numbers, and at the end of the day, we'll want your feedback so we will be returning these. How does that sound, ladies?"

"Sounds like we're being tested, but I will overlook that. I understood when I made this appointment last year, this was a place to be pampered, and treated like a goddess. Is that just a trick to entice people to your spa?"

"Mother!" Samantha said, then turned to Layne. "I'm sorry. She's had too much to drink. We're fine with whatever you all have planned."

"No, we're not! I want to know what's going to happen to me beforehand, don't you? We do have an infant to consider," her mother said, her voice higher than normal.

She had her there. "Can you give us a few minutes to look this over? I'm sure it's all fine."

Samantha skimmed over the paper and didn't see anything out of order. She filled out the form, using her parents' home address and her cell number. Scribbling an illegible signature on her form, she took her mother's and did the same, only she passed it to her mother for her signature. "Sign this," she said, leaving no doubt that it was time to get down to the rough business of getting pampered.

Samantha handed her sheet to Layne. "We'd like to start now. Mom, sign the paper in this lifetime."

Samantha gave her mom a stern look, but she refused to give up her info sheet or whatever they called it.

Sam followed Layne. Her mother finally got the message and trailed behind them. Each room they passed smelled divine. Soft music played, and candles were placed in strategic areas of all the rooms they walked through.

"Your first spa treatment is our detox pool," Layne said, a hint of a smile on her face.

Samantha busted out laughing. "Are you serious? Do all tipsy clients go to the detox pool first? It sounds . . . silly, that's all. Sorry." She wanted to laugh like she had as a teenager, giggle until her eyes watered and her sides ached. Biting the sides of her cheeks to keep all that laughter inside, she tried to distract herself by looking at her mother.

Mistake, *big* mistake.

She'd taken the sheet she was supposed to sign, and on the back side she'd drawn a giant happy face with a tongue sticking out. Quickly, Sam turned away because if she didn't, she would end up humiliating them both. "Mother, please let me have your spa sheet. Now."

Her mother winked at her, then handed over the paper.

She gave Layne her mother's spa sheet, smiley side down, and hoped the woman didn't look at it now. At least let them be in different rooms when she viewed her mother's artwork.

"Very well, now, ladies, these"—she opened a set of heavy wooden double doors—"are our detox tubs."

She'd been expecting anything but this. An Alice in Wonderland moment, she thought, or Disney World. Whatever. Ten or so, and Samantha would swear to this if ever asked, giant *teacups* were spaced evenly apart throughout the giant room. The scent of cucumber was so strong, she wondered if the detox pools had been mistaken for the salad bar.

Stop! Stop! Stop! She was becoming her mother!

Definitely no more alcohol for her.

"And we're the tea bags?" her mother remarked. "Is this a joke? You expect us to relax in a . . . cup? Are we supposed to get undressed? Why, I bet those are filled with all kinds of nasty germs. I think I want a refund. I never signed up for"—she pointed to the cups—"this!"

Samantha wanted to throw herself on the floor in a fit of laughter, but she didn't. Instead, she calmly asked Layne to explain. "I don't think Mother realized what the elite package included."

"Each tub is sanitized and filled just minutes before each client enters. They're made to fit one person, and as you'll see, we have swimsuits for you to wear. They are new and in packaging, so you may take them home if you wish. At Serenity, we like to remove any harmful toxins in the body first. Of course, we'll have you drink plenty of water so you don't become dehydrated. After half an hour or so, you'll be ready for your next treatment, and with the toxins removed from your body, our treatments are much more effective." Layne spoke as if she were explaining brain surgery.

Samantha wondered how many times a day she went through this spiel. "What's in the water that's going to detox our bodies?"

"We add magnesium sulphate, which you'll know as Epsom salt. A bit of baking soda, and Himalayan salt, then we add a small amount of apple cider vinegar. You may choose your favorite essential oil to add, but I always recommend lavender for its relaxation properties. That's it. Most of the things you would have at home in your kitchen cupboard. Nothing harmful, I assure you. When we combine these ingredients, you'll get the full benefit if you stay in our tubs for the whole half hour. I see you both have facials scheduled afterward, so if either of you are suffering with blemishes or any topical concerns with your skin, the detoxification process will aid in this as well."

"Show us the way," Samantha instructed. "This sounds like fun." If her mother thought she was excited, then Samantha knew she would dive into the process wholeheartedly. If this would detox the small amount of alcohol they'd consumed, then she was all for it. And she'd try to remember the recipe the next time she needed a detox. She'd visit the kitchen, then take a bath.

Layne led them to the changing rooms. She had to

admit, they were pretty lush. Stacks of thick, pale green bath sheets, matching terry robes and slippers, and dark green swimsuits in light green cellophane wrap lined a wall. The suits were placed on shelves according to size. "They run true to size," Layne said, watching Sam glance at the shelves.

Samantha couldn't remember the last time she'd worn a swimsuit. "That's good to know."

"I don't suppose we're allowed to try them on first? I have a very small waist, but I'm quite busty," Sam's mother blurted out.

Samantha almost wished she were back in Italy in her crappy apartment. Anywhere but here.

"She'll take a small, and I'll have a medium."

Layne took the proper-sized suits from the shelf, then led them to their private dressing rooms.

"When you're ready, our detox specialists will prepare your tubs."

"Mom, don't say a word. Layne, thank you for your information. It's been very . . . informative."

"Then I hope you'll add this to your spa experience. We all appreciate compliments. It lets our employer know we're doing our job."

"Absolutely. I'll make sure to give you a glowing review," Samantha said. "So, we'll just put these suits on and return to the detox area?"

"And our detox specialist will meet us at the teacups," her mother added from her dressing room.

"Just as I explained," Layne said. "Now, I'll leave you two to prepare yourselves. Enjoy your spa experience."

Layne left the room, and her mother came out of the dressing room. Samantha was mildly surprised when she saw how great her mom looked in the plain green swimsuit. She'd put her up against any twenty-year-old.

"Don't stare, dear. I feel like I'm on display in one of those shop windows on Fifth Avenue."

One of the more luxurious areas to shop in Naples, Fifth Avenue catered to the wealthiest of them all.

"Mom, I don't know what you're doing, but you look freaking fantastic! I want what you're having," Samantha said, stepping out of her dressing room. Her own suit was too loose in the chest area—no shock there. No way she filled it out like her mother.

"Stop, you'll embarrass me."

"No, I won't stop. Now, tell me what you're doing to look like a twenty-year-old in a swimsuit?"

"I go to the gym, and I joined a Zumba class. That's it, and I'm trying that clean-eating thing, not very successfully, but I am trying."

She took a deep breath. "Trust me, whatever it is, it's working. You ready to go get pickled?"

"I've acted horribly, haven't I? It was that champagne! I hope I haven't embarrassed you, and yes, I'm ready. I'm not so sure this spa thing was such a good idea."

"Mother, it's a great idea. I think the Cristal on empty stomachs was a bad idea."

"That's it! I didn't have breakfast. Normally, I can have two or three glasses to drink before I feel the effects."

"Mom, please, the detox specialists are waiting." It was all she could do to say this with a straight face. She would definitely remember her first Mother's Day, and if not the actual spa experience, she knew she'd remember her mother's attempt at comic relief.

They returned to the detox baths. Two women in their

early twenties explained once more what they were putting in the water, then left them alone.

Inside the cups or tubs was a small built-in seat, but there wasn't enough room to stretch out their legs. "Not the most comfortable cup I've ever bathed in." She was reminded of a time she'd been in an actual tank, the feeling of claustrophobia that overcame her. She almost felt that way now. Samantha did not like to be confined.

"Well, I do think the smell is a bit better now they added the lavender oil. I think all this vinegar they're using is what made it smell like a cucumber. Maybe a good scrub with bleach between detoxing would help. I'll make sure to write that on that stupid sheet she kept referring to. Don't you think she went a bit overboard?"

Closing her eyes, Sam tried to summon up a picture of what patience looked like. Her mind remained blank. Then she thought of Caroline. The stress eased from her shoulders, and her impatience with her mother lessened a bit. Leaning her head back on the rim of the tub, she opened her eyes and caught her mother staring at her.

"What? Is one of my boobs hanging out?" She sat up, looking down to make sure everything was where it should be.

"Samantha, I know you've been through a hell of a nightmare. Don't think I can't see those dark circles, the sadness in your eyes. I'm sure you want to talk about whatever it is that's caused this, and I know you're not going to, or you're not allowed to. I do understand. I just want you to know that if you ever feel the need to unload, I'm here. I'm a tough old bird. Goofy, I know, but tough. I just needed to tell you."

Tears filled Sam's eyes, and she used the back of her hand to swipe at them. "You're very perceptive, Mom. I hope I'm as in tune with Caro as you've always been with me. I've had a rough couple of years; career-wise, it's been a challenge. I was getting tired, though. The people—they get to you. I felt horrible sometimes when I'd go on-air, with my cameraman zooming in on the tragedies of war. It was all I could do to speak clearly and not show my true feelings on-air. It got so bad, I started to fear that I would just blurt out the real truth live, on-air. I needed to stop. When another offer came my way, I had to take it."

Her mother got out of her "teacup" and came to sit beside hers. "You won't get the full detox if you don't stay in the tub for the full thirty minutes or so," Sam teased her mother.

"Who cares? I can do this at home. I just wanted us to have the day to ourselves. Granted, when I made the reservation, I didn't know you'd be celebrating Mother's Day as an actual mom yourself, but you're good at this mom thing. Not everyone is. I can't begin to imagine how difficult it must be doing this on your own. Can I ask about the father?"

Darn. Of course she could ask, but that didn't mean Sam would give a truthful answer. Not wanting to be a total fraud, but knowing what she could say, she spoke softly, as though ears and eyes dotted the walls. "Caroline's father was a great man."

"Good. So, I'm going to run with this, and you can stop me if you want. Caroline's father was or is in the military. Most likely he's injured, or . . . no longer with you, and he didn't, or doesn't know he's a father."

She smiled. "Mom, you're good, you know that? All those mystery books you used to read put some fantastic theories in your head. Do you still read them?"

Her mother raked her hand through her hair, the same

as she did when she was stressed or put on the spot. "I do. I'll never stop reading books. I love them. I don't have a Kindle, or an iPad, just so you know. I just like the feel of the book in my hands, the feel of good paper, a sturdy binding. Does that answer your question?"

They both started laughing.

"We do this a lot, don't we?" Samantha said. "I've always loved this about you. Your sense of humor."

"I've learned not to take life too seriously most of the time. People create problems, many don't bother to seek an answer when it's right there in front of their eyes. I've turned to humor because it's all around us. Plus, it's a lot easier to laugh than cry. That's a simple explanation, but it's how I feel. I know there is tragedy in this world that I can't even begin to fathom. I'm sure you've seen that side of the world in your work. I know it's there, but I don't put a voice to it in my day-to-day life. Does that make me sound uncaring?"

Samantha patted her mother's arm. "Not at all. You've discovered what works for you dealing with your life. Many don't even have a clue, let alone a clear sense of why they think the way they do. You're succinct, and that's one more thing I love about you. I always know where I stand with you. Dad, he's a bit harder to crack."

"He's an old softie. That tough cop image isn't all he's about. Anyone who really knows your father knows he's true blue all the way, with friends, family, and even strangers. He's a straight shooter. He does have a humorous side. He doesn't show it as much as I do." Her mother stood and wrapped the pale green towel around herself.

"That's an understatement." Samantha lifted herself out of the small tub, reaching for her towel. "Dad's a winner. I think this grandpa role will be one of his finest, don't you?"

"I do. He'll be as much a father to Caroline as he was to you. Children need two parents in their life."

"I agree, but I also know there are circumstances that often keep one parent out of the picture, and I'll leave it at that. Now, what kind of facial should we have?"

Samantha knew where this conversation was headed, and she wouldn't go there.

She couldn't.

Chapter 7

The sleek white limousine returned at half past six. Inside, Samantha melted into the soft leather. Her first Mother's Day had been awesome. Beyond relaxing; she'd never been so well pampered.

"I take it the elite package is true to its name?" her mom asked from the seat next to her.

Smiling, Sam felt almost drunk, blissfully content, but her thoughts were as clear as Florida's blue skies. "I don't recall ever being this relaxed." Well, maybe there were a few instances, but she wouldn't allow her thoughts to travel down that road.

"Maybe this is a new tradition. Me and you. Spa day. And Caroline, when she's old enough. Poor Stella. Poor Evelyn. No granddaughter to take to the spa."

"Mother! That's awful. They might end up with ten granddaughters each for all you know. Don't act so smug." Adding that she might have ten sons would've opened her up for more questioning, so she kept quiet.

"I know, I don't mean it that way. I love those girls like sisters. We all like a good one-up. Keeps us on our toes."

"Nothing wrong as long as no one's feelings are hurt,"

Sam responded, her head lolling to one side. All she could think about was her bed, crawling beneath the cool sheets, the ceiling fan making that same whirring sound she'd grown used to as a child. "Don't ever change that fan out in my room. Promise?"

"What?" her mother practically shouted. "Are you all right?"

Shaking her head, she sat up. "Of course. Why would you even ask that? We've been together all day."

"You were talking about the ceiling fan in your room."

"Oh. I'm just so relaxed." Which was true. All she could think about was sleeping through the night. Is this what her mom wished for during the three years she'd been unable to sleep? If so, she was now her true hero. "How long before we're at the house? I think I'll just close my eyes."

"Go on, dear. Rest up, you've got time for a quick snooze."

She managed to whisper, "Thanks," before drifting off.

Thirty minutes later, Sam felt her mother gently shaking her awake. She sat upright, raking her hand through her hair. "I'm ready." She saw she was still in the limousine. "Guess I took a nap. That was the best massage I've ever had in my life. My muscles must've been hard as a rock because I feel soft and mushy as mud right now." She leaned against the seat, a slight smile on her face. "Let's do this again. Soon."

The limo driver pulled into the driveway, then got out and opened the door for them. Her mother whispered something to him, then he nodded and climbed back in the long white luxury vehicle.

Inside the house, her father greeted them with a finger to his lips. "She's napping. Finally."

"I take it your first day as a full-fledged grandpa went well?"

"It was quite the day. You've got a dirty but contented little gal sound asleep. She found mom's gardening supplies in the garage and had a run-in with the potting soil. Cleaned her up as best as I could, but she's gonna need a scrub down."

"She was in the garage?" Sam asked.

"Yes, in her walker. I turned my back for two seconds, and she'd pushed herself over to the storage cabinets and opened the door."

"And found a bag of potting soil? I hope there wasn't anything poisonous in there?" she asked, instantly nervous.

"No, dear, just the potting soil," her mother answered. "I keep all the chemicals locked away. Remember, your cousins and their little ones visit now and then. Can't be too safe when they're here, you know?"

That was putting it mildly.

"Speaking of kids, you have an admirer. It's in the kitchen," her dad said. "I'm going to take a quick shower now that you two are here."

Samantha needed to check on Caroline first. Had her dad said *you have an admirer*? "Mom, can you run up and check on the baby? I need a minute."

"Of course," Helena said, and hurried upstairs.

Sam went to the kitchen and saw an enormous vase of roses on the counter. Her hands began to shake. Who would be sending her flowers? No one knew she was here . . . or did they? With trembling hands, she removed the small white card placed at the bottom of the bouquet. Taking a deep breath, she took the card from the envelope.

Love, Gio.

She stared at the plain white card. *Love, Gio.*

Was this someone's idea of a joke? Who would be so cruel? Who knew she was here?

She searched through the bouquet for something—she didn't know what—anything that would prove this was nothing more than a weird prank. "Dad," she shouted, not caring if Caroline woke up. She wouldn't put her down for the night without a bath anyway. "Mom!"

Her parents, along with her sleepy and dirty daughter, stood in the kitchen. "Dad, who sent these?" She nodded toward the flowers.

"I'm not that nosy. I didn't read the card," he told her. A bit of shaving cream was clinging to his face, the spicy scent of his aftershave reminding her of *him*.

"Do you remember the name of the florist that delivered these? That's what I meant." She wanted to jump up and down, and another part of her wanted to fall to the floor in a heap of despair. Not yet, she thought, not yet.

Her father rubbed his cheeks. "No, they were on the front porch when I came in from the garage. I can find out who delivered them if it's important to you."

It was, but she didn't want to let him know exactly *how* important. She needed to calm down. No one knew she was here, other than Maria. She hadn't told her exact plans to those she worked with. All they knew was that she was suffering from major burnout on the job, had a new baby to care for, and had quit her job as a reporter. That much was true.

"You're upset," her mother said, stating the obvious. "What can we do?"

She needed to think. "Uh, let's bathe Caroline. Here in the sink if that's okay. I didn't have a bathtub in Italy. Just a small shower. She's used to sinks. I'll just run upstairs to get her things." Before either could ask why the flowers caused such a drastic change, she raced upstairs to her room. She closed and locked the door. Spying her tote on the bed, she dumped the contents into a pile in the center of the bed. After searching for the card with the number she was to use in a life-or-death emergency, she sat on the bed and stared at the number, which she'd memorized just in case she lost the card. *Calm down. Take deep breaths.* She closed her eyes, forcing herself to focus. Flowers weren't life and death. She needed to take that bouquet apart to look for any possible clues but couldn't do so in front of her parents.

She heard Caroline's cries from downstairs. Bath supplies. That's what she'd come for, and a few minutes of privacy. One thing at a time. She found the bottle of baby wash, grabbed a bath toy she'd picked up in Target, a diaper and a set of pajamas from her luggage. Her mom and dad probably thought she was losing her mind or suffering from postpartum depression. Her behavior was anything but normal.

Before they came looking for her, she crammed the contents of her tote back inside but stuck the card in the pocket of the yellow shorts she still wore.

Hurrying downstairs, she took another deep breath before returning to the kitchen. "Here we go," she said in an overly cheerful tone.

"Mom, could you get me a washcloth and towel? I forgot baby washcloths when we were at the store." She'd never had baby washcloths, only the thin muslins she'd purchased in Italy. Her lies were pathetic. "Actually, I've never used a real washcloth on this little girl," she said as she washed out the new farm sink her parents had added when they'd updated the kitchen. *It's huge,* she thought. "Mom, get an extra towel. I have a feeling this is going to get very messy."

Love, Gio.

She couldn't erase those words, no matter how hard she tried. *Focus, Samantha!*

"Would you like me to take over?" her mother asked. "I think you need to take some time for yourself. I was going to say you needed to relax, but we had enough of that today."

"You didn't say—how was the spa?" her dad asked as he took Caro's bath supplies from her.

"We took a bath in a teacup," her mother piped in. "Other than that, we plan to make this a habit. It was eye-opening. That champagne you ordered was a bit much, but we managed to sober up." She shook her head, "Charles, let's focus on getting this baby into the sink."

"Mom, Dad, I've got this, really. I appreciate the help though."

She filled the sink with warm water and moved a bottle of dish detergent and a scrubbing sponge out of her daughter's reach. Holding her arms out for her baby, she realized she hadn't undressed her.

"Let me," her mother said, taking Caro's onesie off with one hand, the other encircling her daughter. Then she whipped the disposable diaper off in less than ten seconds. "Now, little miss, let Grammy get to work." With expert movements, her mother placed Caroline in the sink.

Gurgles and hands splashing in the water assured Samantha that Mom had this.

"Hand me the baby wash."

Sam did as told.

"And that squeaky thing."

Squirting a small amount of the golden baby wash into the sink, her mother sloshed one hand in the water while holding Caro's arm. "Bubbles! See the bubbles?"

The baby's eyes grew in size, and she began splashing her little hands in the water. When it splashed her face, she took in a couple of quick breaths, then giggled out loud. Sam relaxed a bit, seeing how much fun her daughter was having while Grammy bathed her. Caroline spent the next fifteen minutes splashing about while her grandmother gently washed her and her dark curly hair. When Helena took her from the sink, she adjusted the taps and rinsed her with clean, warm water.

Wrapping Caroline in the giant bath towel Charles held out, they took her into the front room and placed her on the sofa, diapering and dressing her in the pink-and-white pajamas. The two of them looked like pros; then she remembered they'd been through this with her. Once the baby was dressed, her dad went to the kitchen and returned with a fresh bottle.

He took Caroline to the rocking chair, placed her in his arms, and began feeding and rocking her, singing a lullaby Sam had never heard.

Caroline's eyes drooped, her little mouth lost its suction on her bottle, and her father gently placed her against his chest, continuing to rock her. "Why don't you tell us why those flowers upset you?"

"Can you really find out who delivered them? It's important," she said.

"I can. Let's get this little gal to bed first, then I'll make a few phone calls." Samantha followed him upstairs to her room and watched as he gently placed Caroline in her temporary bed. Before heading back downstairs, she turned on the night-light and left the door open so she could hear her if the baby woke up.

Downstairs, her mother had cleaned up and made a pot of coffee. Seeing the roses again sent Sam's mind racing. She should've taken them to her room.

"Coffee? I have a key lime pie if either of you want dessert," her mother said. "Or leftover cake," she added.

Samantha was too keyed up for sugar or caffeine. "I'm okay," she said.

"Charles?"

"I'll have a cup of that coffee. Never had a chance to make a pot this morning after you girls left. The little lady kept me on my toes all day, but I did manage to heat up a can of chicken noodle soup for lunch. Caro loved it."

Sam just shook her head. "Good to know when I'm out of baby food."

Seated around the table, her dad took the house phone, a notepad, and a pencil. Before he spoke, he took a sip of coffee. This reminded her so much of her dad's days as a police officer. Organized and patient, all that she wasn't.

"Can I see the card?" he asked.

"No."

He nodded his head. "Okay. I take it the message is private."

"It's just strange," she said.

"It would help if you could tell me, but if you can't, I can call Roger."

"Roger from across the street? How can he help?" Samantha asked.

"He's the nosiest man in the neighborhood," her mother reminded her.

How could she have forgotten? He'd spotted her on more than one occasion slipping in through the garage when she'd missed curfew. Always called her parents, too.

"Then let's see what he knows," she said, becoming impatient with the entire situation. She felt anger toward whoever had sent the flowers. Knowing they couldn't be legitimate hurt more than she wanted to admit. But she'd keep those thoughts to herself.

Her dad dialed Roger's number, and Roger picked up immediately. "Rog, how's it going? Good, good. Listen,

I was wondering if you were home today, say around two, two thirty? Yes, I was in the garage, and there was a floral delivery. I wondered if you happened to see the name of the florist."

Samantha listened to her dad's end of the conversation.

"Okay, pal, I owe you one. Thanks." Charles ended the call.

"Did he see who it was?" she asked, not caring that she sounded overanxious.

"He did, but said it wasn't a florist. A black car. Said he couldn't tell if it was a man or woman, but he did see a black car. That's all. Does this help?"

A jumble of thoughts slammed through her head. "Did he happen to see what make the car was?"

"Sam, are you being stalked? If so, we need to file a report. This isn't something to mess with. People can do crazy stuff," her dad said, and she heard in his voice how seriously he was taking this.

Was she being stalked? It was possible, but if that were the case, why leave a note? Didn't stalkers like to remain anonymous?

"I'm sure I'm not being stalked, but is anyone ever sure? I don't have a clue who would want to stalk me, or why. Remember, I've been out of the country for three years. If I had a stalker, I would think . . . I don't know what to think, honestly. Let's just say the card has information on it that only I would know."

"A name?" he probed. "A clue?"

"Dad, I've told you I can't talk about certain things, and this is one of them. At least I think it is. I need to make a phone call." She didn't dare tell him she'd need a secure phone. "Are you and mom okay keeping an eye on Caroline while I take a drive? I need to think. I do my best thinking when I'm driving."

"I don't believe this is a good idea, Sam. We don't know what you're thinking. And not knowing is alarming. Can't you just walk around the block or something? There's a convenience store a few blocks over, maybe go grab a soda or something?" her mother suggested. "At least we'll know where you are."

"That's a good idea. I'll have my cell phone, so call if you have to, but whatever you do, just check on Caro."

"Samantha, if that child is in danger of any kind, I want to know. Now. Not after the fact."

"She isn't, I'm sure of it. This is what I can't talk about, but she's okay. Just keep an eye on her. She might wake up and want another bottle or something. I'll be back as soon as I get this sorted out. I need to get some cash. Be right back."

She needed to see Caro. She took three twenties out of her wallet, gave her daughter a light kiss on the cheek, then headed downstairs, where her parents waited in the front room, each as white as the walls.

"Mom, Dad, listen. I'm fine, and Caroline isn't in any danger. I need to handle this now. I won't be long, and I've got my cell phone." Before she slipped and said something she shouldn't, she hurried out the front door, heading for the convenience store. She jogged as fast as she could without attracting the attention of drivers in the cars that passed. She was thankful that joggers were accepted as normal, even at night in this muggy heat. When she spotted the lights of the store, she stopped, got her breath, and entered the store. She smiled at the cashier, a young guy, in his early twenties with tattoos covering all visible parts of his body.

"Help ya?" he called out in a deep Southern accent. "I can direct ya to whatever ya need."

"Uh, sure. I need some"—she felt like an idiot, but what

the heck—"feminine things." That was the only way she was going to get out of here fast. "And a cell phone. You have those little disposable ones? Mine broke last night, and I haven't had a chance to get a new one." If someone were to question this guy, he'd have enough detailed information to identify her, which shouldn't be a problem, but she knew better than to reveal too much. She really had no reason to hide her whereabouts.

"Aisle two on the lady stuff, and I got the phones here at the register."

"Thanks," she said as she located a box of tampons and placed them on the counter. She'd added a chocolate bar, and a Coke, too.

"You want to take a look at what we got to offer? There are four different models."

"I'll just take the least expensive. As I said, I'm going to get mine repaired or replaced, whatever." She shot him her best smile.

"Then you'll want a Tracfone. They're just over twenty bucks, plus tax. You get a full hour of free talk time, then ya gotta buy a card with extra minutes if ya want to talk longer. I'd go with one of the better ones, but hey, it's a free country, so ya get whatever you want."

"Just the cheap one, please. I need to uh, get home. I had this"—she pointed to the box of tampons—"happen." Hopefully, he had enough sense to put two and two together.

"Uh, sure, but I got a ladies' room if ya need it," he said as he tried to pull a plastic bag apart.

"No, I'll be fine, but thanks. Just this," she said, sliding the chocolate bar and the Coke closer to him.

"Sure thing," he said as he scanned the items. "Twenty-six dollars and seventy-eight cents, that's your total, ma'am. Biggest purchase I've had all night."

She pulled two twenties from her pocket and slapped them on the counter. She wanted to tell him to keep the change, but that would most likely bring on another round of questions she didn't need or have time for. He counted out the change and said, "Hope ya don't mind a few ones, or I'll have to get some tens from the safe."

"That's fine." She held out her hand, then stuffed the ones in her pocket, snatched the bag, and raced out of the store before he had another reason to keep her there.

As soon as she was a couple of blocks from her parents' house, she ripped open the hard plastic and took out the phone. She used the flashlight on her iPhone to read through the basic instructions. The phone was charged. She only needed a few minutes. Before she could stop herself, she punched in the number she'd memorized, then checked it against the paper she'd written it on before hitting SEND. Unsure who would answer, she hit the SEND button and hoped for the best.

"What?" an angry male voice asked.

"Uh, I was given this number—"

"I know. Why are you calling?" the angry voice shouted.

She wanted to scream into the phone, wanted to relieve herself of the twenty-seven months of worry she'd endured. Samantha was through dealing with this mystery.

"I'm calling because I received a bouquet of flowers with a card that said, 'Love, Gio.' I realize that isn't life or death to you, whoever you are, but I need answers!" She was shouting now and didn't care.

"Shit," the voice replied in a much calmer tone.

"Shit? That's all you've got to say?" Her breathing became rapid, her heart racing. "Who are you?"

"Gio didn't tell you?"

"Tell me what?"

"Man, this is messed up, but you have this number, so you need to be told."

No! No! No!

This wasn't the way it was supposed to end, not like this. On the phone with a stranger. She refused to accept it. She would go back to Afghanistan, leave Caroline with her parents, then she could search for answers herself. It's what she knew best.

"Lady, are you there?"

"Yes," she answered. Any hope she had was gone.

"If you can tell me how many flowers were in the bouquet, I can answer your questions."

"What?"

"How many?" he pushed her.

"I don't know! Why would I count them?"

"Then this conversation is over," he said.

"Wait! Wait, don't hang up. I can tell you the number, just give me a minute, please, I'm begging you." She pleaded as she dialed her parents' number on her iPhone. Her dad answered on the first ring. "Dad, listen, I don't have time for questions, I'm okay, but I need you to go count the exact number of flowers in the vase. Please, just do it, and I'll explain why later."

She held the Tracfone to her ear. "Are you still there?"

"Not for long," he said.

"Please, just one more minute." She definitely did not like this man.

"Not a second more," he replied.

"Samantha, are you there?" Her father's voice was coming from her iPhone.

"Yes, Dad. How many?"

"Twenty-seven," he answered.

She put the Tracfone back up to her ear. "Twenty-seven," she said.

Silence. "Are you there? I said twenty-seven!"

"Yeah, just had to check something. So, yes, that's the right number. There's one last thing," he said. "You're supposed to know the significance of that number."

"It's the number of months I've known Jonathan Giovannozzi. Is that the answer you're looking for?" Damn, this man, she would strangle him if she knew where to find him.

"Yep, looks like you've answered all the magic questions. We'll be in touch, so don't call this number again." Click.

Sam hit RESEND, but all she heard was a recording telling her the number was no longer in service. She dropped down in the grass, her hands shaking, her iPhone ringing. "What?" she shouted into the phone.

"Sam, I'm coming after you, stay where you are," her dad said, then hung up.

Needing to get ahold of herself, she stayed put. More confused than ever, she wished she'd left well enough alone. Why had she been given the number if it wasn't meant to be used? Yes, they'd said life and death. A note with Gio's name could mean life or death to her. Confused, she tried to remember what the man who had given her the number had said.

Call only in life or death? Can confirm life or death?

She didn't remember the exact words! It'd been so long, and her life completely changed once she found out she was pregnant with Caroline. She'd forgotten what she'd been told to forget and took the job with the Associated Press. Practically lived as a hermit in Italy. Felt like she'd been watched though she didn't know why or who it could've been. And now she hadn't accomplished anything other than upsetting her parents, who probably thought she was losing her mind, and she'd left her child to chase . . . what? An anonymous voice? Drawing in a deep breath, she closed her eyes and didn't try to stop her tears.

Chapter 8

"Don't skip one word," her dad repeated. "Start over, from the beginning. I realize there are issues you can't disclose. Now, focus on the day you learned whatever it is you can't discuss."

Samantha had spent the past two hours sobbing, trying to explain what had happened without breaking her word. "It's been so long, and there were so many days, they all seemed the same. I'd learned some intel that I knew had to be reported, but I didn't know who to trust. This is the part where you're both going to hate me, but I told my . . . husband."

Her parents looked at her, then at each other. "Say that again," her father said, his tone letting her know he wasn't going to take "no" for an answer this time.

"I told my husband." There, now they knew.

Silence hung in the room like an old odor.

"Mom, Dad?"

"Sam, why didn't you tell us? Is this man Caroline's father?" Her mother's eyes filled with tears. "I need to understand why you wouldn't tell your family. Not only did you hide our grandchild from us, now we learn you've a husband hiding out there somewhere, too."

"It wasn't supposed to be this way. I know that's not the answer you both want, but it's the truth. Wartime, life and death. It was crazy over there. I met Gio not long after I went to Afghanistan. We fell madly in love, really. He's a good man—was a good man."

"Why are you speaking of him in the past tense? Do you know for a fact that he's dead?" her dad demanded.

"I think that's what the phone call meant."

"You think, but you're not sure? Sam, put that damned reporter's hat on and think! Let's track the number. I'll go door-to-door and see if anyone can identify the vehicle that delivered those flowers. Between the two of us, we can figure this out. Never give up on someone until you have proof of death. I learned that many years ago, and you should know better, especially in your line of work. Now, get that number, and I'll see what I can find out."

She pulled the rumpled paper from her pocket and gave it to her father. "Good luck," she said.

"I need to check on Caroline," Sam said, as soon as her father picked up his cell phone. She wasn't sure if she wanted to know more than she did already. Jon—*Gio*—knew how to find her, knew where she was from, who she worked for. If he'd needed to contact her, it wasn't like her life was a secret.

Like his.

She saw that Caroline was sound asleep. *Poor baby,* she thought. What a crappy start she'd given her. But she hadn't had a choice. When Gio disappeared, she knew that he must have thought that their quick marriage was a mistake.

And this was right after she'd told him about . . .

Before she could change her mind, she raced downstairs. Her mother was still sitting on the sofa, her dad in the kitchen talking in harsh whispers to one of his buddies in the police department.

"Mom, I might've figured this out. I need to talk to you and Dad. Now. Can you get him off the phone? Please?"

Her mother hurried into the kitchen and yanked on her dad's shirt. "Charles, I need you to put the phone down right now." He placed his hand over the phone. "Lena, this better be important."

"Sam thinks she's onto something. She needs to talk to you."

He returned to his call. "Get back to me ASAP," he said, then tossed the phone on the table.

"What?" was all he said when he looked at her.

"The intel that I discovered, I told Gio about it. It wasn't too long after I told him that he disappeared. I hung around, waited, but after a few months, I knew the marriage didn't mean anything. Then I found out I was pregnant. I had to focus on my baby, my health. I stopped reporting then. I had to get away from the front lines, the bombing, the horror of it all. I had to think of her, and I moved to Italy."

"Why didn't you return to the States?" her mother asked.

"Jon said he had family in Italy. I thought if I could locate his family, I would find him. I went to Rome, Venice, used what knowledge I had to search for his family. Nothing. I spent a few weeks in Florence and Milan, but if he had family there, I couldn't locate anyone who knew him, so I went to Verona, and that's where Caroline was born. Italy was beautiful—it's Caroline's birthplace—but after all that time, I knew I had to come home. I wanted Caro to have a normal life, and the tiny apartment we lived in was so small, it barely held our clothes. I had money, but that didn't matter. I knew I had to come back to Naples. Life was so jumbled, and confusing, and now I've made it even worse. I didn't know what to do, I still don't. I trusted Gio, I would swear he was a good man." She broke down in tears again.

"Caroline Renee, sit," her mother directed.

She sat down in the kitchen.

"Charles, can you check on the baby?"

"Sure," he said, and headed upstairs.

"She's fine, Mother. I just checked on her."

"What was Gio's place of employment? Where did he go to college?"

"He studied law. At Harvard. I think he . . . he was writing a novel when I met him."

"Why write a book in Afghanistan?"

"He said it was part of his main character's history. You of all people should know how authors research locations, working all those years in the library."

"Did you ever read any of his work?" her mother asked.

Samantha realized that she hadn't. "No, I thought it was too private. I was a writer, too, a different kind, but I didn't like having my colleagues read my reports until I was about to go live. Writers are funny that way, so I never pushed him."

"What can you remember about him that is significant? Anything he liked, disliked, his favorite books, TV programs, his political stance, anything besides that he went to Harvard?"

She thought over these simple everyday-life things, and the only concrete answer she could come up with was his alma mater.

"Charles, you can come downstairs now," her mother said.

As soon as her dad returned to the kitchen, his cell phone rang. "Stewart here," he said. "Absolutely. Send it now," he said into the phone, then pushed the END button. "Raymond thinks he's got information on the phone number."

Sam jumped out of her chair. "What kind of information?"

"Charles, before you say a word, Sam's Gio is a Harvard Law School graduate."

She looked at her mother. "Why does that matter?"

Her dad sat down. "Your mom is right. It matters. It's starting to make sense now."

"Then please fill me in. This is my life and my daughter's father we're talking about. If you know something, don't hold back, I need to know."

"Raymond is sending an e-mail attachment."

"Okay, and what is in the e-mail?"

"We're about to find out," he said as he used his cell phone to check the e-mail.

He read the e-mail, then opened the attachment. It was a photo. He looked at her mother, nodded, then gave his phone to her. "Do you recognize this man?"

Epilogue

One week later

"She looks just like her daddy," Gio said into the phone. He looked at Sam and winked, holding Caro in his arms. He'd barely put her down since he arrived. "Mom, trust me, she's beautiful. You're going to fall in love with both of them, I promise. Yes, I will. I promise."

"I can't stop staring at you," Sam said. Gio did not look like the heavily bearded writer she'd married and had a child with. "You look so . . . normal, but handsome."

"You didn't think I was handsome when you married me?" he admonished her, pulling her close. "You can't imagine the hell I went through trying to get word to you without blowing my cover. The phone was the key. It was my only way to keep you safe."

It was simple, he'd explained last night to her parents. He'd been recruited by the Central Intelligence Agency after college. He'd been around the world, but hadn't really made his claim to fame until Samantha told him where three of the Taliban's top militants were hiding. She was in danger if her discovery could ever be traced back to her. He convinced his superiors to allow him to infiltrate as an undercover operative, which took months. The details were sparse, and he'd told his wife and in-laws that there was little more he could say, but they should just watch the news over the next few weeks.

"I can't believe I didn't figure this out. As soon as Dad traced that phone, I knew there was hope that you were alive, and you better have one damn good explanation for leaving me."

"I'm sorry, Sam. I counted the months, and thought you'd know when I sent the twenty-seven roses. I'm so sorry that I missed our daughter's birth, all this *life* I missed. I am going to try and make it up to all of you, I promise."

Gio was tall, his olive skin an exact match to Caroline's, his eyes as dark as she remembered. Sam couldn't get enough of him. A week ago, her world had gone spinning out of control. And look at her now.

"You know, Samantha and I have been discussing a wedding," her mother informed Gio. "You missed Mother's Day, but what about a Father's Day wedding?"

Samantha hadn't discussed this with him yet, but what a gift it would be to all of them, most of all to their daughter.

"A June wedding on Father's Day, huh? Not a date I'd forget, that's for sure. I'm all yours, sweet girl. Whatever you want," Gio cooed to the infant in his arms.

Charles cleared his throat. "I know this isn't about me, but when I thought you'd abandoned a pregnant woman, I wanted a piece of your rear end, but knowing what you were doing, and why, I just want to shake your hand."

"Absolutely, sir," Gio said. "What is this now, the tenth time?"

"Dad likes you, so you'd best shake his hand anytime he asks," Samantha teased.

"I'll shake hands, anytime, sir. Now, back to that wedding we were talking about. I'd want a small wedding," he said, his tone serious. "Just our family. Then we can have a big celebration later if you want," Gio said, his attention focused totally on Samantha and Caroline.

"I thought you would want a big Italian wedding," her father said to Gio.

"I don't have family, just me and Mom. Dad passed when I was in high school, and Mom never remarried. Being only children was one of the things Sam and I had in common. We both knew we wanted a family, a large family. Maybe five or six little ones," he said, his dark eyes sparkling.

"I think we'd better talk about that," Samantha said. "Let's enjoy this little one for a while, then we can work on starting a brother or sister for Caro."

"Did you tell your parents about the name?" Gio asked.

"I didn't! With everything going on, and the way I introduced them to her, they never asked, and I never told them. Mom, Dad, Caroline is Gio's mother's name, and, of course, we all know where Helena came from. If we'd had a boy, he would've been called Jonathan Charles. Gio's father was Jonathan, too. We talked about this right after we married. I really didn't think we'd have kids so soon, but I wouldn't have it any other way."

All the nights alone, the fears, the worry seemed nothing more than a distant memory. Life for their daughter had started out a bit shaky, but now that Gio was home, and she was really home, Caroline would only remember these times. Someday, when she was older, she would take her to her other home country, show her where she had been born, the little apartment she'd spent the first few months of her life. Though Gio was an American by birth, his roots were as important to him as hers were to her. They planned to teach Caroline Italian when she was old enough, and Sam had a feeling this little sprite would be a fast learner.

Though Samantha had spent Mother's Day at that ritzy spa with her mother, having a little too much champagne and way more pampering than she'd ever wanted, she knew she would always remember the week *after* that day as much as her first Mother's Day.

"Hey, where is my bride?" Gio asked, pretending he couldn't find her though she stood next to him.

"Don't you dare sneak off and make me hunt you down."

"No way, Mr. Giovannozzi. I promise you, I'm not going to let you or our daughter out of my sight."

"I'll hold you to that, Mrs. Giovannozzi," he said, then passed Caroline to Charles. Not caring who saw them, he pulled her into his arms and kissed her long and hard. There was no way she would ever let this man get away from her again.

Always and forever, she thought, as his kiss made her dreams come true.

Blue Hollow Falls: New Beginnings

DONNA KAUFFMAN

To the newlyweds, Mitch and Alissa
May your new beginning
lead to many wonderful tomorrows

Chapter 1

"**O**ut!" Katie MacMillan herded her brother and her brother-in law's eldest sibling to the door of the sunroom. She kept going until they were all out in the great room of the lovely mountain A-frame her sister now called home. "Pippa's on bed rest. What part of that needs further explaining to you lads?" Her Irish accent was more crisp-edge than lilt.

"Well, to be fair," Cassian MacMillan said, smiling and utterly unrepentant as was the norm for her charming older brother, "our dear sis is presently reclining on a lovely padded longue, so I don't see how our visiting is causing any undue stress." He raised his voice so Pippa could hear him all the way in the sunroom. "We bring only joy and good cheer wherever we go!"

Katie hustled Cash and Aiden across the great room. "Along with a constant stream of chatter and flipping television stations, arguing whether Manchester United will beat Liverpool—"

"As if that's in question," Cash said with a snort. "I'll be taking that twenty off you this time tomorrow, mate," he added, shooting a confident grin toward Aiden.

"Oh, you think so, do you?" Aiden replied good-naturedly. Aiden Brogan was the only brother of Pippa's husband, Seth. There were four sisters as well. Thankfully, not all of them were visiting at once, though each one had managed to "pop in" at some point during her sister's pregnancy. As if casual visits were possible, given none of them even lived in the same state, or on the same coast.

There were a lot of Brogans, it was true, but there were just as many MacMillans. Pippa and Katie had three other brothers in addition to Cash. They'd each managed to drop in over the past trimester or two as well. All the way from Ireland, in fact, along with other assorted cousins and her parents. Seth's parents had come out, too. *You'd think this was the first baby in this generation for either family, not the dozenth or so*, Katie thought as she continued nudging the two men toward the front door.

"All I know is I've been here less than twenty minutes and you've exhausted my patience," Katie told her brother.

To be fair, her family had thought Pippa would be in Ireland for the last few months of her pregnancy, and for the birth, so the visits weren't entirely unexpected. No MacMillan in their line had been born on anything other than Irish soil. But Pippa's health, and the baby's welfare, had, of course, come first. So, they'd simply hopped a flight. Or two.

Or ten.

The equally expansive Brogan clan was mostly located across the country on the West Coast. When Pippa had been put on travel restriction by her doctor with four months still to go, they'd also made a habit of suddenly finding reasons to hop a flight to the Blue Ridge Mountains of Virginia. Loving gestures all, but even when it was family, and they did their best to help, there was still an additional strain put on the hostess.

All of which had prompted Pippa and Seth to finally call in the cavalry. A cavalry of one. Namely her. Katie might be the youngest of her clan, but she was arguably the toughest of the lot, given she'd had to contend with all five of her siblings from birth onward. She wasn't the least bit intimidated by the prospect of sibling-wrangling, hers or Seth's. She also happened to be the personal assistant and best mate to her world-renowned folk singer sister, a job she'd held since graduating university just as Pippa's star had risen with unexpected swiftness.

Even when Pippa had started splitting her time between Ireland and Blue Hollow Falls after she and Seth had tied the knot, Katie had mostly performed her duties from their home base in Dublin. However, when Pippa's pregnancy hit a few health snags, Pippa and Seth had ultimately decided to stay in Blue Hollow Falls and have the baby there. The thought being that Pippa would have a better chance of the peace and quiet she needed if she was tucked away from both of their clans.

That had been two months ago. The visitation situation had gotten completely out of control since.

Katie had only just arrived. And given the scene she'd walked into, none too soon. If Aiden had been surprised to see Pippa's baby sister all but physically remove him and Cash from the room, he hadn't shown it. Katie hid a private smile. With four sisters of his own, she was pretty sure Aiden knew better.

Aiden turned to Cash as Katie swung open the front door. "Just because I'm new to your beloved soccer teams doesn't mean I don't know—"

"Football, mate," Cash corrected.

"No," Aiden countered with a grin. "That's what the Seahawks play. You come back to Seattle with me and I'll show you some football."

"You want sport, mate, rugby is the real men's game." This came from the kitchen behind them.

Katie whirled around to discover Hudson Walker stationed in front of the big, stainless steel Wolf stove there. He was the head chef at a local gastropub owned by one of Seth's best friends, and Katie knew, firsthand, just how good Hudson was at his job.

"Oh my God," Katie said. "There's more of you?" He must have come in and made himself right at home while she'd been trying to get Cash and Aiden out of the sunroom.

Hudson merely held up his hands, a spatula gripped in one of them. He was grinning, too. Apparently, not a single one of them realized the delicacy of her sister's current situation. "I got permission," Hudson said, his Aussie accent adding even more of an international flavor to the conversation. "Seth knows I'm here. I heard you were arriving today, and I offered to stop by and whip up a little something for you all to have for dinner, on my way in to the mill. One less thing for you to contend with while you settle in."

Her annoyance dipped at that lovely bit of news. "That is incredibly thoughtful of you," she said, and meant it. She'd forgotten how much Blue Hollow Falls was like Donegal, where all of the MacMillans had been born and raised, and where many of them, her parents included, still lived. Everyone pitching in, everyone looking out for one another.

She'd been in the Falls the Christmas before last for Pippa and Seth's wedding, and again eight months ago, over Christmas, to play maid of honor when Moira Brogan and Hudson had gotten married. Katie couldn't wait to catch up with her former college roommate. Moira was actually the reason the Brogans and MacMillans had crossed paths in the first place.

On the flight over, Katie had been thinking how it felt

like ages since she'd been there. Now, standing in her sister's lovely mountain home, overlooking their vineyard, seeing Hudson again, it felt like just yesterday she'd watched him say the most romantic of "I do's" with her best friend. Blue Hollow Falls had felt like Katie's home away from home since the first time she'd visited.

It's your permanent home now, she reminded herself, excited by the change in her circumstances, even while feeling the expected stab of homesickness, all at the same time.

Cash put his hand on the doorframe to temporarily prevent his ejection from the house and turned in time to drop a noisy kiss to the top of her head. "We're glad you're here keeping the peace for our Pippa, Katie Kat," he said, all cheerful grins and sparkling MacMillan blue eyes. "It's happy I am to see your pretty face."

"Stop being adorable," she groused, but with a grudging smile. Cassian had only to flash those dimples and her defenses were gone. Only eighteen months apart in age, the two of them had always been close, despite her wanting to strangle him half the time. She kissed him on the cheek, then impulsively gave him a quick, tight hug. "It's good to see you, too, Cazzie," she said, feeling even more nostalgic after hearing him use her childhood nickname and using his in return. "It's been ages."

He nodded. "Since we were here together for Pippa's wedding."

It was hard to believe, but true. She leaned back and took a moment to truly take him in. "Well, whatever it is that's taken you on a gallivant this time, it looks good on you. I want to catch up on all of it before you go."

"I could say the same about you," he said. "Stop growing up on me so fast, will you?"

"Well, at least my age still starts with a two," she teased, then scooted sideways before he could give her a pinch.

"And it's fine I'd be to keep it that way," he replied. "If only because it makes me feel less ancient knowing I'm just a wee bit older than the youthful beauty that is you."

Katie rolled her eyes. "Only you could find a way to compliment yourself in the guise of complimenting me."

Aiden just shook his head. "Hey, I've got more than ten years and a handful of kids on both of you. I should head out before you two have me using a walker to get to my car."

They all laughed, and Cash said, "I'm going to head down to the stone barn and see if I can give my brother-in-law a hand for a bit." He smiled at his sister. "Don't worry. I'll be bunking up at Pippa's cabin. Seth told me you're staying here till the blessed event and offered me her old place." He leaned in and dropped another kiss, this time on her temple. "Don't worry, Katie Kat, I'm only here for a few days and I promise I'll call before dropping by."

"See that you do," she warned, but was so thrilled to hear she'd get to spend a little time with her favorite brother, the warning held little heat.

Cash offered his hand to Aiden. "You can leave my football winnings with the sheriff here," he said with a cheeky grin. "Give my best to Mary and to your delightful daughters. They're probably old enough to drive already, so it's just as well I didn't get the chance to see them."

Aiden flattened his palm on his chest. "Don't give an old man a heart attack now. I'm having a hard enough time with them gone in school all day. I may be the only parent alive who was happy when summer vacation finally got here."

"Aw," Katie said, and smiled. "That's a lovely thing to say. If only more men were like you."

Aiden grinned. "We can't help it. It's in the Brogan DNA. We'll see how the vineyard fares once Seth has a wee one so close by."

After a quick handshake between the two men, Cash was out the door and heading toward the old stone barn that doubled as the winery's tasting room.

Katie smiled up at the towering man who filled the doorframe. Aiden was like his brother in that way. A family of Vikings, the Brogans were.

"Are you, Mary, and the girls staying for dinner?" Katie was there to keep the traffic flow down, but given Aiden and his family were already in town, she felt she needed to at least be hospitable. Besides, she loved all the Brogans and could handle any necessary hostess duties from now on. Pippa could remain out of the fray. Katie nodded toward Hudson in the kitchen. "You must be enjoying not having to play chef while you're away from your restaurant. And your brother-in-law puts on quite a spread, himself. I'm sure there will be plenty."

Aiden chuckled. "You'd be right about that on both counts. We all shared a big breakfast together this morning and I doubt I'll have to eat again until I'm back on the West Coast. I think we've been in your hair—or your sister's hair—quite enough. I dropped Mary and the kids off down at the cidery. Once I round them up, we'll be heading to the airport." Now it was his turn to flash a charming grin in the face of her disappointment. "They've been by already to say their good-byes, so you'll have fewer troops to marshal at any rate." He winked. "Until the next batch arrives."

She leaned in closer, and with a wry note in her voice, said, "As the eldest Brogan, I don't suppose you could help me out and cancel any future flight plans for your various other family members, at least until the baby arrives?" She wasn't without her own skills and smiled winningly up at him. "Take one for the team, as you Yanks say?"

He laughed and nodded. "I'll see what I can do. We're not heading home just yet. We're making an adventure out of this. We travel from here to visit Mary's folks in South Carolina for a week. Will be the girls' first time seeing the Atlantic Ocean." He chuckled. "This is the longest I've been away from the restaurant since my honeymoon."

Katie beamed approvingly. "Well, good for you, then. I'm sure your wife and the girls are thrilled that you're getting to do this all together. It sounds quite marvelous." She gave him a quick hug. "Seth and Pippa said you were planning to come out in a few months for Thanksgiving. So, we'll all be together again soon enough." Her smile deepened. "Even better, Baby Brogan will be here by then."

Aiden nodded. "I think Seth and Pippa are planning on being in Ireland for Christmas, so the timing is good all around. And everyone gets some time with the newest member of the family."

Hudson joined them just then, and gave his brother-in-law a handshake that turned into a quick back-slapping hug. "I'll follow you out," he said to Aiden. Turning to Katie, he added, "Stew is on the stove, rolls in the oven on warm. There's a breakfast casserole I made earlier cooling on the counter for tomorrow, and some fresh greens and vegetables in the fridge." He winked. "And Pippa's favorite orange sherbet in the freezer. I picked some up on the way here."

Katie gave him a quick squeeze. "You're a prince among men." She kissed his cheek. "Thank you. And tell Moira I'll be calling just as soon as I'm settled in. I texted her on the way from the airport but haven't had time to see if she replied."

"Give her a call later," Hudson said. "I know she wants to see you as soon as you can make time."

Katie could have sworn there was a note of urgency in Hudson's voice, but his expression was as open and friendly as usual. She nodded. "I will make certain we touch base today."

"Great," he said. He turned to Aiden. "I'll follow you down to Mabry's, say one last good-bye to your flock. I know Moira has really enjoyed getting to play auntie to your girls the past few days."

Katie waved and watched as the two men continued their conversation on the way out to their respective vehicles. A quick glance toward the stone barn and the rows of vines beyond showed that things seemed to be moving along normally there as well.

Katie took a moment to breathe in the fresh mountain air, then closed the door and turned to lean back against it, appreciating the equally delicious scent of Hudson's stew. She let out a contented sigh. She was really here again. *And not just for a visit*, she reminded herself. She barely resisted the urge to hug herself and dance a little jig.

With the exception of her years at university in California, she'd spent her whole life living in Ireland. Aye, it was true she'd seen a goodly part of the world while touring with her older sister, but that wasn't the same as truly being in a new place. Settling in. Putting down roots. She'd loved her time in California, but nothing compared to the feeling she'd had the first time she'd come to see Moira in Blue Hollow Falls. "Something about this place," she murmured.

"Everybody gone?" Pippa asked as she slowly shuffled into the great room. "Something smells heavenly."

Katie smiled. "Hudson was here."

Pippa's eyes closed, a blissful expression on her face. "Bless that man."

"Bless your husband," Katie said. "I think he had a little something to do with that." She crossed the room and gently rubbed her sister's back as Pippa rested her elbows on the counter that separated the kitchen from the living and dining area and dipped her chin. Katie knew better than to scold and urge her back to bed. Pippa was not one for sitting still, so the past few months had been particularly challenging for her.

From their long phone conversations, Katie was well aware her sister was going stir-crazy, even while doing everything possible to make sure the baby stayed right where he or she was until her due date, which was still seven weeks away. "I'd ask how you're feeling, but . . ." She hadn't missed the swollen ankles or the fact that her sister's tiny frame looked as if it was presently housing half a football team inside it.

Pippa turned her head and smiled up at her much taller sister, looking weary. "I swear they delight in tap-dancing on my spine when I'm down or wrestling on top of my bladder when I'm up." She sighed as she straightened, lifting a hand when Katie went to help her. "I'm just up for a trip to the loo." Her smile was wry. "I've gotten doctor's permission for that much."

"Do you want to go back to the sunroom after?"

Pippa shook her head. "I thought I'd come lounge on your bed whilst you unpack. Catch up a bit." She shifted closer and slung an arm around her sister's waist. "I'm so very happy you're here, Kat."

Katie pressed her cheek on top of her sister's head, her heart filling with so many emotions, all of them good. "Me too."

Pippa's cell phone went off and she slid it from the side pocket sewn into the floaty, flowery pullover dress she had on. She glanced at the screen and sighed. "I already sent my response to the promo campaign for the new single," she grumbled, then squeaked when Katie slid the phone from her hands.

"You, go to the loo, then go lie down. I'll handle this."

It was a mark of how tired her sister was that she put up zero argument and started toward the guest bathroom located in the short hallway between the great room and the sunroom. Seth had built the glass-enclosed solarium onto the back of the house after their wedding, creating a space where Pippa could play her fiddle and guitar, and write music. Pippa had bought and kept the small cabin she'd stayed in when she'd first come to the Falls, with the intention of using it as a private studio and creative space. Instead, she'd found herself happier and more inspired staying home on the vineyard, so the addition had been built.

Pippa had offered the cabin to Katie once the baby arrived and she was out of any health-related danger, and Katie was admittedly excited to have a wee place of her own. Apparently, it looked like Cash was going to be staying there for the next few days at least, but that worked. With Pippa's pregnancy being so closely monitored, Katie and Seth had thought it best to keep the three of them under one roof.

Pippa had moved down from the master bedroom that dominated the upstairs loft, to the largest of the guest bedrooms at the far end of the house on the main floor. Katie would be staying in the room across the hall for the time being. She'd work from the small office area that had been set up off to one side in the solarium, which was where she headed now, Pippa's phone in hand.

She'd only gone three strides when she stopped dead in her tracks as what Pippa had said earlier fully sank in. Katie whirled around and stalked straight to the closed bathroom door. They'd been raised in a house with nine people—two parents, six kids, and their grandmother— and only two bathrooms to accommodate all of them, so modesty was not something any MacMillan had the luxury of indulging in. It was a measure of her hard-won self-control that she didn't simply walk right in and demand Pippa clarify.

Instead, she waited until Pippa opened the door. "You said 'they' were tap-dancing on your spine. What do you mean *they?*"

After a brief moment of surprise at finding her sister all but leaning on the bathroom door, Pippa didn't bother trying to pretend she didn't know exactly what her sister was referring to. "I wanted to tell you, I swear," she said, excitement and a healthy dose of trepidation lighting up her heretofore tired blue eyes.

"Oh my God," Katie said, her mouth dropping open, then snapping shut. "So . . . you are? Having twins? How could you not tell me? I mean—wait, Seth knows, right?" Her mind was scattering in a dozen different directions and she couldn't seem to organize her thoughts. *Twins!* She and Pippa were best-friend close, but that didn't mean they shared every last detail of their lives. Still, it was impossible to think her sister had kept something as big as this from her.

"Of course he does," Pippa said with a laugh. "But we haven't really told anyone else. Not our families, anyway. Seth has confided in his two closest mates, and I—"

"Told someone other than me?" Katie shouldn't be hurt

to hear that. It was her sister's prerogative to tell whomever she pleased.

"Addie Pearl knows," Pippa replied, and Katie immediately relaxed.

"Of course she does," Katie said with a laugh. "What doesn't Addie Pearl know?" Addison Pearl Whitaker, who was in her late seventies, was like the patron saint of the Falls. In this case, a patron saint who favored tie-dyed T-shirts, wore her steel gray hair in a braid that fell below her waist, and was rarely seen without a funky, hand-carved walking stick.

"Don't be mad that I didn't tell you sooner," Pippa said, sounding sincerely apologetic. "I just—it didn't feel right, telling you over the phone. Then there were the complications, and we were a bit scared to tell anyone anything until we were on sturdier ground. By then I knew you were coming." She took Katie's hands. "I wanted you here, I wanted you to know this way." She placed Katie's hands on her distended abdomen. "Like this."

Katie's eyes widened with amazement as she felt movement under her palms. "That's amazing."

"That's one way to put it," Pippa said with a tired laugh.

"It's no wonder you look like you're carrying an entire football team in there."

Pippa grinned. "Well, at the very least a decent center-forward and goalkeeper, if they have anything to say about it." She made a sudden grunt of discomfort and pressed her hand to her side. "Speaking of which."

Katie had already lifted her hands, but even through the softly pleated sundress she could see the way Pippa's stomach bulged and shifted. It was like witnessing that moment in a horror movie right before the monster erupts. It was also an utterly fascinating and unbelievable human life happening, all at the same time. Katie immediately started to steer Pippa back to the chaise longue in the sunroom, which was closest, but Pippa shook her head. "Your room."

"I don't think you need any more chitchat today," Katie said. "I'm here to play Sheriff Katie and maintain crowd control, but I'm also still your assistant and that means my job is to take care of you, too."

Pippa laughed at that, then gasped when one of the twins—*twins*—jabbed her again with a foot or an elbow, and she quickly opted to allow Katie to steer her back to her own bed in the main guest room.

"Honestly, I'm used to it now, mostly. I won't lie, though, it's still exciting and terrifying, like every other minute," Pippa told her. She had one hand pressed to her side, and the other gripping Katie's forearm as they both shuffled along. "I mean, on the one hand I can't wait to meet them and get started on this grand adventure. On the other, I can't help but wonder what in the world are we getting ourselves into, you know?"

"It's a little late to have second thoughts now," Katie said with a short laugh, still trying to take in the stunning news. "Ma and Dad don't know?"

Pippa shook her head. "Do you think we'd be able to keep all of them from moving in then?"

Katie laughed at that. "Good point." She helped Pippa up the little set of steps someone—Seth, probably—had built to make it easier for Pippa to maneuver herself onto the tall, deep mattress bed, only to have her sister's phone buzz yet again. Katie had forgotten she was still carrying it. Annoyed, she jammed the mobile into the hip pocket of her jeans and took a moment to make sure Pippa was comfortable, or as much as she could be, all things considered. Katie propped up the pillows behind her sister and handed her another one to put under her knees, then spread the crocheted throw their mother had made over her sister's bare legs and feet.

The phone vibrated once more as she took it from her pocket and Pippa went to reach for it, only Katie held it out of reach. "Sit," she told her sister sternly. "Stay. I'm going to the solarium, so you don't have to hear me haggle with Braxton over this ridiculous ad campaign." She turned Pippa's phone off and put it on the nightstand. "I'll call him back from my phone. Emergency texts only," Katie told her. "I'll come back and check on you when I'm done, then get myself unpacked and settled in." She'd boxed up everything in her flat in Dublin but had come with just two pieces of luggage. For now. The rest was in storage until she decided what she wanted. "It won't take me long."

Now Katie's phone started buzzing and the sisters both shared a rueful laugh. Katie was reminded of the parts of her job she didn't like. Wrangling with aggressive promotion managers being one of them. She was quite good at it, but that didn't mean she enjoyed it, and Braxton was about to get a piece of her mind. Seeing her sister's discomfort firsthand, knowing the stress she was under worrying about carrying the babies to term— babies, plural—only made Katie that much more determined to do what she'd come here to do. Other than Seth, anyone who wanted to so much as glance at Pippa was going to have to go through her.

She was still reeling from the stunning news that she was going to be an auntie to two brand-new wee babes, and at the same time, annoyed about Braxton's aggressive pestering, and now also worrying even more about her sister. She made a mental note to talk to Seth, find out if there was anything else she didn't know about, given she was going to be Pippa's frontline caregiver while Seth was out running the vineyard.

So, Katie was completely unprepared for the second shock she got when she turned to leave . . . the sight of a large, black-and-white photo hanging on the far wall of the room. There were several in fact. Though the others were in color. Rich, vibrant color. The vineyard was the subject, each one reflecting a completely different viewpoint. They were captivating, stunning even.

And Katie would have only needed to see one of them to know who had taken them.

She felt as if all the air had suddenly been sucked from the room. Or her lungs, anyway. She turned to Pippa, her expression slack, like she'd been sucker punched. Because she had been. "What are those?" she asked, when what she meant was, *Why are those?* As in, *Why are those here? In Blue Hollow Falls? Inside your house?*

The resigned and regretful look on her sister's face said it all, and Katie didn't want or need to hear any actual words after that.

"That was the other thing I wanted to tell you," Pippa said quietly, though she didn't otherwise apologize.

Nor should she. Declan MacGregor was a member of their family, even if he hadn't been born to it. An orphan and an outcast as a child, the misfit Scot had been left to pretty much fend for himself in the Irish countryside, seeing as the family who had taken in the ten-year-old boy saw him as little more than a pair of hands to work their farm chores. Until Cash had found him, that was. From that moment on, Declan had become part of the MacMillan clan. He was welcome anywhere they happened to be, because he was one of them. Including Blue Hollow Falls.

No, this wasn't about Declan. This was only about her. Not even Pippa truly understood all the undercurrents going on where Declan was concerned. Katie had kept her share of secrets, too, she supposed.

Katie lifted a hand to stop her sister from saying anything else. "Rest. I'm going to deal with Braxton and unpack. Then I want to hear every last detail about the babies. Babies, Pippa," she added in hushed awe. "And I'm not upset at all that you waited to tell me about them. I understand why you held off. Truly. And I'm thrilled for you both." She laughed. "All four of you. Wow." She didn't so much as glance at the wall behind her. "I don't need to know about those," she added, quite certain Pippa knew exactly what Katie was referring to. "He's an amazing photographer. Always has been. They're gorgeous. No one could capture this beautiful place so well as he did. It's fortunate that you get to enjoy his mastery, and I mean that." *And why wouldn't she*, Katie thought. Declan had never done a single thing wrong, not to her, or anyone else. It was hardly a crime not to love someone back now, was it?

Katie put a bright smile on her face and tried to look like she meant it. Part of her did mean it. The part that was trying hard not to allow the cavalcade of . . . everything to crash in on her at the mere mention of her first, and pitifully only, true love. Pitiful for so many reasons. Only the very least of which was that it had been unrequited. "And they have nothing to do with me," she added, which was painfully true. "So, it's none of my business." Seeing Pippa's worried expression, Katie walked back to the bed and quickly leaned down to kiss her sister on the forehead. "I mean it," she said, looking Pippa straight in the eye. Then she smiled again as she straightened, and it came naturally this time. "He came, he took photos, spent time with the fabulousness that is you, and left again."

"That's just it," Pippa whispered, regret filling her eyes

now. "He . . . well, he actually came with Cash the last time he was here."

Katie straightened now, trying to ignore the sick ball of dread curling up in her gut, wanting to deny where she knew this was going. This was her fresh start, her new place in the world, her very own life. One that came with just enough family members milling about for her to feel at home . . . and none of the parts of home she'd be just fine never seeing again. "Cazzie has been here before? I mean, since you've been pregnant?"

Pippa nodded. "I didn't tell you, because, well—"

"Because Declan came with him," Katie said, then slowly shook her head as if that alone could make it not true.

"Rather than talk around that fact, I—I just thought it best, all around, to, you know, not mention it," Pippa said, looking miserable.

"He was a . . . sore spot once upon a time," Katie acknowledged. He was that. A sore spot on her heart. "But that was a long time ago. We're all adults now. You could have just told me. I'm not that ridiculous." Well, she was, just not for reasons Pippa knew anything about.

"I didn't think you were," Pippa said. "If I did, I wouldn't trust you to handle my whole life. Which you do, Kat, brilliantly. I wasn't on bed rest when they first came, and you've been so slammed trying to take care of everything so I can just focus on getting ready for the babies. I just . . . didn't see the need to add that to the mix. Like you, I assumed he would hang out a bit, take a few photos, then head on out again." She let out a deep sigh and sank back into the pillows. "So, I had it all planned. The moment you got here I'd tell you straight off. Like a good news, bad news kind of thing." She reached for Katie's hand, grabbed it, and held on with surprising strength. "I knew I wanted you to be here, to hear the news of the twins firsthand, and I don't regret holding that until now. The other . . . I guess I was hoping it would rectify itself before you arrived. I mean, from the time he finished his senior cycle, when has Declan MacGregor ever stayed in one place any longer than, well, any longer than our darlin' brother, Cassian?"

"Only he didn't leave," Katie said, not needing confirmation. "He's here. Now."

Pippa nodded, clearly regretful. "I didn't know how to tell you, because I know how excited you are to move here. I am, too. For you, and for myself. This time, it wasn't him simply popping by."

"So . . . he's staying here," Katie said hollowly, all of her excitement and anticipation slipping out of reach, as if she'd been having a marvelous dream she was certain was real, only to awaken to a cold, damp, storm-swept morning.

The thing Pippa didn't understand, couldn't understand, because Katie had never spoken of it, was that it wasn't that she was embarrassed by her past feelings for Declan. Or that he'd found out about them in the most humiliating way possible. Humiliating to her. She wasn't hurt or mortified that he'd gone out of his way to avoid her from that time forward. Not any longer, anyway. She'd been eighteen then. More than a decade and a life filled with amazing experiences had occurred since then. For both of them.

As adults now, they were well beyond any mortification expiration date. Their paths simply had no reason to cross, and each seemed fine with that arrangement. She was confident in who she was, happy with how things were going in her life. She loved her work, loved working for Pippa, and the wondrous life both of those things afforded her. Not the least of which was getting to live in Blue Hollow Falls full-time. Yes, it had been an inordinately and somewhat ridiculously long time since she'd seen him. Even with their very different life trajectories, the MacMillans made time for family, always. She and Declan had just managed to do that at different times. For a long while. But she wasn't afraid to see him again, to speak to him, or have the opportunity to put this awkward breach mercifully behind them both.

No, what she was afraid of, nay, terrified of, was that she'd take one look at him, and it wouldn't matter whether it had been twenty years or fifty since she'd last laid eyes on him. What she didn't want to know, could go the rest of her life without discovering about herself, was that no amount of time, no amount of life lived, would change the one thing that had been true since she'd first laid eyes on him.

That he was it for her. The one. Period. Full stop. She'd understood that on some level even when they were children. She remembered, as a fanciful eight-year-old, feeling that a spell had been cast, some mystical magic performed, the first moment he'd appeared and looked her way. That feeling never changed, even when she grew past the age of fairy tales and enchanted imaginings. Lord knows she'd tried her best to prove herself wrong as the years passed. Because it had been made quite painfully clear that the cruelest part of this enchantment was that it only worked for her. He'd left her no doubt that she was not the one for him and never had been. Never would be.

And she very much doubted that had changed or could change. There was no way to even begin to describe how he made her feel.

That much she knew for a fact. From that one day forward, that one day when she'd blurted it all out to her dear brother, tried to explain what it felt like, to know with such clarity what was meant to be, to feel so strongly about someone, in ways that went so far beyond a silly crush or even mere lust, only to discover Declan had heard all of it, from that afternoon onward, she'd kept the knowledge to herself. Held that certainty close, the utter lunacy of it—because what else could it be but a certain kind of madness, to still affect her so acutely, even now?

She objectively understood that it should be a simple case of unrequited love. She'd loved someone, and he hadn't loved her back. It happened to people all the time. Move on. And God knows, she wanted to. Had tried to. Repeatedly.

Only, the truth of it was that no one had come close to making her feel what he could, just by standing in the same room with her. She'd seen a good part of the world by now, and she'd met charming men, serious men, strong, bold, silent, sexy   add any adjective, she'd met them, and a few had even lain their hearts at her feet, or would have, if she'd encouraged them. By rights, any one of them should have made her heart swoon. And maybe it would have. Surely it would have. If she hadn't already met Declan.

Quiet, serious, smart, dry-witted, big-hearted, dead-sexy Declan. No one had come close to matching the utter wholeness she felt when he was near. Not simply in her heart, but in the whole of her being. Even before she'd understood the more adult aspects of her attraction to him, it was the absolute feeling of peace, the beautiful, grounding sense that everything had found its perfect balance, its perfect pitch, when he did nothing more than merely look at her. Look into her, as only he ever had. As only he ever could.

And that had been when they'd hardly experienced

anything of life, of the world around them. She couldn't begin to fathom how much more intense it might be now. Now that they were truly adults, with the experience required to understand the depth and breadth of what the heart could want.

That was something she could have gone a lifetime without knowing. Only now he was here. Now she would have to face the truth of it once more, feel it, confront it. *Hunger for it.*

Every single day. Every time she saw him.

Saints have mercy.

Chapter 2

Declan MacGregor gently squeezed the remote shutter release, easing the pressure slowly, so slowly, waiting, waiting, until . . . *now*. He pressed, heard the satisfying sound of the shutter opening, then closing again, and smiled.

He could have turned off the sound, but he was old-school. Most of his targets were landscapes, or people who knew their photos were being taken. Nothing to be scared away by the gentle *whirr-click*. It satisfied him to hear it, to know he'd captured something.

He'd spent a solid hour waiting for that one moment, that one shot. He'd wanted to preserve forever the exact moment when the very first sliver of gold light pierced the horizon, then shot like a laser beam, straight at him. He would have —and had—waited far longer for a payoff. Would have come back and done it all over again if he wasn't satisfied, if he knew there was a chance to get something even better.

This time, he knew he'd gotten it. He hadn't looked yet, but he knew it would be there when he did. At the age of thirty, he'd spent over half his life looking at the world through crystal-clear optical glass. Much better glass these days.

Years spent behind the lens had honed his instincts, and he was rarely wrong. If anything, he was more often pleasantly surprised when things turned out better than expected, or simply different, compelling him to develop whole new angles, different sequences, fresh settings.

He took several more shots anyway, because he wasn't a fool.

He dipped his chin, then chuckled. Okay, so he was no longer the fool. Or as often, at any rate. Early on, after his first surge of success, he'd gotten so chuffed with himself, so certain of his genius, that he'd decided he'd only ever take the single shot. And he would either capture perfection, his vision of it, at any rate, or he'd miss. If it was the latter, then he didn't deserve to have it anyway. He was either good enough. Or he was not.

"A bloody arrogant eejit you once were," he murmured under his breath, his grin wry. He took his camera off the tripod, removed the lens, then began methodically packing up his gear. He didn't look at the shot. At any he'd taken during his predawn outing. He'd do that when he was in his studio, with the right lighting, the right editing equipment, and start working from there. Today he was working digitally, but he also had a darkroom and loved, almost more than anything, shooting with traditional film, going through the developing process, watching the images emerge. Most of his black-and-white photography was done that way. He just liked the look of it better, loved the primal feel of clipping up actual printed photos.

He loved all of it, actually. He was a born observer and couldn't imagine doing anything else. God willing, he'd never have to.

He collapsed and packed the tripod last, attaching it

through the loops on the bottom of his pack. He slid the gear pack on his back, then turned, and simply took in the scene. Some people would only ever view the things he saw by looking at his photos. He was fortunate to be seeing it with his own eyes, so it was important to him to always do just that. Take time, no camera, no thoughts of angles, lighting, apertures, or shutter speeds, and simply look at the world.

The irony of his chosen profession was that it made it harder to get his photographer brain to experience the moment in and of itself. But he made sure he tried. To empty his mind, and just live, let that be his memory of the place.

Smiling, he watched two hawks circle lazily over the ridge where he stood as the sky slowly grew lighter, the mauves and grays turning to dusky blues. He shifted his stance and looked down. Firefly Lake spread out down below, still quite a bit above the Hawksbill Valley, well beyond his line of vision. Fingers of water at either end of the lake penetrated the wilderness and pine forest that crowded around the shore, tucked in as the lake was, amongst the rocky ridges, high up in the Blue Ridge.

Declan knew the lake area was being developed now, a lodge was being built, cabins and such, trails were being tidied up and additional docks built. Once complete, visitors would be able to enjoy the beauty of the lake and the surrounding area up close, right outside their door. He was too high above to see any of the construction work with his bare eyes. It was just past daybreak and quiet still reigned supreme, except for the sound of birds wakening and calling to each other. He tracked Firefly Creek from where it fed the lake, on up into the hills. He'd heard there were waterfalls along that trail, and he thought that might make for the perfect addition to the series he was creating.

The first series, he thought, taking in a slow, deep breath, then letting it out again, appreciating and acknowledging the feeling of contentment that filled him in that moment. He'd traveled to some pretty far-flung places, some considered exotic, others simply unknown. Most often, it was the textures and colors of the vistas that pulled him in.

He had no idea why this place grabbed at him with such ferocity. It was far from exotic, or unusual, or unknown. So very many photographers before him, amateur and professional both, had scoured the timeworn hills of this ancient mountain range, and captured its beauty in what seemed every way imaginable. It wasn't even the challenge of trying to impose his own point of view onto something so often captured by other lenses. He couldn't say what it was. He only knew he felt . . . settled here. At peace. There was no sense of urgency to hurry up and document it, so he could move on to the next place, as was his norm. The world was so very, very vast. He'd never see it all. There was no time to waste.

Here, he felt none of that. It made no sense, but it felt so good, he'd decided to just go with it. He smiled. Cash thought it was simply a sign of getting older, of being ready to transition from one phase of life to another. Declan wasn't so sure. Whatever the case, it would sort itself out in due time, and he had whatever time was needed. Thanks to Pippa MacMillan's bringing his work to the attention of her massive, worldwide fan base, he had the luxury, as very few in his line of work did, to work at his own pace, when he wanted, where he wanted. He was hardly raking it in, but his needs were simple, and he lived simply. He was forever grateful to her for providing the foundation that had launched a career, a life he so loved and fully enjoyed. Yet another debt to the MacMillans he could never repay.

He finally turned away, lifted his hiking stick from where he'd tucked it in a crook between two boulders, and started along the ridge trail.

It was midmorning when he finally emerged from the trail, about fifty rock-and-boulder-strewn yards or so from Pippa's cabin. She'd been kind enough to loan it to him short-term in exchange for doing some much needed maintenance to the cabin and surrounding property.

When Declan had decided to stick around, he'd worked it out with Addie Pearl to get his own studio space at the mill, create a darkroom there, as the wee cabin wasn't conducive to that kind of thing. An old silk mill down by the falls that had given the town its name had been converted several years back into an artisan enclave of sorts, where members of Addie Pearl's Bluebird Crafters Guild took up residence. It was quite the space and he loved the energy, the vibe of it all. He'd been made an honorary member for the duration of his stay. He could display and sell his photos if he liked, but he hadn't gone that far as yet, though he was slowly assembling what he thought of as his first Blue Hollow show.

He should have found a more long-term place to live by now, but he'd been putting it off. He liked it up here, and the cabin was perfect for his needs. Cash was bunking in with him for a few days, and the two had enjoyed sitting out on the small porch the past few evenings, sipping locally brewed ale and catching up.

Pippa wouldn't need the place back until after the baby came, so he still had time. He also knew who would be moving in when he moved out. Knew she'd be coming to stay with Seth and Pippa any day now. He needed to come to grips with that, with . . . all of it. But he hadn't even begun to grapple with his feelings.

He heard her laughter before he saw her, and for a moment thought he'd merely conjured it up. Conjured her up. Just from thinking about her. It wouldn't have surprised him in the least. None of the things he felt for her should surprise him any longer. Yet they always did.

He stopped beside a copse of scrawny pine once the cabin came into view and did what he was best at. He observed. And there she was, talking to her brother Cash. *Their* brother Cash. Cash wasn't *like* a brother to Declan, he *was* his brother. *So, what does that make her?*

Exactly.

Declan hadn't seen her in ten years, five months, two weeks, and four days, in case anyone was counting. More than a full third of his life. The last time he'd seen her he'd been toying with the idea of university, only he didn't know what he wanted from it. Cash already knew he was bypassing secondary education, planning to let the world at large educate him. That day, in the garage, had resolved the question for Declan. He'd tied his star to the tail of the comet that was Cassian MacMillan and they'd both lit out of Donegal shortly thereafter. Shortly after he'd heard all the things he should never have heard. She was supposed to be his sister. He'd felt so connected to her from the moment they first met. A shared glance, a nod, a quick smile in response to something they saw, something they heard, was all that was needed to communicate entire thoughts. They did it instinctively. Searched each other out. Always had. He'd never felt so closely in tune with anyone, even as a child. Yet, even then, she had never once felt like his sister.

Girls liked Declan. A lot of girls. And they weren't shy about expressing it. Katie wasn't like any of them. She wasn't one for histrionics, silly crushes, over-the-top displays, exaggerated drama. Neither was he. She'd grown somewhat aloof around him when they'd reached their teens. When she'd been around him at all, which had become more and more rare. Back then he'd thanked God daily for that. It was the only way he could manage himself. Knowing that all the things he was feeling for her, all the things that felt so wonderful and good and true, wouldn't be seen that way. *She was family, for God's sake.* So, it had been a blessing that she didn't seem to want any of those things. That realization held him in check, even as he waged the battle to rid himself of the absolute knowledge of who she was to him, who she would always be to him. The one.

Then she had to go and tell Cash, explaining to him in shaky, trembling words, that she'd been doing exactly the same thing he had. Trying to pull back, trying not to feel what she felt. But it wasn't working, because she'd known, had always known, the same thing he had. They were meant for each other. She'd been so damn vulnerable, wide open, and completely undone by it, by him. He'd wanted to go grab her hand and run. Just . . . run. Away. Anywhere. Everywhere. Together.

Then she'd seen him, realized what he'd heard. And he knew from the look on her face, from what she'd revealed to Cash, that it was far more than mortification that had her crumpling. His Katie didn't crumple. She was a damn warrior. He'd done that to her. Kicked the solid ground out from under her feet. She didn't want their connection to be true any more than he did, but perhaps not for the same reasons. He didn't know. All he knew was that wanting him was destroying her.

So, he'd run, but not with her. He'd taken off with Cash,

mercifully far, far away from Donegal. From Katie. From all the things that had felt most right in the world to him.

All the exact same things he felt now, in Blue Hollow Falls. Where they both had landed. Together. In the same place. Once more.

He shook his head, feeling the fool for thinking he could outrun what was meant to be. What had always been meant to be. *Okay, Fate. You win.*

He hadn't come here for her. He'd never have done that. He was a pro at being anywhere she wasn't. He'd come twice already, once before Pippa's wedding, to photograph the two in advance of their big day and again with Cash earlier this year to see Pippa. Blue Hollow Falls had cast its spell on him the moment he'd set foot in the place. He'd never expected to find Katie here. She worked for Pippa, yes, but she did it a continent away. She did it on tour buses and via phone chats and all the ways that had her safely anywhere but here.

So, he'd let the pull of the place lure him back once more, then twice. And it had felt exactly the same each time. Perfect, calm, solid. *His.* None of which made sense, and none of which he cared about in the least. It was what it was, and it felt so damn good—why the hell not give in to it and stay?

The answer to that stood not twenty yards away.

He slid his backpack from his shoulders, aching to get his camera out, hide behind the lens. He could never capture her. He'd tried hundreds of times over the years. Thousands. He'd destroyed every last photo of her before he'd left Ireland. It wasn't healthy, carrying her around with him like that, no matter how good it felt in truth. He shook his head. Like he didn't have every last one of those images embedded in his brain, anyway. In his heart. *Eeejit then, eejit now.*

He didn't hide behind the camera. He let himself look
at her, hear her, watch her. Forced himself to do it, with no
filter, no barrier. And it rocked him. Hard. The years
hadn't just been good to her, they'd been wondrous. He
had no hope, none, of girding himself now. More than a
decade of time hadn't lessened all the things he felt for
her, knew about her, knew about himself, not one whit.
They were amplified, and standing in this place, in these
ancient hills, it all felt as if it had come full circle. That no
matter how far he'd run, no matter how hard he'd worked
to keep his orbit separate from hers, all along it had only
been a matter of time before they landed in the same spot,
their lives intersecting once more.

There was no escaping it. No escaping her. No escap
ing himself.

*So what are you going to do about it? Running doesn't
work. It only postpones the inevitable. Only postpones this.*

What he wanted to do, what he felt compelled to do,
was step out into the clearing, make his presence known,
until she turned and saw him. Until their gazes met, connected, and the life he was supposed to be living finally
began anew. Then he'd simply open his arms, open himself, to her. She'd come to him, he'd go to her, until they
were as entangled as two people could be. Until they were
where they were supposed to be all along. Together.

Who's all dramatic and histrionic now? He smiled at
that, too. He'd stopped trying to make sense of it, make
it fit with the logical world around him. It simply was.
Like his connection to this place. He'd stopped trying to
make that be anything but what it was. It had felt so good,
giving in to it. Stopping, breathing this place in, and feeling
the peace.

How did he do that with her?

Did he just walk up to her and announce how he felt?

"Oh, hullo, Katie. Long time. So, about fate and mystical connections that can't be explained and that bit about feeling bonded to someone for all eternity? Turns out you're not the only one who felt that way. So, what say we give that a go, eh? Do you fancy a wedding?"

Did she still feel it? That certainty of what was meant to be? Or had she found a way to flip that magical switch to OFF? Did he want her to teach him?

Where did he begin? What did he want?

"Declan."

He lifted his gaze from where it had shifted, unseeing, to the ground, as he battled with himself. How had he not felt her approach, with every fiber of himself? "Katherine Elizabeth," he said, and saw her tremble.

Their gazes held, and maybe he trembled, too. He had no idea where Cash was, nor did he care. The world might as well have fallen away, except for the short space between them.

"Why are you here?" she asked. Not accusingly, not fearfully, simply wanting to know.

He didn't know if she meant here at the cabin, or in Blue Hollow Falls. It didn't matter. *For you, apparently.* "I owe you an apology."

That surprised her. He took a moment to just look at her. The pleasure in being able to do so was palpable. She was exactly the same and yet entirely different. More beautiful, yes, stronger, he could see. Confident and whole. Maybe they'd both needed to go off and do that for themselves.

He didn't feel strong or confident in the least in that moment.

"For?" she asked.

For not stepping up and telling you that you weren't alone. For making you feel like a fool when I was the fool.

I was the one who was too weak, too afraid, too unsure of his worth to reach for it, to reach for you.

Could he just say that? Would she laugh in his face? And what if she did? Wouldn't he deserve that at the very least?

He couldn't read her. That much had changed. He'd always been teased about being the inscrutable, hard-to-read one. Only, at the moment, she was doing a damn sight better job than he was at masking whatever was going on inside her head. Not that it mattered what she thought of him now, but he didn't want to say anything, or do anything, to bring back so much as a shred of what he'd seen on her face that day in the garage.

It's been ten years, Dec. Perhaps, unlike your sad, sorry self, she's gotten past it. She's over it, over you. Just say it then and get on with your life.

"I avoided you, after that day," he began. "And that was wrong."

From the stark expression in her eyes now, she knew exactly what day he was referring to.

"You don't have to —" she began, and he knew he'd already done exactly what he hadn't wanted to do. She didn't look mortified. That much time had healed. She looked . . . afraid.

Maybe he should tell her he felt the same.

"I do," he said. "I didn't have the words then." A smile teased the corners of his mouth. "I don't have them now. And I've had all this time to practice."

He saw her lips twitch, too, and the light returned to her eyes. The ache that bloomed inside his chest in that instant was so swift, so fierce, he had to fight to keep from pressing his fist against it.

"It was a long time ago, Declan. I was a kid, and . . ."

She let that trail off, glanced away, and he wondered why she didn't say the rest of it. *I don't feel that way anymore.*

But she didn't.

What she said, instead, he did not see coming.

"I'm the one who's sorry," she said. "For disappointing you. I think that was the worst part." Before he could ask her what on earth she meant, she went on. "It leveled me, having you find out that I was no different from those brainless girls you were always complaining to Cash about." She lifted a shoulder, as if to say it was all water under the bridge.

But he saw beyond her nonchalance, as their gazes connected once more.

"You were nothing like them," he told her, hearing the hint of ferocity in his tone as he defended her.

She must have heard it, too, because her brows lifted in surprise. "Worse, then?" she said with a little laugh.

It took everything he had not to reach for her. How had he so screwed up the one good thing, the perfect thing he'd been fortunate enough to find even once?

"Hardly," he said, and realized he'd sounded harsh. The scorn hadn't been directed at her, but at himself. She thought he'd rejected her. *What other conclusion could she have drawn?*

He hadn't just vanished from her life that day, that single afternoon, he'd played cat and mouse for more than ten years—ten years—to keep from confronting the truth. *To keep her from knowing the truth? Well, here's your chance.*

Before he could find the words to begin, pick a place to start, she said, "Will you be staying? In the Falls? Long-term, I mean?"

"Yes," he said, without even having to consider his

answer. He might have dissembled a bit if he'd been asked even ten minutes ago. Before he'd seen her again. Now? There was only certainty. He knew now why he was here. Why it had felt right. He wondered if she did.

"Can we at least agree that we no longer need to avoid each other?"

"Katie—"

She'd said it lightly. Her eyes, however, continued to search his. He wished he knew what she hoped to find there.

"I don't know if Pippa told you, but I'm moving here. Full-time." She nodded toward the cabin. "She's giving me the cabin. I'll be at the house with Pippa and Seth until the bab—ah, the blessed event occurs. So, I'm not booting you or Cash from the place now. I just . . . thought you should know."

"How is she doing?" he asked, as if it was perfectly normal to chitchat about family and lodgings, and simply avoid talking about the very gigantic elephant in the room.

"Good. Stir-crazy," she added with an affectionate smile. "She and Seth are at one of their regularly scheduled doctor appointments today, and hopefully that will be all good news. So, I thought I'd come here and catch up with my brother. I didn't know that you were staying here . . . Pippa didn't mention . . ." She let that trail off; then the wry grin surfaced in full and his heart skipped several beats. He'd have waited the rest of his life for that perfect shot. "So, I'm sorry if I just ruined the whole separate orbits thing. It wasn't intentional."

"I wasn't trying to—"

"Ten-plus years of holidays, family birthdays, weddings," she added archly, and he knew she was referring to his not being at Pippa and Seth's wedding. "And our paths don't cross even once?" She tilted her head. "You were trying."

"Katie—"

"You didn't have to, Dec. I mean, I know how ridiculous I sounded that day, and I clearly freaked you out. I'm sorry about that, truly. But I was young," she reminded him.

"You were eighteen," he countered. "Going on thirty. You were born going on thirty. Even as the youngest, you were somehow always head and shoulders past the rest of us."

She laughed then, and he marveled at how well she was managing what, to him, felt like a life-altering moment. Maybe she really had grown past it. Maybe he'd blown up the whole fantastical thing. Only he knew he hadn't. The proof was standing right there before him. Proof was his heart beating so hard inside his chest, he wasn't sure how she couldn't see it. Proof was his desire for her not dimming at all, but being light years beyond what it had been when they were mere teenagers.

"I'm the youngest of six—seven counting you. It was survival of the fittest." She shrugged. "I'm a survivor."

He looked into her eyes then, wanting to see everything, wanting to know everything. Either this was an amazing performance, or she really had put it all to the side. Left it in her past. Left him there, too. He'd certainly given her no reason to tend her devotion, to keep it alive. Quite the opposite. But could he truly be the only one who still felt it? Who still knew it?

She doesn't know you feel it, too, remember? Did you really expect her to just fling herself at you a second time? After ten years of complete and utter avoidance?

"I shouldn't have," he said. "Avoided you. Then or now. It seems ridiculous, after all this time, I know."

"And yet?" she said softly, and he could tell she regretted the words as soon as they were out.

Tell her. He tried to find the words. None of them seemed sufficient to the enormity and the delicacy of the task. "It wasn't because I was disappointed in you or trying to keep from hurting your feelings."

"Thank you?"

He smiled at that; then the smile faded, and he held her gaze for the longest moment, and finally let the walls fall completely. Let her see what he'd worked for ten years— his whole life really—to hide.

It was an enormous relief. It was exhilarating. Freeing. It was terrifying. Utterly. It was one thing to never try, and simply never know what might be. It was another thing entirely to put it all out there and fail. And know you could never have what you desperately wanted.

"Those things you said that day," he said quietly, and he felt her, saw her, pull back. He wanted to reach for her, but that wasn't his right. "I wasn't disappointed, Katie." He waited for her to look at him, look into him. "I was terrified."

Her eyes widened, and he knew he'd shocked her.

"Maybe I should have told you then. Or found you at some point since and explained. Laid myself bare like you did. It's only fair."

"Bare . . . how?" she said, the words hardly more than a whisper. She was trembling. He could see the quiver along her jawline. And he knew then that she hadn't forgotten a damn thing, hadn't put any of it aside, hadn't let it go. Hadn't let him go.

His heart soared. As did his panic. Panic that he'd ruin this, say the wrong thing, do the wrong thing, as he had all those years ago.

"You . . . Cash, all of you, were my family," he began.

She blanched. "So you thought I was some kind of— because to you we were related and I had feelings for—" She started to turn away, looked like she might be sick.

He swore under his breath—he *was* ruining it. He did reach for her then, only to drop his hand away when she all but leapt back from his touch.

"Not you," he said, when she turned away. "Me."

She froze. She didn't turn back. Didn't look at him. She simply stood there, and he felt like his heart was a living, beating, pulsating thing filling the chasm of space between them. She had the power to take it, hold it, cherish it. Or stomp on it. Worse maybe, to ignore it. Walk away from it.

"I didn't know that you felt it, too," he said, his voice ragged. "I always knew, from the time we were little, that you were special. In ways I couldn't truly understand then, but couldn't deny, either. Then, as we got older, you grew so . . . aloof around me. So, I fought our connection. For years. Because it had to be wrong. I had to be wrong to even think about it, much less want it. Want you."

"No," she said, shaking her head, her back still to him, the single word not a reply, but a denial of all that he was saying.

"I was a kid, too, Katie. I didn't have the words. Not the way you did."

He moved finally, walked around in front of her, not touching her. He dipped his chin until their gazes caught once more. "I wasn't brave, or strong, or . . . any of the things I should have been. You put it out there, tried to make sense of it," he said, so quietly only she could hear him. "And your confession so stunned me, flipped everything I'd been thinking, believing, about you, about us, about myself completely upside down . . . I panicked. I ran."

She finally lifted her head, and what he saw on her face wrecked him.

"You let me think . . . all this time—" She didn't finish. She just looked away, then tried to walk past him.

"I am sorry for that. That is my biggest regret. But . . . what would have happened if I'd been as forthright as you?" he challenged, and she stopped again. "If I admitted that it wasn't just you? That I felt it, too? We were supposed to be a family. We are family. Then what?"

She turned to face him, and her expression was walled off, sealed up tight, done. "I guess we'll never know."

Chapter 3

Katie didn't begin to shake in earnest until she was safely in her room back in the A-frame, behind a closed and locked door. *What the hell had just happened?*

It was so much, so very, very much, she couldn't even begin to let it all in, much less process any of it.

That it wasn't just you? That I felt it, too? Then what?

All this time, all these years, she'd thought he'd been disappointed in her, embarrassed for her, had been preserving her dignity by staying away. So she wouldn't have to be reminded of what she'd said, what she'd revealed, how utterly insane she'd sounded. It hadn't just been a confession of love. She'd gone on about fate, and twin souls, and was it possible that her destiny was predetermined. She'd wondered if there could only be one perfect mate for her in the whole world, because that was how certain it had felt.

It had never, not one time, felt wrong to her that he all but lived at their house. Yes, he'd become a part of her family, but he was not her blood relative. She'd never once felt conflicted on that score. It hadn't even occurred to her. That he'd thought his feelings for her were wrong, or worse, the sign of a sick mind—she'd never thought of it from his viewpoint. She'd had the luxury of knowing she'd been born into her big, loving family, never questioning her place in the world. Declan hadn't had any of that. So, of course he'd be cautious and very aware of doing anything to upset this place he'd finally found himself in, surrounded by people who truly cared for him. Developing feelings for her, understanding the depth of their connection, must have been horribly conflicting for him on so many levels.

The more she thought about it, the more her anger and hurt faded. This wasn't just about her feelings, her struggles; it was about his, too. She'd never truly considered the situation from his side. Of course, she hadn't known he had feelings for her all this time.

He had feelings for her! All along. She couldn't think past that simple and insanely complicated truth. She'd worked so hard to set their relationship aside. To set him aside.

Then she'd been standing outside the cabin, and there Declan was. It hadn't been strange, or awkward, or any of the multitudinous things she was certain it would be. It had been . . . a relief. Like *finally. What took you so damn long?* She'd expected to feel nervous, scared, annoyed even, at being thrust back into the midst of that unquantifiable, yet undeniable *thing* she'd had only with him. Instead, she'd felt buoyant, almost giddy. *There you are.* And oh my, had he been.

He'd been a devilishly handsome lad, with the sort of dark, broody looks that made girls sigh, scribble his name in notebooks, and write bad poetry. Time had only enhanced those looks, in every way possible. He'd always been a quiet sort, but he'd certainly been aware of the effect he had on the opposite sex. It would have been impossible not to. Girls' attention seemed to annoy him more than anything. He wasn't like Cash, who used his charm to further his lot in life. Not in a bad way, but Cash was well . . . Cash. Heart of gold, soul of a gypsy, spreader of joy. Conversely, Declan had been steady, forthright, observant. He hadn't been much of a talker, except maybe with Cash, but when he spoke, it was always with purpose, and his insights were always spot-on.

He had more than a few inches on her own five-foot-seven self and his frame had gone from that of a somewhat lean young man to a bit more of a brawny adult. His shoulders seemed impossibly broad, his jaw impossibly rugged. Maybe it was simply the passage of time, but more likely, she thought, the result of his world travels.

His voice was still deep and a bit rough, his Scottish brogue adding that extra edge to his braw self. His face was more mature, more angular now, though his hair was still a thick, dark unruly thatch. He sported the hint of a beard and she knew, from their childhood, that he'd started shaving earlier than any of her brothers. Only now that dark shadow on his jaw made him look worldly rather than brooding. Or maybe a bit of both. His sea-green eyes were as laser-focused as ever, and if anything, she expected he was even more observant now than back then. All those years spent looking at life through a lens could have only strengthened that quality in him. Having seen his work, she knew she was right.

Had he used that laser focus to keep from looking at the bigger picture? She'd thought avoiding her had simply become habit for him, that he couldn't possibly think she still pined for him.

Only she did. And he knew why.

All this time, she thought fate had played her for a fool. How had she not even considered that it might be the opposite, if only she'd looked.

She thought back to that day in the garage, still crystal clear in her mind, from the mingled scents of motor oil and the freshly cut grass still clinging to the mower blades, to the summer sun trying to get in past the dirty windowpanes, even the position of every last dust mote filtering in and out of those soft beams of light. Cash scoffing at her as only big brothers could when their female siblings were being emotional, brushing off her explanations of why she couldn't be nicer to Declan, making her that much more determined that he understand, until she was shouting at him and all of it came out.

She thought about the expression on Dec's face when she realized he'd been standing behind her and recognized now the disgust she'd seen had been self-directed. She had feared that maybe Cash was right, that the whole thing was her wanting to believe in fairy tales. Declan, on the other hand, thought he had an unhealthy attraction to a girl he should think of as a sister.

Only he didn't. And she wasn't.

What *would* she have done if he'd blurted out his truth that day in the garage? If she was honest with herself, Declan had a point. Given the dynamics at play and the opposite way they were looking at their feelings, what would have happened? Even if they'd come to terms with how they felt, then what? Go out on a date? It was all so much larger than that.

She sank down on the side of the bed. She was angry and hurt that he'd let her live her life feeling rejected by him. Only the more she thought about it, it was becoming clear that maybe he'd done the only thing he could at that time. The only thing that either of them could have handled.

Maybe not then. What about now?

The light knock at her bedroom door startled her badly and made her jump to her feet. Her first instinct was to cover up what she was feeling, shove Declan MacGregor back inside that dark box she'd kept him in all these years. If only she knew how. Her entire world had been quite literally turned on its side. Everything she'd thought she knew, was utterly certain of, about herself, about Declan, about who and what they were to each other, about how crazy it was to be so certain of something even after he'd proven it to be patently false . . . all that had been trashed and it was going to take some time to truly recalibrate. *A lot of time.*

She wiped her damp palms on her pants legs and pushed her hair back from her face, feeling the heat emanating from her cheeks as she did. She was flushed and cold all at the same time, and honestly wondered if she'd ever feel normal again.

I fought it. For years. Because it had to be wrong. I had to be wrong to even think it, much less want it. Want you.

His words wouldn't stop echoing through her mind. She couldn't stop hearing him, hearing all the things she'd wanted to hear him say for so long. Had never thought she'd hear him say.

"Katie?" Pippa said, her voice hushed, as if she suspected her sister might be napping.

Katie wasn't ashamed to admit she considered pretending she was doing just that. Only it wouldn't matter if Pippa saw her now or hours from now. Katie didn't imagine the shell shock was going to wear off anytime soon.

"I'll be right there," she called out. "Just changing clothes."

She escaped into the bathroom that was connected to her room and to the hallway and locked the hallway door. She splashed cool water on her face but avoided looking at herself in the mirror. She didn't want to know what she'd find.

I wasn't disappointed, Katie. I was terrified.

She wrung out the washrag and hung it up, then sank down on the edge of the tub, her knees still feeling wobbly as his words pelted her again and again. It was all too much, too different, surreal. She'd spent her adult life not just thinking she understood the playing field but knowing it with absolute certainty. And now she had to throw her understanding out and consider . . . *what?*

She stood up and resolutely walked out of the bathroom and across the hall to Pippa's room. She didn't just put it all aside, she shoved it there. "How did it go?" she asked Pippa as she walked through the open doorway. She could hear Pippa in the walk-in closet at the back of the room.

"I hope I didn't wake you," Pippa said, her voice muffled. She walked out wearing an oversized T-shirt dress that hung past her knees. "No more bra," she said with a sigh of relief. She cupped her boobs and jiggled them. "You'd think I'd be chuffed to finally have a pair that would fill one, but I could barely wait to get the thing back off." She grinned and nodded to her naturally more well-endowed sister. "Honestly, I don't know how you girls do it."

Katie laughed, relieved by the distraction Pippa never failed to provide. "Well, I suspect if they weren't resting on the cathedral-sized dome of your abdomen, you might feel different."

"Good point." Pippa pressed her palms to either side of her belly and let out a deep sigh. "As much as I hate being confined to bed, I admit that I have thought of nothing else the last hour but climbing back in and passing out. I'm knackered."

Katie crossed the room and helped Pippa up into the

bed and went through the pillow and blanket routine they'd perfected over the past few days.

"What did the doctor say?" Katie asked as she fluffed and arranged, perhaps more than was strictly warranted.

"She said I'm doing really well. Nothing negative, no surprises. Just keep doing what I'm doing and push toward the finish line." She smiled. "I'm officially at thirty-four weeks now. That's longer than she feared I'd be able to go. She said that I've made it to the point where the babies would have a really good chance, even if I go into labor early."

Katie went still, then looked at her sister. "What do you mean, 'a really good chance'?"

"Well, if I was just carrying the one, being almost through my eighth month, things would be on the positive end of the scale for a premature delivery. But since there are two, they aren't likely to be the size and weight of a single babe."

Katie put her palms gently on the mound of belly that rose up under the crocheted throw and let a wry smile cover her worry. "Are you sure about that?"

Pippa laughed. "I know, aye?"

"I know you and Seth said early on you didn't want to know the sex—sexes—but, does the doctor know? Could she tell from your ultrasounds?"

"I didn't ask. We just asked her to tell us if she saw anything that was of concern or we should be alerted about." She beamed. "So far, so good."

"Will they be identical? Or—"

"We don't know."

Katie sighed and sat gently on the side of the bed. "I'm still just so dazzled by the thought of it all. Twins."

Pippa laughed. "I got past the dazzle stage early on. Right about the time Seth and I had to order a second set of everything." She motioned to the two small cradles that sat in the corner of the room where the sun shone in through the window. Right below Declan's photos.

"They look so tiny," Katie said, and got up to walk over to them, knowing it was the pull of those photos, not the cradles, that had her wanting to feel close. She smiled back at her sister. "I'm so happy I get to be here to help with them. I hope it makes it seem at least a little less overwhelming."

Pippa smiled and gently massaged the sides of her abdomen. "You have no idea. I told Seth on the way to the doctors that I may not want you to move to the cabin right when they arrive after all."

Katie's gaze went unerringly to the photos, then quickly back to the tiny cradles, but not quickly enough.

"Ah," Pippa said softly. "So, you've been up there today, then." She didn't really make it a question, but Katie nodded.

"Since you were going to be gone with Seth a good part of the day, I went up to spend some time with Cash and catch up. I didn't realize he wasn't there alone. I should have, I guess."

"No, I should have thought of that." Pippa shook her head. "Declan knows he has to be out by the time the baby is born, so I just . . ." She sighed. "I am clearly in the running for suckiest sister ever. I'm sorry, I'm the worst. I feel like I'm brilliantly in control and on top of things one minute, and totally out to sea the next. It's not an excuse but—"

"It's every excuse," Katie said, turning back to face her sister. "And I'm a big girl. I knew it would happen at some point."

Pippa nodded, smiling in gratitude for the understanding, then tilted her head. "And?"

"It's fine." Katie managed an easy shrug. "We talked, cleared the air. So much time has passed, it's really not—"

"Who is it ye think yer talkin' to here, lass?" Pippa broke in, adopting the stronger accent of their grandmother, but saying it gently all the same. She patted the bed. "Come, sit. Tell me all."

Katie put a smile on her face. "Maybe later." The very last thing she wanted to do was talk about Declan Mac-Gregor. If only she could stop thinking about him while she was at it. "You need rest. I'll bring in some crushed ice and lemon water. Is Seth back to work outside?"

Pippa nodded, and Katie saw her eyelids were already growing droopy, despite her clear interest in what had happened up at the cabin.

"Okay then." Katie walked to the side of the bed and leaned down to kiss her sister on the forehead. "Rest a bit." She looked at her sister's belly and added, "You two behave and let Mama get a wee kip in." She smiled back at Pippa. "I'll come in and check on you before dinner."

"Okay," Pippa said, covering her mouth to hide a yawn.

Katie made sure Pippa's phone was within reach. "Text if you need me. I think I'll wander down and look around the barns, walk the vines. I haven't been out there once since I got here. I want to see the changes you've made. And I want to see Dex." Dexter was the llama that had come with the winery back when Seth had purchased the place.

"He'll love that," Pippa said, the words a bit slurred as her eyes closed and she let out a soft sigh.

Katie primped the covers one last bit, then quietly left the room. Her phone buzzed and she was delighted to see it was Moira. She took the call and immediately invited her friend up to stroll the vines with her and catch up.

Moira agreed and Katie ended the call and pocketed the phone. At this rate she might be able to put off thinking about what had happened at the cabin today all the way till nightfall. At least Cash hadn't been a witness this round. He'd gone back into the cabin and given them their time to talk. Katie had been saying her good-byes when Declan had shown up anyway, so she'd simply fled.

Cash had only commented on that afternoon in the garage one time. He'd apologized for being dismissive and asked her if she wanted him to talk to Declan, about . . . any of it. She'd begged him to leave it alone. And he had. He and Declan had taken off shortly thereafter and though she knew the rest of the family was well aware of what had happened, they'd let it lie. She'd left for university in the States not much longer after that, at the same time her oldest brother, Garrett, had been busy giving her parents their first grandchildren . . . and life had gone on.

As she tugged on a pair of barn boots and sat on the edge of the porch, waiting for Moira, Katie wondered what her family would think if they found out Declan hadn't timed his visits so carefully because he was preserving her dignity, but because he'd wanted exactly what she'd wanted.

Moira's arrival thankfully took her from her own thoughts. She wasn't sure if she'd talk about Declan, or how to even start if she did. It was a measure of how firmly Katie had needed to keep Declan and all the stuff that came with him tucked away that through four years of college and another half dozen years after that, she'd never told her best friend about him. Being an ocean and a continent away from home had given her exactly what she'd needed back then, and she'd grabbed on to it with both hands and held tight. Studying, parties, more studying, dating, focusing on her future—her future without Declan MacGregor—had been priority number one, and Katie had excelled at it. In every way except finding Declan's replacement.

Katie slid off the porch and met her friend as she got out of her car, giving her a tight hug. "I can't believe we're both here, again," she told her.

"I can't believe you'll be staying here," Moira said with a smile that bordered on giddy.

Katie laughed. "Who would have thought your little scheme to spend time in my hometown studying for your bar exam would end up with our siblings married, *you* married, and now us both living here?"

Moira shook her red curls back from her face, buffed her fingernails on her shirt, then blew across them. "Pro level. What can I say?" She looped her arm through Katie's and they headed toward the fields. "I have some other news I've been dying to share, but I had to wait for you to get here."

"That's more on trend than you could possibly know."

Moira's brows lifted. "Oh, really? Tell me more."

"Oh no, you first," she said, then slung her arm around her shorter friend's shoulders and pulled her in for an impromptu squeeze. "I'm so happy you're here. Tell me everything." And she was happy. A sense of hopefulness bloomed anew inside her. There was so much in Blue Hollow Falls that made her happy, fulfilled her, excited her. She had her family here, her best friend, work she loved, and soon, new nieces and/or nephews to dote over. She'd figure out where Declan fit into that landscape. Ultimately, he had no real ties here, not long-term. Given his passion, his art, his work, he couldn't be planning on any long-term stay. Thinking about that objectively, she started to feel a bit steadier.

Knowing how he'd felt about her back then changed so many things. What didn't change—wouldn't change—was the fact that they were following very different orbits. What was past was past. Maybe now that they'd confronted what happened, admitted it, reckoned with it, she could finally let go of him.

"You sure?" Moira asked on a laugh. "Because you are definitely not listening to anything I'm saying."

Pulled from her thoughts, Katie had the good grace to look abashed. "I'm sorry. I am. It's been . . . an interesting day."

Moira slowed their pace, looked up at her friend. "Is Pippa okay? I mean, it's none of my business, but—"

"No, it's fine, and she's doing great. Tired of being on bed rest, yes, and I'm sure tired of being kicked and elbowed from the inside every other second, but she's really handling it all like a pro."

Moira nodded, and Katie didn't miss the way her friend's free hand slipped briefly to caress her own stomach. Katie stopped them both on a dime and turned Moira to face her. She looked her friend right in the eyes, then her own widened. "Oh my God."

Tears instantly sprang to Moira's eyes. Katie's momentary stab of worry, that her friend wasn't happy about the news, was immediately relieved when Moira's face broke into the most beatific smile. She nodded. "We just found out. A week ago." She pressed both palms to her flat belly. "I'm eight weeks pregnant, Katie." She shook her head and let out a giddy laugh. "Gosh, it feels so crazy to say it out loud."

Katie tugged her into another hug, albeit a gentler one this time. Then she leaned back, resting her hands on Moira's shoulders. "So . . . had you started trying? Last we talked about it, I thought you both wanted to wait a bit." Moira and Hudson had only been married for eight months, and together for an additional year before that.

"We did." Moira shrugged, still smiling. Beaming, really. "I guess fate had other plans."

Katie remembered the urgency she'd sensed in Hudson the day she'd arrived. "Hud, is he happy about it?"

"Oh my God, Katie, he's over the moon. We just found out, and he's already out there scouting tiny caboose cars to add on just for the baby."

Katie laughed at that. Hudson and Moira lived in several old train cars that Hudson had completely renovated and retrofitted into a home. He'd even gotten Moira a caboose car that now proudly sat on the town square in Blue Hollow Falls and housed her little law office. "That is adorable. I love every part of it." She looked at Moira's tummy, then back up. "Do you know what you're having?"

She shook her head. "Not yet. We won't get the first ultrasound for a while longer. But we've decided we do want to know when the time comes." She smiled. "I still haven't really wrapped my head around it, but I want to plan and enjoy all of it, and knowing the sex will let us really do that the way we want."

"You're doing okay otherwise?" Katie asked. "Morning sickness? Pippa suffered with that something awful."

Moira shook her head. "No, nothing, thank goodness. Honestly, I feel wonderful." She sniffled suddenly, then laughed as she dabbed at the corners of her eyes. "Except for being exceptionally prone to sudden tears—happy ones—I wouldn't have even known if I hadn't missed a period. I never miss them. Ever."

"Yeah. I remember from when we lived in a tiny dorm together." They laughed. "I'm so happy for you both." Then another thought occurred to her. "Oh my God. This means the Brogan clan is—"

"Expecting another baby," Moira said with a laugh. "I know."

Three of them, Katie thought. "Have you told them?"

She shook her head. "Pippa doesn't have too long to go, and we don't want to take anything away from her. I'll just barely be in my second trimester when her baby comes. We can wait till then."

"Pippa would love to know you're expecting," Katie told her. "In fact, it might even ease her weariness a bit, being happy and excited for you, and for Hudson." She laughed. "Having a sister-in-pregnancy wouldn't hurt, either. You can swap stories and she could probably share some tips she's learned. Of course, it's up to you and Hud, but I honestly think the whole family will just be that much happier and have more to rejoice over."

"I don't know if we can keep it a secret that long anyway," Moira said, then laughed again. "Hudson is already bursting at the seams." She held Katie's gaze. "If you really think Pippa would want to know—I'll talk to Hudson tonight. Then you can let us know when you think would be a good time. She's supposed to rest, so I don't want to—"

"Trust me, you'd be the one visitor who might actually help," Katie said with a grin.

They continued their stroll, each in her own thoughts, until Moira broke the comfortable silence with a softly spoken question. "So . . . have you seen him?"

The question caught Katie completely off guard, but she quickly discarded the notion of pretending ignorance. Moira was far too sharp for that. "What do you know about it?" she countered, not defensively, but truly curious.

"Well, you go on and on about your family, but you don't—"

"I included Declan in those stories," Katie said.

"I was going to say you don't talk about them the way you talk about him."

Surprised at that, Katie said, "Meaning?"

Moira gave her friend a sideways glance, her lips curving in an affectionate, if wry grin. "In case no one has told you, you're a terrible actress." She slipped her arm through Katie's again. "Also, you didn't compare every boy you dated in college to Cash, or Garrett, or your other brothers. No, they were all measured against the one and only Declan MacGregor."

"That's not—that can't be true."

"How else would I have known?"

Katie thought about that, thought back to her days with Moira in California. Had she been so utterly transparent while trying so hard to be mature and over it? *Probably.* She grinned at that, because, at this point, what else could she do? "Well, the last person I'd have compared any guy to is wild child Cassian, and God help them if they turn out to be overly serious like Garrett."

"Point taken," Moira said, having met both men at her brother's wedding to Katie's sister. They continued in silence another bit, then she said quietly, "You don't need to fill in the backstory. It's not my business, and given all we've shared over the years, you'd have told me by now if you'd wanted me to know."

"Moira—"

"I don't mean that as a rebuke, gentle or otherwise." She glanced up at Katie as they continued walking the long rows of vines. "I mean it sincerely. We're all allowed our personal, sacrosanct places, and I get and respect that he occupies one of those for you. I only bring it up because we're all living in the same place now, and I wanted you to know that I . . . well, I don't *know* know what it's all about, but that I at least understand he holds some significance for you. And . . . I'm here for you, if you ever want to talk."

Katie slid her hand down Moira's arm, took her hand, and squeezed it. She gave her a side glance and a smile. "You're going to make a great mom," she said, and there might have been a little damp sheen fogging her vision just then, as well.

They strolled yet another long row as Katie searched for the right words. "Declan is special to all of us. But . . . he's always been special to me in a different way. We shared an immediate connection, even as kids." She cast a whimsical smile Moira's way and let the lilt in her accent become a slight bit exaggerated. "I come from the land of faeries and mystical things, ye ken, where it shouldn't have felt so odd to have such an . . . elemental connection to someone. On a level that wasn't remotely like anything so pedantic as what most mere mortals experience."

Moira laughed. "Ah, is that all, then."

Katie laughed with her. "Dramatic, I know. I wish I could explain it better, but I can't. I always just . . . knew it. As I matured, that connection deepened, on every level. Mental, emotional, spiritual. Sexual. I loved him so fully. When it became clear he wasn't under that same spell, I tried to let it go, to find the same magic with someone else. It's just . . . supposed to be him. I can't explain it."

"You never told him? Maybe he just didn't know."

She shook her head. "Not directly. I explained it once, tried to, with Cash. I was eighteen, Dec was nineteen, almost twenty. I didn't know he'd heard the whole thing until I turned and saw him standing there." She let go a long, soft sigh. "He avoided me after that."

Moira's expression fell. "Aw, Katie. I'm so sorry."

"He and Cash took off to see the world shortly thereafter, so it wasn't quite so dramatic as all that. Not at first. But he's stuck to that decision ever since."

Moira stopped then and turned Katie to face her. "Wait. You haven't seen him, not once, since you were eighteen?"

Katie shook her head. "It's not as odd as it sounds. Well, okay, it is, but to be fair, we've been traveling ever since. I went off to the States, then went to work with Pippa, and we traveled all over. We both go home, see everyone; we just do it at different times." She lifted a shoulder. "Years pass more quickly than you'd think. It's not like I haven't tried to find someone else."

"You didn't sit home on Saturday nights when we were in school," Moira agreed with a smile, which then softened as she added, "But I knew your heart was never in play. Not once. And you had some really worthy candidates." She sighed. "I mean, they heard your Irish accent and all but fell over themselves to do your bidding. If I didn't like you so well, I'd have been jealous as hell." She grinned. "Okay, I might have been a wee bit anyway. But I didn't hold it against you."

Katie laughed. "Like you had time for dating, Ms. Pre-Law."

"I liked to tell myself that was the case, too," Moira said with a laugh. "Anyway, I figured you must have someone back home you were still hung up on, and then you'd talk about your family—Declan included—but you always had this sparkle when you told stories about him. I think that's when I put it together."

"You never said anything."

She lifted a shoulder. "It was your story to tell. I respected that. I'll admit I always thought that, when you went back to Ireland, maybe things would work out."

She slipped her arm back through Katie's, her voice quiet when she said, "So, I ask again, have you seen him? Since you've been here?"

Katie glanced down, caught Moira's gaze, then nodded. "And?"

"I was wrong," Katie said simply. "About why he left. Why he stayed away."

Moira looked surprised, but the hopeful look that stole into her eyes dimmed when Katie shook her head.

"I thought he was embarrassed for me, disappointed that I'd turned out to be like all the other foolish girls who chased after him. I thought he was helping me maintain my dignity, out of respect for my family." She cleared her throat, still trying to work through the actual truth. "It, uh, it turns out maybe fate had it right after all. It seems I wasn't the only one who knew we shared a special kind of bond."

Moira's mouth dropped open, then snapped shut. "And that's not a good thing . . . because?"

Katie stopped and turned to face her. "Because the reason he was fighting it was that he thought it was wrong. Like lusting-after-your-sister wrong."

Moira made a face. "You're not his blood sister."

"I know." She sighed and started walking again. "But it doesn't change the way he felt. That he was bad, or wrong, or devalued, in some way, because he wasn't respecting the gift my parents gave him, being accepted into our family, by lusting after their baby daughter."

"Oh, Katie."

"I never thought about it from his perspective. This orphaned kid who'd been pulled into my big, huge, wonderful family and shown love and support and loyalty, like he'd never before received, and how does he repay them?"

"That's awful," Moira said. "But I get how he was seeing it."

"And then he heard me blurting out all the things I was really feeling, and he panicked. Because he had nothing to hold on to then. He didn't know what ground to stand on."

Moira stopped again. "You were both so young. And that's a lot of confusing stuff to sort out." She took Katie's arm and turned her until their gazes met. "So, are you saying he still feels that way? Do you?"

"I'm saying we can't not feel that way," Katie said. "But I don't know if I see a path forward. It's too . . . clouded now, and weird and—"

Moira shook her arm gently. "What was the very first thing you felt when you saw him? First reaction, before any of your ten-years-of-overanalyzed mental stuff got in the way."

Katie lifted her eyebrow at that last part but answered truthfully. "Joy." She sighed then, and relented, and let down what defenses she had left. "And this soul-deep relief. Like I could finally breathe again."

Moira nodded, looking satisfied. "And him? What did he look like, when he saw you?"

"Fierce," Katie said softly, thinking back on it now. The way he'd defended her. "Like he was looking at someone who mattered. Mattered more than anything in the world."

"Then what else is there?" Moira asked gently, but directly.

Katie thought about that. The corner of her mouth kicked up in a smile. "I understand now why you're such a good lawyer." She smiled fully then. "Also, your kid has no chance when it comes to skipping class, busting curfew, or pulling one over on mom and dad."

"From your mouth to God's ear," Moira said, and clasped both hands in front of her as if in prayer.

They both smiled, then laughed and hugged each other again.

"So, go get him already," Moira whispered in her ear as she squeezed her friend tight. "Ten years is long enough to wait."

Chapter 4

He should have taken her picture. Declan looked around his studio space in the mill, more than a little annoyed with himself for even considering packing things up. *Enough with the running, laddie. Apparently, the world isn't big enough for the two of ye to get lost in, after all.*

He sat down at his computer and opened the file containing the photos he'd shot that predawn morning a week earlier. He'd been useless since. Done nothing but obsess over what he was going to do about things. About Katie. About himself. He'd managed to bollocks it all up once again, but when he'd finally shoved his frustration aside, he knew at the very least they weren't done talking about it yet. That was all he'd allowed himself, the hope for a conversation, or ten if that's what it took to get them to a place where they were, at the very least, at peace with each other.

And at best?

He refused to think about that. To let himself want more. He'd gone back into the cabin that morning without any sense of what Cassian would do or say. He was still grappling with the enormity of what had just happened, of seeing Katie, talking to her, finally, after so many years. He wouldn't have blamed Cash for pretty much any response he cared to give. He'd hurt the man's sister. Again, quite obviously, from the manner in which she'd departed. Even if it wasn't intentional either time.

To his surprise, Cash had merely shaken his head and said, "Don't be a horse's arse. Fix it." And then he'd headed out, his bag already packed.

"Any advice?" Declan had called out as Cash walked to his car.

Cash had tossed his bag into the back seat, then leaned on the open driver-side door. "Stay. Talk. Then keep talking until you figure things out."

Declan could have pointed out that Cash was the worst at following his own advice, especially right at that moment, but the timing seemed a bit off. So, he'd given his brother-in-arms a nod, and the two had parted. Declan had gotten a short text from Cash later that evening, from the airport.

Whatever you do, don't leave.

Declan could swear the "her" at the end was implied, but he might have been projecting.

He'd spent the rest of that day, and the five following it, and all the nights in between, trying to decide what he should do next. He'd heard nothing from Katie and was fairly certain, given how she'd concluded their one and only conversation, that she wouldn't be the one reaching out.

In the end, he'd decided to take Cash's advice and talk to her. Set a predetermined time and place to meet, then sit and talk it out. Put it all out there, until there was nothing left to say. At least he would. He could only hope she would, too. Somewhere out of the public eye, but somewhere she'd feel comfortable. His choice would be someplace neutral, but frankly he wasn't so sure she'd agree to see him again at all, so wherever worked for her, worked for him.

Now he just had to decide how to reach out. Cash had left a piece of paper on the kitchen counter with Katie's phone number. Declan wasn't thinking she'd be all too thrilled with that breach of her privacy. Which left going to see her in person. To ask to set up another time to see her in person. Also awkward.

"Which is why your sorry arse is still sitting here, dithering over this like an untried lad looking for his first date." If only it was that basic. That inconsequential.

It was anything but. He knew he had one shot left to get it right. To give himself a chance. Give them a chance.

He'd stopped pretending he didn't know what he wanted from this. He wanted all of it. He wanted her. In his life. In his world. As his other half, finally right there next to him, where he could reach out and touch her. Make her laugh, hear her sigh, breathe in her scent. Challenge her and be challenged by her. Discover her intimately. Taste her. Finally. And fully.

Be claimed by her.

He wanted her like he wanted oxygen to breathe.

"So, you know," he muttered, "no pressure."

He opened the folder on the screen, then immediately closed it again. He wasn't seeing anything clearly and likely wouldn't until he sorted this out. He definitely didn't trust himself with editing software. He pushed his chair back and grabbed his gear bag. He'd do what he always did when the world wasn't making sense. Figure it out from behind the lens. Search, and keep searching, looking, focusing, and shooting, until things started to fall into place once more.

He'd just slung his bag over his shoulder when his phone buzzed with an incoming text. Half-expecting it to be Cash looking for an update, he was surprised to see it was from an unknown number. Only he knew exactly whom it belonged to. It was the same number Cash had left on the notepad on the kitchen counter. He slid the gear bag to the floor, then swiped his phone on to see the full message.

Where in the Falls have you not gone as yet, but is next on your list? K.

Declan sat down on the nearest stool. His palms instantly went damp. She was reaching out. Giving him his chance. He replied: Firefly Creek Trail. First waterfall up from the trailhead.

He watched the little rotating dots as she typed her reply and thought his heart might not be able to take the waiting.

Do you have time for an evening hike?

He almost dropped the phone in his haste to reply.

Trailhead, 5PM?

Bring a blanket. I'll bring dinner.

Done.

He waited, but no floating dots. His fingers hovered over the keypad as he debated saying anything more. Then he decided the time for not putting thoughts to words was over. He typed Thank you.

For?

Knowing where to start.

See you at 5.

He frowned then but decided not to read anything into it. If she'd just wanted to tell him off or request he go back to leaving her alone or even leave Blue Hollow Falls, the Katie MacMillan he knew would have just come right out and said so.

Instead she'd invited him to dinner. He wondered how she'd gotten his number, then grinned. Cash might have pulled his standard operating procedure of cutting out when things got emotionally messy, but he hadn't been content to leave them completely to their own devices. It was a measure of just how important this was, that Cash had waded in as much as he had.

Declan read over the brief text conversation again, then pocketed the phone. "I'll do my best not to let any of us down this time," he murmured, then grabbed his gear bag and headed out of the mill.

He found a note wedged between the two boards that made up the trailhead sign telling him to meet her up at the base of the waterfall. Apparently, she'd decided she didn't want to have their conversation while walking up a narrow, single-file-wide trail. *Fair point.*

It was a testament to how distracted he was that he literally looked at nothing but the trail in front of him, focused solely on getting where he needed—wanted—to be. He had his gear bag with him, and the requested blanket, but for perhaps the first time ever while in the great outdoors, his mind was not on photography.

He could hear the falls long before he got to the base area. According to the trail map, he still had a few tenths of a mile to go. He slowed as he finally saw the clearing ahead, then stopped at the edge of the trees. She was wearing soft green shorts, a light, flowery blouse, and sitting cross-legged on a large flat rock about ten or fifteen yards in front of him, a large wicker basket beside her. Her back was to him as she looked across the big pool of spring water formed at the base of the falls.

He couldn't have described the falls if asked. He hadn't even glanced at them. Instead he slid his gear bag and the blanket to the ground and pulled his camera out. He framed the shot, then lowered the camera again, and waited.

She turned almost immediately, though she couldn't possibly have heard him approach over the sound of the falls. She looked right at him, then at the camera in his hand.

He lifted it again, but paused and held her gaze, waiting for permission. She gave a slight nod and he immediately positioned the camera—an old one, one of his favorites—against his eye and looked through the viewfinder. Old-school. He zoomed in, and his breathing stilled as he connected with her direct gaze. As if she was looking directly into his soul. And he had no doubt she was, or could, from any distance.

There was no way to keep the camera steady, no way to relax the slight tremor in his hands. All his training, his knowledge, his muscle memory when it came to shooting film, fled. There would be no tripod, no remote shutter release. He held the frame until her lips twitched, and the light entered her eyes. He instantly depressed the shutter release, heard that *whirr-click*, then lowered the camera.

There would be no second shot, or third, and no editing the shaky result later. Not because of any sense of arrogance. The opposite of that. Whatever he'd captured, however it turned out, was the truth of that moment.

And he wouldn't be destroying that shot. Ever.

He stowed the camera, picked up the gear bag and

blanket, and headed toward her as she stood. There would be no more picture taking today. He was in this moment, and all the ones she would allow him to be in going forward, no filters, no barriers.

She'd pulled her shoulder-length dark hair back in a messy ponytail. Her hair was too wispy-curly for it to be anything else. He stepped up on the same rock and set everything down. Her eyes were an exact match to every one of her siblings'. An azure blue so vivid, the depths so rich, he'd have sworn they were a shade that didn't exist in nature. Set off by her dark eyebrows and apple cheeks, her cheeky grin, they always pulled him in, chest first.

She wasn't smiling now, but her expression was open. She was studying him, much as he was her.

"So, it occurs to me that we don't really know each other," she said at length. "Not truly. We've lived our adult lives on very different paths that are nothing like our childhood. The part we shared of it, at any rate."

He'd tried to anticipate where she'd start. He could have guessed all day, and it wouldn't have been that.

"True enough." If she was referring to external things, ephemeral things. *Who* she was hadn't changed, not the part of her who mattered to him.

She lifted her hand in a brief, cheery wave, then lowered it, clasped her hands and let them dangle delicately in front of her, like a royal. *Fitting*, he thought. She was every bit a princess to him.

"Hello. I'm Katherine Elizabeth MacMillan. I hail from Donegal, Ireland, originally, big family, loads of sibs. I'm the youngest, but don't let that fool you. Went to uni here in the States, got my degree in communications, made a lifelong friend. Of late I traipse about the globe with my older sister, who sings a wee bit. Keep her in line, that sort of thing. She's a pretty responsible lot, so it's an easy job, and one I love. Of course, she's gone and gotten herself knocked up, so—" She lifted a casual shoulder. "Handsome devil of a bloke, though, and she did marry him." Her smile had that wry twist he'd always loved. "Like I said, she's tiresomely responsible. He also happens to be the brother of that lifelong friend I mentioned, so that was handy. He lives here in these beautiful mountains, and now so does my sister, and, as of a few weeks ago, so do I."

Her eyes were twinkling, and if he hadn't already been certain he was going to do every last thing in his power to get her to agree to marry him, any lingering doubts had been erased.

"Pleasure to meet you, Katherine Elizabeth." He had the absolute pleasure of watching her pupils expand when he said her name. He couldn't remember now why he'd taken to calling her by her full name. He supposed he'd just liked the rhythm of it. That and she'd been quite annoyed with him when he'd first used it. Had told him, rather imperiously, that only her parents could call her by her full name, and only when she was in trouble, which, as the baby of the family, she most certainly never was. He'd used it every chance he got from that moment on, and he knew she'd secretly grown to like it quite a bit.

Seeing her very adult response to it now did all kinds of things to him he hadn't expected. The kinds of things that made him decide he wouldn't be changing his mind on using it anytime soon.

"And you?" she asked, and he loved the ever-so-slight husky note that had crept into her voice.

Her unexpected introduction had done what he'd thought impossible. It relaxed him. Her humor, her whimsy and easy manner had restored his confidence that she was truly giving them a chance to, at the very least, clear the air. She'd forgiven him for the mess he'd made of things during their last conversation, and he'd be wanting to know why, what had changed her mind. But for now, he'd follow her lead. She'd already proven to be miles better at this than he was.

"Hullo," he said, utterly incapable of keeping himself from grinning. He wasn't much for talking about himself. Ever. Quite decidedly the opposite. And yet, he knew he'd tell her his entire life story in excruciating detail if she wanted to hear it, without so much as a pause to catch his breath. Traveling the world as he had, he'd learned to be more present when needed, and he was never so thankful for that than now.

"I'm Declan MacGregor. No middle name, and I'm none too certain I came by the last one honestly, either. I hail from God knows where in Scotland, though the rumor is 'twas somewhere around Inverness." He lifted his shoulder in a matching casual shrug. "Paperwork wasn't strictly maintained, so I'm not entirely certain how, but I was orphaned as a bairn, left to the care of a group of nuns who had absolutely no idea what to do with me, seeing as they weren't running a home or orphanage of any kind."

Her eyes went soft, and a bit sad at that, but she let him continue.

"I got passed around a bit and somehow ended up in Donegal with a family I don't remember around age four or five. They were the first of a few."

His eyes might have been twinkling a bit when he added, "I'm certain it wasn't anything I did. I was an angel."

She lifted a skeptical brow at that and there was a decided twitch at the corner of her mouth. The sympathy was gone, however, and that had been his aim.

"Eventually, around age ten, I landed with the Douglas

clan, also from Scotland, but living and operating a commercial farm in Donegal, because I suppose someone thought putting Scots together made sense. They weren't the best foster parents; they weren't the worst." He left it at that. Some things couldn't simply be glossed over and were best left alone.

"Then I met a lad born right there in Donegal, came from a big family, like what you mentioned in fact." He smiled. "They provided safe harbor and I'm not ashamed to say I took advantage of it. I like to think I contributed as well, or I tried to, at any rate. The father of that family gifted me my first secondhand camera on my twelfth birthday." His smile deepened. "It was love at first sight," he said. He wanted badly to hold her gaze on that particular point, read her expression, but thought it might be too soon.

"I went on to become quite good at it, at least so the locals led me to believe. I decided to see if I could make a go of it, did some traveling with that same lad I spoke of earlier. Turned out he has a sister who can sing a bit, and she passed my work around to the handful of folks who followed her. Gave me my start, for which I'll be forever grateful. I am to the whole lot of them, actually." He saw her expression shift at that comment and thought maybe she'd come to realize how conflicted he'd been back then, about her feelings for him and his for her. That would explain why she'd reached out to him.

"I went on to have a fair amount of success. Enough to allow me to do what I love. I came here with that same lad to see that singing sister of his. Turns out she's also pregnant, just like *your* sister. Must be going around."

"You have no idea," he thought he heard her murmur, but she merely nodded for him to go on, her eyes soft now, affection openly filling them, whether for her family or for him, or both, he didn't know. Regardless, it steadied him, and that was enough.

"I've been here twice before. I felt a connection like I've never felt anywhere else the very first time I set foot in Blue Hollow Falls. One that compelled me to come back not once, but twice. I don't repeat any of my journeys. There are too many places yet left to explore, and though each one has filled my soul in a way that is hard to express—"

"You express it," she said softly. "For all the world to see."

He dipped his chin then, for a moment, and nodded in gratitude. She understood. Of course, she understood. "And yet," he went on, "I was always left hungry for more. Partly from curiosity, partly . . . because I haven't found the place that fills that last empty spot." He lifted his gaze to hers and held it intently then, his expression serious, his tone quiet, sober. His soul laid bare. "This time, I've had no desire to plot my next course. The pull here is even stronger than before," he added more quietly. "So, I gave in to it."

Her gaze was searching his, and he caught the slight trembling of her lower lip. "Pleasure to meet you," she said, the words soft, barely above a whisper.

"Wait," he added, knowing he owed her the rest. At the very, very least. Owed himself, too. "I left out a very important part of the story."

"Declan," she whispered, and he saw a hint of very real fear enter her eyes.

"The most important part," he said, then waited. *Trust me*, he thought, and wondered if they really did share that kinetic link, because he no sooner thought it than she nodded for him to continue. "From the time I learned to read, I always had a stack of books stashed somewhere, from wherever I could find them. I was an avid reader, still am. It was my escape, my way to learn about worlds other than my own, dream of what might be. So you can imagine my delight, the first time I went home with that young lad—Cassian was his name—and discovered he lived with this little faery sprite. Right there under his own roof. It was an enchanting discovery for this quiet, misfit Scot. She was like something right out of the pages of one of my favorite mythical tales, quite something, really, and I was captivated. Entranced. I was instantly convinced, despite all logic to the contrary, that she was there just for me. I couldn't explain how I knew that, but I simply knew it like I knew I would see the moon and stars at night, though I had no idea how they'd gotten up there, either."

Katie had been shaking her head slightly, as if not wanting to risk hearing what else he might say. Her pupils, however, had begun to expand as he'd continued. The insouciance that was pure Katie was also a defense mechanism, he knew, when she was nervous, or unsure of herself. As he spoke, it had faded, until she was right there with him, wide open, no walls. He knew that, because while he might not know every moment of the life she'd lived in the past ten years, he *knew* her.

"It turned out to be better than any tale I'd read in a book," he assured her. "Of course, there was a bit of adversity, adventure, and uncertainty, as all good quests have. I envisioned myself her knight errant of sorts. We shared a special friendship, a bond unlike any I had with the rest of the mere mortals who resided in that magical realm, known as the MacMillan residence. Or so it always felt to me. Even without a word, we were always in tune, always in sync." His expression shifted then. "As I grew older, I grew concerned that my feelings for her—which were pure—wouldn't be seen that way by the lad, or his lovely family, who had provided me with shelter, with love. I couldn't do anything to disrespect them. So I pulled back, as did she. I told myself that was a good thing. Grown-ups didn't believe in childish fairy tales, and it was good that she was shedding those faery wings and me my pretend knight's armor. It was childhood magic, after all, something to be left behind, for the next generation to believe in."

He took a step closer, then another. "Only, try as I might, I never could stop believing. And, as a young man, my feelings for her were no longer remotely childlike. When I overheard her confessing she felt all of those same things, and was bewildered by them, questioning why she felt them, but so certain of them all the same, I'm ashamed to say that rather than prove I was indeed still her knight errant, worthy of her love, I fell victim to my own doubts about my worth, my value. My fear that I'd do something to displease the people who had quite literally given me everything. That was no way to repay them."

She was trembling now, and he closed the remaining distance between them. "I've regretted hurting her every day since, even as I convinced myself that I'd ultimately done the right thing. Because I couldn't see a future where the misfit boy and the faery princess could find their happily ever after. But I knew if I stayed, knowing how she felt, there was no way I could have stopped myself from trying to be with her." She dipped her chin then, and he gently, very gently tipped her face back up to his. He let the story go and spoke directly from his heart. "I was afraid I'd lose the respect of your family, who meant everything to me. I thought showing my true self to you would ruin everything, my home—the only one I'd ever had—your home, ruin the entire foundation my life was built on . . . and in trying to prevent that from happening, I ruined us."

He started to lower his hand, knowing he needed to step back, give her space to take in all he'd said, all he'd laid bare, but she surprised him—shocked him—and caught his hand with hers.

She held his gaze, quite tremulously, as she shifted his hand and cupped his palm to her cheek, then shocked him further by turning her face into his palm and pressing her lips there.

He felt his knees unlock a little at the touch of her soft skin, her warm lips. The other parts of his body, however, went full-tilt rigid. Her eyes were glassy when she slipped his hand to her cheek once more and held it there.

"You didn't ruin us," she whispered, the words rough. A watery smile rose to her lips then and his vision might have blurred the tiniest bit, too, when she said, "You just gave us a chance to grow into who we needed to be, so we could see the rest of that tale through."

"Katherine Elizabeth," he said, the words hardly more than a rasp as his throat closed over at her words. Instead of stepping back, he did what he should have done all along. He stepped up.

She moved into his arms as if she'd been there a hundred times before, a thousand. A lifetime. *Or three.*

"Declan MacGregor, errant knight of the realm," she said, surprising a hoarse laugh out of him. Her eyes sparkled with unshed tears as her gaze dropped to his mouth, making his throat go dust dry. She looked back into his eyes, and what he saw in hers was everything he'd always wanted. "I think I can say with absolute certainty that this is the part of the story where you finally kiss the girl."

"Your wish will forever be my command," he said roughly, and lowered his mouth to hers.

Chapter 5

Katie was trembling so hard as their lips met for the first time that she reached for his shoulders to have something to hold on to. They were hard, and unexpectedly densely muscled, and that discovery added a quiver to muscles she hadn't used in a very long time. A deep ache bloomed inside her with a swift, primal ferocity.

This wasn't how she'd thought the day would go. She'd hoped to clear the air, maybe find some common ground where they could be more comfortable around each other . . . and see where that might take them.

This is so, so much better. This is everything.

His lips were warm, firm perfection and he claimed her mouth like he had been kissing her forever. *Lifetimes.* He knew her mouth, knew how to take it oh-so-beautifully, and wasn't shy about proving it. Add in his shower-fresh scent, the surprising feel of his body, the delectable taste of him, and all of her senses were swimming.

He pulled her deeper into his arms, until she was pressed fully against him, the intimate contact making her gasp. He slid his hand to the nape of her neck and angled her head so he could take the kiss deeper still. *Finally*, was all she could think as he claimed her again, and again. She slid her hands across his shoulders, traced her fingertips up the back of his neck, then threaded them into those thick dark waves she'd wanted to touch for longer than she could remember.

She felt his body harden as her nails raked his scalp, which made that deep ache tighten into a painful knot, even while other parts of her softened, opened, wanting him everywhere he could be.

He took his time, seducing her slowly, and quite deliberately. He wasn't aggressive or demanding, but quietly confident. Perfectly Declan. Everything about it, about him, was heady and thrilling. He invited her to join him every step of the way . . . and she gladly took him up on each and every offer. Hearing his guttural response when she gently nipped his bottom lip had her trembling all over again.

That they were taking their time, doing nothing more than kissing, didn't lessen the building sense of urgency. If anything, it amplified it. After so many years of waiting, of longing, it was hard not to want it all, all at once. This alone was more satisfying than any lovemaking she'd ever experienced.

She moved against him, her body yearning for all of its pleasure points to be taken care of, and his response, that low growl at the base of his throat as his body leapt even more rigidly to attention, excited her as much as what he was doing to her.

He finally left her mouth but didn't stop his steady assault on every last one of her now hyperaware senses, until she couldn't press her thighs any more tightly together to assuage the ache. She was all but clinging to him, just to remain upright, when all the rest of her wanted was to lie down and pull him right down with her. The need to feel his weight on top of her went beyond needy to downright primal.

He nipped her earlobe, making her body jerk against his.

"I don't want to stop," he murmured, his lips next to her ear. "Every last part of me wants to make up for the time we missed, all right now, all at once," he said, echoing her exact thoughts.

His voice was a deep, guttural hum that vibrated along her skin, making her need for him that much more visceral. He lifted his head, and her knees went wobbly at the almost ferocious desire she saw in those now dark green eyes.

"But this isn't something to be rushed." He cupped her cheek and tilted her lips to his again. "I want to savor you."

I want to strip naked right this very second and beg you not to stop. "You're making up for lost time just fine," she managed, her voice not much more than a rasp.

He smiled at that, looking sweetly surprised and pleased, and that was the Declan she'd known her whole life. His sweetness, combined with the wolfish desire in his eyes, did all kinds of things to her insides. Things she was pretty sure he was going to take care of in the most wonderful, delectable, screamingly amazing kinds of ways.

"Maybe we should spread that blanket," he began; then the corners of his mouth kicked up as her body jerked against his once more. "And have that dinner you brought," he finished.

She wasn't even remotely embarrassed. He had worked her up into quite a state, which he darn well knew, so he only had himself to blame. And he was looking quite pleased about that.

"You're hungry?" she said, unable to even contemplate food at the moment.

His eyes darkened further, and his gaze dropped to her mouth. "Oh, I'm starving."

Katie squirmed against him. Ten years hadn't changed his quiet, deliberate demeanor, but boy-oh-boy was he surprising her with the delicious layers of how he utilized it these days. She wanted to reveal, then revel in every single one of them.

He was looking at her now, an amused smile on his face.

"What?" she asked, smiling back at him. She slid her arms around his neck, thrilled to be exactly where she was at that moment. Why hadn't she been standing in his personal space like this her whole life? She planned to spend as much time right there as possible for all the time to come.

"I was just thinking, this 'kiss the girl' part is pretty nice."

"Yes, well, please know I'm also a big fan," she said, her smile deepening along with his. "Who knew a knight errant could kiss like that?"

"Well, once we take the armor off, things go a lot more smoothly."

She wasn't sure if he was just being wry, or if there was a double meaning there, but knowing Declan—and boy, she knew a lot more about him now—he'd meant it on every level.

"Probably easier for having picnics by waterfalls, too," she teased, then regretfully let him go, already missing his touch and anticipating his next sweet savoring of her. *Hopefully with something soft and comfortable to lie on nearby*, her little voice offered, and Katie did nothing to quiet it. "If you'll grab the blanket, I'll get the picnic hamper."

Just as she turned toward the basket, her phone buzzed. She slid it out of her pocket and checked the screen. It was from Seth. She froze the moment she opened the message. "Oh my God," she whispered. She looked at Declan. "It's happening!"

He'd walked to the edge of the flat rock where he'd dropped the blanket earlier, but turned to look back at her, frowning at the urgency in her voice. "What is happening?"

"The babies are coming," Katie said. She looked around, dazed, having a hard time switching her mind from what she'd been doing for the past twenty minutes to the fact that her sister was in labor. Five weeks early. "I have to go."

She closed her eyes and took a moment to slow her brain down and focus. When she opened them again, Declan had draped the blanket through the handles of the picnic basket, which he held in one hand. His gear pack was once again on his back. "Ready, Auntie Kate?" He smiled and held out his free hand to help her down from the rock.

"I'm sorry," she said. "About the picnic, and—"

"I'll drive," he said easily, his steady demeanor helping to steady her, too. "We can come back for your car later." He gestured for her to take the lead.

She nodded, her mind on Pippa and how she was doing, how the twins were going to fare, making such an early arrival. "That would be wonderful." She paused and turned to face him. "Thank you." She searched his face. His lovely, handsome face. "For . . . all of this. For telling me your story. For being willing to start over, for understanding about—"

He stepped in, dipped his head, and kissed her so softly, so sweetly, it made tears spring to her eyes. "I'm exactly where I want to be."

"And where is that?" she whispered.

"Right where you are."

She smiled and nodded, dashing at the corners of her eyes. "Same," she told him.

As they started back through the woods, he said, "I do have one question, though."

She glanced over her shoulder. "Anything."

"What did you mean, 'babies'?"

"They're so very wee," Katie said, sitting beside her sister's hospital bed, holding her hand, and looking at the photos the nurses had taken of the babies.

Michael Sawyer Brogan and Aileen Pearl Brogan had already been well on their way to arriving as Katie and Declan had raced through the lobby, and had made a very speedy, and not slightly alarming debut. Pippa had barely made it to the hospital in time.

Katie hadn't seen them in person yet. The twins were in the Neonatal Intensive Care Unit, NICU, doing well, but still under observation and awaiting the results of a few tests that would help determine their development and any issues they might be facing. Seth was outside calling the family and letting everyone know the big news.

"I'm so sorry I wasn't there," she said, but Pippa hushed her.

"Seth was with me when my water broke. He brought me straight here. It wouldn't have made any difference." She smiled tiredly. "In fact, if the two of us had dithered for even a few minutes, I might have delivered in the front seat of his truck."

Katie smiled, still trying to fathom what her sister had just been through. "You did great," she told her, smiling proudly. "So, they're okay?" she asked.

Pippa nodded, relief mixed with the worry that was still there. "They can breathe on their own, which is the most important part. We still have a lot to figure out, but they were at the high end of the weight scale for preemies."

"That's good news," Katie said, then stood and leaned down, kissing her sister's cheek. "They're MacMillans so they're fighters," she whispered, grinning as she sat back down. "And Brogans, so of course they're a hearty lot."

"True," Pippa said with a laugh even as she yawned.

"I should let you rest. Did the nurses say when you could be back in with them?"

"Soon," she nodded. "So, I'm actually trying to stay awake. I already can't bear to be apart from them, Katie. How is that possible?"

Tears prickled at the corners of Katie's eyes. Happy ones. She couldn't seem to stop them since she'd heard the news that the babies had officially arrived, and everyone was safe. "Because you're a mom, now," Katie said. "And such a good one already."

They both sniffled and laughed as Katie grabbed more tissues from the box on the table next to the bed.

"So, distract me by telling me why you and Declan arrived together?" Pippa said, wiggling her eyebrows. "And I've seen both your faces now, so don't even bother trying to tell me you've just been talking."

Katie blushed, but she was too blissful about all the events of the day to even try to pretend otherwise. "I don't know how to explain it, but I think we've finally gotten it right, Pippa," she said. "And it's more wonderful than I could have ever imagined."

Tears immediately sprang to her sister's eyes, and Pippa held out her arms for a hug. Katie leaned down and hugged her back; then they both laughed as Katie just took the box of tissues and put it right on the bed within reach of them both.

"I'll want to hear it all," Pippa said. "But it makes this day even more special. All is right with the world now, as it should be." She sighed, then added, "I hope." She looked at the clock on the wall, then the door.

"I'll go talk to the nurses," Katie told her. "See what the plan is. Declan should be back in a moment. He just went down to the cafeteria to get coffee." She stood and took Pippa's hand again. "We'll talk tomorrow or the next day, or whenever you and Seth are ready, about how you want to handle announcing the happy news to the rest of the world."

"Okay, good," Pippa said, "and thank you, for taking care of all that, for making sure things went so well here. I can't tell you what a relief it's been."

"Of course," Katie said. "Everyone here has been pretty amazing about respecting your privacy, so that helped." Katie was doubly happy they were in the Falls, and not in Dublin, where Katie would have had to deploy far more rigid security measures to keep the news from getting out. Pippa's fans were lovely and well-meaning, for the large part, but the sheer number of them created its own set of worries.

In Blue Hollow Falls, folks took care of their own, and everyone had been wonderful about giving Pippa some space for the duration of her pregnancy. Katie smiled, thinking it had only been their own family and Seth's who'd needed monitoring.

Even though the closest hospital was a good thirty minutes outside the Falls, down in the valley in Turtle Springs, Pippa and Seth had had meetings with the hospital administrators and set up a plan to handle the blessed event.

Katie had followed up on all of that upon her arrival and taken over as point person, so she knew each and every security protocol that was in place, from keeping the news private, to keeping anyone but family from getting anywhere close to her sister or the babies. Not that anyone had tried, which in and of itself was a relief.

Turtle Springs might be bigger and more developed than Blue Hollow Falls, but Katie had been pleased to discover it was still a small town at heart, and so far, everything had gone perfectly. From the doctors on down to the orderlies, they were a close-knit family, too, and Pippa and the babies were now a part of that family. Yet another reason her sister had made Blue Hollow Falls her full-time home.

Katie stepped out in the hall just as the nurse came to get Pippa. Katie stepped back inside as the nurse helped Pippa from the bed to a wheelchair.

"I can walk," Pippa said, looking at Katie, who took a step closer, prepared to carry her sister to the NICU if needed.

"For now, you'll ride," the nurse told Pippa with a kind but no-nonsense tone. "You'll be runnin' after those little ones soon enough, and wishing you had someone to wheel you around. Enjoy it while you can."

They all shared a laugh, and Katie helped spread a thin blanket over her sister's legs. She kissed her on the cheek. "I'll go get Seth."

"We've got that covered, too," the nurse said, and then out they went.

Declan came in a moment later, and Moira was right behind him.

"You just missed her," Katie said after giving her friend a tight hug. "Auntie Moira."

"Auntie Kate," Moira replied, already sniffling.

Declan handed them each a box of tissues that he'd snagged somewhere between the cafeteria and Pippa's room.

They both laughed and gratefully accepted them, then settled in the chairs in Pippa's room.

Declan handed a coffee to Kate. "Can I get you anything?" he asked Moira.

She shook her head. "I already spend half my life running to the bathroom," she said with a laugh. "Thank you, though." She looked back at Katie. "Have you seen the babies yet? Seth is ridiculously adorable about them already. I ran into him outside. We came in together just as one of the nurses found him and took him back to NICU."

Katie shook her head. "Just the pictures the nurse took."

Moira nodded. "He showed them to me. Proud papa holding his babies. They just look so impossibly small." She laughed. "Of course, given the size of him, any baby would."

"I know, right?" Katie said, and they were both laughing and sniffling again.

"Seth said they were doing well, but I know he'd never worry me, especially now," Moira said, and Katie saw how she protectively covered her own abdomen.

Katie reached over and took her hand. "They'll be fine, and so will you."

Moira nodded, then sniffled a bit inelegantly, making them both laugh, and Declan smile. "I guess I won't have to worry about when to tell them our news," she said on a watery laugh.

Declan's eyebrows lifted in surprise and he instinctively looked at Katie, just the way they used to when they were younger. Entire conversations had happened between them with nothing more than a look, an expression. It was clear he knew exactly what news Moira was talking about and had put together now what Moira had meant about her frequent runs to the loo. They shared a quick smile. She'd missed their silent communication more than she realized. He held her gaze a moment longer, and she knew he was thinking the exact same thing.

"We haven't really told many people yet," Moira told him.

"Your secret is safe with me." He smiled. "Congratulations."

"Thank you," she said, and Katie thought it was true what they said about expectant mothers glowing. Pippa had, too. Before her stomach grew to the size of Wembley, anyway.

"We're excited," Moira went on. "We just didn't want to shadow Pippa and my brother's big event." She looked at Katie. "How long have you known?"

Katie didn't have to ask what Moira meant. She expected both sides of the family to be more than a little miffed about being kept in the dark about there being two new arrivals rather than just one, though she doubted a single one of them would say as much to the new parents. Especially given there might be obstacles yet to contend with.

"She didn't tell me until I arrived here in the Falls," Katie said, then laughed at the shocked look on Moira's face. "So not much before you. I'm sorry I couldn't tell you when we had our little walk and talk, but I promised—"

"No, no, I understand. I know how worried they must have been, with Pippa on bed rest. I respect any decision they had to make." She laughed. "Seth knows I'd have been horrible at keeping that secret. I understand it was important for Pippa, so word wouldn't get out. It was nutty enough with her fans just finding out she was pregnant."

Katie laughed. "Tell me about it. The twins could have a new stuffed animal every hour of every day from the loads that arrive daily at our offices back in Dublin." She grinned. "We announced that they were all being donated to local hospitals, shelters, and other wards, but I'm guessing we'd already blanketed those places before she'd even hit her second trimester."

"Her little video, asking her friends to donate any gifts and joy they wanted to share with their local hospitals and shelters all around the world was a brilliant way to handle it, and so sweet," Moira said.

"That was Seth's idea, actually. It slowed the influx a wee bit, anyway," Katie said with a laugh. "And please know, they wanted to tell everyone, especially family. When they first found out, they were overwhelmed, as would be expected, but excited. Pippa told me they'd actually been talking about some fun way to break the news to both sides of the family. Then Pippa started having some problems, which we all learned about when she was put on bed rest, and she really didn't want to add worry on top of worry. And there was keeping it mum from her fans to consider as well. I can't believe they pulled it off, actually—"

"I truly understand," Moira said. "I know we'd have all wanted to help in any way we could, but I also know both sides of the family had already become a bit suffocating."

"A bit," Katie agreed dryly.

Moira smiled. "You're right about one thing. Her fans are going to be over the moon. That might be kind of fun, actually, when the time comes. She and Seth are already like peak adorable and I love how supportive her fans have been since her return to the music scene, then her wedding, and now add in twins? Are you kidding me?"

Katie's smile was soft but edged with worry. "I just want them all to be healthy and okay, first." She didn't even want to think about what her job was going to be like in the very immediate future. "Once everyone is out of the woods and declared healthy, we'll worry about that." Even then, and despite all the support from the hospital and the folks in the Falls, Katie was well aware the timetable might not be theirs to control.

The nurse stuck her head in the room just then. "I'm afraid we're asking all family members to head on out," she said. "Mom and Dad are doing well and will be staying with the twins for a bit." She smiled. "You'll be happy to hear all four of them are dozing. You may want to call before coming tomorrow. Maybe offer to help out at home in some way?" Which was the nurse's nice way of telling them to let the new family be a family for a bit.

"We will absolutely do that," Katie said, standing. "Thank you and thank everyone who helped with the delivery, and the NICU staff. Again," she added with a laugh, when then nurse merely smiled and nodded, as she had the last three times Katie had said the exact same thing. "I'm just . . . so thankful."

On cue, Declan handed her the tissue box and took her empty coffee cup, and they shared a smile.

"We're just doing our jobs," the nurse said, then smiled fondly. "But we especially like the jobs we got to perform today. I'll be sure to pass along your gratitude. We appreciate the good thoughts. You all have a good night."

Declan, Katie, and Moira exited through the lobby. "It feels like a lifetime ago when we first raced through here,"

Katie said. "And now there are two new MacMillans in the world. It's hard to really believe."

"Two new Brogans," Moira said, and they all shared a quick grin.

"Drive safe," Katie called out after they'd hugged good-bye. Moira headed in the opposite direction, to where she'd parked. "Call me tomorrow."

Moira turned and gave her and Declan a pointed look, then shot a dazzling smile at Katie. "Oh, you can count on that," she said. "Glad to see you took my advice," she added, before climbing into her car.

Declan took her hand as they crossed the lot. She liked that, too. When they reached his car, Katie turned to him before he could open her door. They hadn't really had time to talk, other than conversation relating to the new arrivals. Katie had spent most of her time talking to the staff and making sure the privacy measures were in place for Pippa and her new family. *A new family.* Katie was still so dazzled by the reality that the babies were here, that her sister was now a mother of two. "Thank you," she told him, "for staying."

"Well, I am your ride," he said dryly.

"I know, but I've spent the whole time running all over the place. Moira could have—"

He stepped in closer to her. "It's my family, too, Katie," he said gently, quietly, but with purpose.

"Of course," she said quickly. "I know that, but you've been here for hours and hours—"

He pushed her hair from her cheek, where it had long since tumbled out of her ponytail, then drew his thumb down the side of her face, along her jaw. She took in a tremulous breath at his caress, at the utter pleasure of it, the newness, loving that this was just the beginning.

"We haven't talked about that part yet," he said. "Your family, my extended family. Now isn't the time, I know, but—"

She covered his hand. "I can tell you that Pippa is happy, Dec. About us. Really happy."

He looked surprised. "What did you tell her?"

"Nothing," she said with a laugh. "Even though she's got a few other wee things on her mind, she didn't miss that we'd arrived together." Her tone turned wry, even as she knew she was beaming. "I guess I must look a little happy or something."

"You're beautiful," he said. "Auntie Kate."

She flushed with pleasure. "It's not even like they're my first niece or nephew, but it just feels so different."

"You and Pippa are so close, it's different."

She nodded, then slid her arms around his neck, delighting in the simple but new feeling such an ordinary act brought her. To him, too, given how he immediately bracketed her hips with his palms and drew her closer. She liked how they fit together. "Well, she's excited about the change in our relationship status. Happy for me, for us." She nodded toward the other parking lot. "And Moira is clearly dying to hug us both."

Declan nodded, but Katie wondered what he was thinking. For once he was hard to read. "Are you worried?" she asked.

He immediately shook his head. "We're all adults now, old enough to know what we want, and how to take care of each other. I think that's all anyone needs to know." He looked into her eyes, and she saw he fully believed that and relaxed. "The rest they'll see for themselves."

She smiled up at him and let all the love and affection she felt for him, had always felt for him, show in her eyes. Even in the dimly lit parking lot, she could see his response, and that thrilled her, too. "So, will you be stayin' here, Declan MacGregor, putting down roots in the Falls?" *In my life.* "Or will I be traipsing around the world after ye?"

"There might be some mutual traipsing," he said with a smile. "I'll show you my world, you show me yours."

That slow grin of his did remarkable things to her equilibrium. Especially now that she knew how those curved lips of his tasted. "And we'll always come home to Blue Hollow Falls?"

He nodded, then tugged her into his arms. "Like I said. I'm exactly where I want to be."

"Where we were always meant to be," she said with a sigh, leaning in until their lips were just barely brushing. "What took us so long?"

"Oh, I think fate got it just right," he murmured, and kissed her.

Epilogue

Declan sat on the porch of the wee cabin, his camera
resting on his knee, and watched the little tableau
sprawled out before him. It was well into fall now with
winter on the horizon, but the surprisingly warm weather
had lured them all outside for the day, and somehow the
MacMillan-Brogan caravan had landed in his front yard.
He couldn't be more pleased about that.

Blankets had been spread on what patches of grass
there were. Pippa sat between her husband's legs, leaning
back into his chest, a blanket across her legs with two wee
bundles nestled in her lap. The twins had ended up staying
in the hospital for two weeks. No major problems, just
giving them time to grow and get nice and strong.

They were almost six weeks old now and Declan still
thought they looked like the tiniest of nuggets. Nuggets
with a surprising shock of hair sprouting from their itty-
bitty noggins. Aileen with the dark curls, like her mum,
and Michael, with a shock of straight-up ginger, like his
namesake grandpapa.

When Declan wasn't photographing them, he was
framing and taking shots of the rest of the Brogan and
MacMillan clansmen, and women, and children, and pets

presently dotting the landscape around him. As Katie had predicted, they'd all flocked to the Falls the moment the news was announced. No waiting for Thanksgiving, though Declan wouldn't be surprised if they were all still here when the turkey was served another six weeks hence.

He took a photo of Hudson, who'd walked over to where Moira was watching Aiden's girls play with one of the pygmy goats that had shown up with the caravan for reasons entirely unknown. Declan caught the moment when Hudson wrapped his arms around her, his hands resting on the slight swell of his wife's stomach as she smiled up at him. Declan still wasn't sure who'd brought the wee goaties, but they seemed right at home. Not to mention surprisingly cute. He might have taken more than a few photos of them, too.

Hudson had set up a grill and a few tables, and he, Aiden, and Garrett, all three pub chefs, had turned out the most amazing food Declan had ever eaten.

His gaze kept wandering back to the nuggets. He felt surprisingly paternal about them. To the point he found himself worrying if they'd catch a chill, or eat a bug, slip or be dropped, or . . . something. Anything. Everything. He hadn't held them yet. He wasn't sure why as they'd been passed around, and around. He had endless photos of them already. At turns sweet and content, their so-serious eyes bright, observing everything with their inscrutable expressions, when they weren't yawning, eyelids drooping, their cherubic little lips pursed as they nodded off. They had every single heart within his current viewing distance wrapped around their impossibly tiny fingers, his included. Maybe he worried that if he actually held them, felt their sweet weight in his arms, he'd just become more of the Uncle Worrywart Pippa had already nicknamed him. *Or maybe it's because you're feeling that clock start to tick a bit yerself*, he thought. He ignored that possibility, even though he knew it was absolutely true.

He was home now. Truly home.

His gaze shifted back to Pippa and Seth, and he shook his head, even as he smiled. It was impossible not to. While he sat there and fretted about the sweetlings that weren't even his, his sister and her husband already looked as if they'd been raising kids their whole lives. Relaxed, happy, and so charmingly, soppingly in love with their wee ones, and each other, it never failed to move him. *Lucky wee ones*, he thought. But then, any child born to the MacMillan clan, or claimed as their own, would be inordinately fortunate. He knew that to be true.

And now his connection to them had merely strengthened further, as if that were possible. Katie had been right, of course. News that the two of them had found their way, finally, to each other, had been welcomed unanimously by the entire extended family. Cash, naturally, had taken all the credit.

He'd made sure to get photos of each and every family member, MacMillan or Brogan, who was with them today, thinking maybe he'd talk to Addie Pearl, see if any of the crafters at the mill would know how to take his photos and do them justice in a family album or scrapbook. A small book for each family grouping, and a bigger one, holding all the photos, for the grandparents. Something to put under the tree this Christmas.

A Donegal Christmas for the MacMillans this year, and he was looking forward to going home in ways he never had before.

Katie came outside just then and sat down beside him. She leaned into him and rested her head against his shoulder, as she often did, and as he'd already come to love. He leaned down and kissed the top of her head, and she glanced up at him, her smile letting him know she loved that, too.

Without a word, she took his camera and gently set it aside, then took his hand. "Come on. Let's go outside and play."

She was great at letting him do his thing and took her own joy in watching him recording life as he saw it from behind the lens. She was even better at knowing when to get him to stop playing observer and be fully in the moment.

He caught her hand as they stood and turned her toward him; they were standing so close she had to look up to meet his gaze. "I've been wondering something," he said, all the love he had for her there for the world to see. He still marveled at how wonderfully freeing that was.

"Have you?" she said, smiling up at him, all the very same things there for him to see. She tipped up on her toes and stole a quick kiss, blushing delightfully when the peanut gallery out in the yard responded with whistles and calls of "get a room." So, being the warrior faery princess she was, she kissed her knight errant again, with flair this time, just for good measure, then stuck her tongue out at them, making them all laugh. "What have you been wondering?" she asked when she looked back up at him, eyes dancing, cheeks flushed, MacMillan dimples winking.

"I am so in love with you," he said, knowing he'd never tire of looking into those eyes.

"As I am with you," she said, looking as thrilled as she had the first time he'd told her.

"Maybe I need to up my game if you had doubts," she teased.

He shook his head. "That I know, and delight in daily."

Her smile softened. "You say the loveliest things." She squeezed his hand, then slid her fingers more fully into his. "So, what is it you're wonderin' about, Declan MacGregor?"

He looked into her pretty blue eyes, eyes he planned to look into for the rest of his days, through all of his lives. "Would you fancy a wedding, Katherine Elizabeth?"

Instead of being shocked, or dismayed by his less than flowery proposal, she laughed as she pulled his mouth down to hers. "I thought you'd never ask."

And all the realm erupted in applause, hoots, and cheers as Declan bent her back over his arm as he kissed his future wife, the mother of his children, as only the best knight errant could.

And somewhere in the ether between this world and that, the Fates nodded, satisfied with their result. They could turn their attention away from the MacMillans and the Brogans now, knowing things were nicely settled there. They looked instead, back toward the ancient, timeworn hills that rose up all around this special enclave. Their work in this lovely little hollow wasn't finished. Not quite yet.

Bring Me Home

MELISSA STORM

Chapter 1

Hazel Long had always loved that her mother named her after a color. Granted, Hazel wasn't the prettiest color in the rainbow, but it did match her father's eyes, and, to her, that meant something special.

Her family always joked that she'd come out of the womb already a daddy's girl, but—truth be told—she could have just as easily turned into one of those women who becomes best friends with her mother the moment she hits adulthood. Sadly, that was never meant to be. Although she didn't have many memories of Mom, she clung to the few she still had like precious gems in need of protecting.

She'd been three when forced to say good-bye. Children that age have no concept of forever, and yet she not only had to figure out a way to wrap her young mind around the idea, but also how to accept that her mama had gone to Heaven and wouldn't ever be coming back. And so, both she and her father had no recourse other than to adapt their concept of family right then and there. They became everything to each other, two halves of one mismatched, incomplete whole.

That's how life had been ever since she could remember,

and that's how it remained now. Whenever Hazel had great news to share, she'd call her father before anyone else. Even now, with Hazel rapidly approaching thirty, they still took their summer vacations together each and every year. This year they planned to head to Honolulu for their sixth return visit, and Hazel had already begun picking up new summer dresses in anticipation.

In fact, she'd been shopping her favorite online boutique over a quick lunch hastily eaten at her desk when her father called to ask her to come to his house for some important catching up that evening.

She agreed, albeit hesitantly. For as close as they were, it seemed very out of character for him to extend an impromptu invitation like this, especially at the end of the week. They both had their rituals, and Fridays were generally reserved for Hazel to catch up on her recorded shows for the week with nothing but a pint of Ben & Jerry's and her favorite spoon to keep her company.

Besides, they always met each week on Sunday, and what kind of news couldn't wait a day or two to be shared? Especially when they were both sticklers for routine and order.

No, it couldn't be good news—or at least not *welcome* news.

Hazel ran through a worryingly long list of possibilities as she drove toward her childhood home. Maybe his stable of return customers had cleared out and he needed to borrow some money. Well, she could handle that. Her interior design consultancy boasted a waiting list nearly fourteen months long, and every single one of those clients paid in advance.

Hazel had her father to thank for that, too, in a way. He'd supported their family of two as a well-respected architect in and around Anchorage. He'd always made it his business to design good-looking and soundly structured buildings for both commercial and residential use. And little Hazel had figured at some point, "Well, if he's going to design the outside, then I'll take care of the inside."

She booked her first gig before she'd even finished high school, such was her aptitude and her passion. Looking back now, her aunt had probably been humoring her more than anything, but that didn't stop her from putting together a new family room that worked equally well for relaxing at home or hosting small get-togethers. And her aunt had been both surprised and delighted by the result. All these years later, the crisp feel of that check for one hundred dollars as it passed from her aunt's fingers into her own was still one of Hazel's favorite memories.

These days she made far more for her services, and she'd worked hard to get here. The passion never lacked in her work, such was Hazel's love affair with her chosen profession.

So, yes, if her father needed some monetary assistance now that he was getting up in years and his core client base had mostly moved on to retirement, she could certainly afford to help out.

That is, unless he'd called her over to announce his engagement to that wretched Meryl. They'd been dating for several months now and had begun to appear at an increasing number of social events as each other's plus-one. Just last week, Meryl had joined them at one of Hazel's cousin's weddings and even caught the bouquet.

Oh, she hoped the couple hadn't read too much into that!

Even though Hazel hadn't known her mother well, she

knew enough to see that Meryl could never, ever fill that specific empty spot in her father's heart.

Then again, maybe she herself was the one reading too much into things.

Perhaps the poor man just missed his only daughter. Yes, that could be it. After all, why did his unplanned invite have to signal trouble? Hazel's overactive imagination and tendency to worry had caused her difficulties before, and that's probably what was happening now.

She settled on this line of thinking, as it was the one she liked best, and it quieted her mind for the rest of the drive through the snowy Alaskan suburbs until at last she found herself standing outside on her father's stoop.

"It's open!" the scratchy baritone voice she knew so well called from somewhere near the back of the house.

Hazel took a deep breath and pressed forward, more than ready to find out which of her theories would prove correct. She found him dressed in his favorite churchgoing outfit and waiting for her with hands folded in his lap.

At least Meryl was nowhere to be seen.

Yet still, worry clenched Hazel's chest.

His voice sounded the same as always, but her father's posture and mannerisms were all wrong.

"Thanks for coming," he told her, pausing to lick his wind-chapped lips, then smiling up at her from his perch on the old love seat. "I know it's not our usual day, but I needed to talk to you as soon as possible."

Normally, he'd stand and hug her. He didn't on that night.

She shoved her hands into her coat pockets to hide their worried shaking and did her best to feign a smile. "No problem, Dad. Got some big news?"

It was at this moment she noticed the glint of tears shining at the bottom of each eye—tears that could spill at only a moment's notice, tears that were completely uncharacteristic of the strong, stoic man she'd known her entire life, that told her before his words could that everything would soon change and not for the better.

"Yes, I do," he said at last, licking his lips yet again. "I have cancer."

Chapter 2

Chemotherapy was not well named. There was nothing therapeutic about it for either Hazel or her father. In fact, they both found it downright distressing.

No one appeared to talk them through the harrowing process as the word "therapy" suggested. Instead, they were left mostly on their own with a stream of different medical professionals passing through the room occasionally to check that everything ran smoothly.

Unresectable pancreatic cancer, that was the official diagnosis.

It meant that they'd already moved past the opportunity to operate and excise the diseased cells. The doctor suggested they start with chemo and then consider adding radiation, depending on how her father's body responded to the side effects associated with treatment.

The goal was to stop the cancer from spreading and thus extend his life as long as possible.

Extend.

Not save.

In less than a year, she would become a full orphan—and probably much sooner than that, knowing her luck when it came to keeping parents around.

Of course, Hazel would never be ready to lose her father, but she had to make the best of what precious time they had left, all the while hoping for the impossible, praying for a miracle.

"You don't have to sit here with me the whole time. I'm sure you have other things to do," her father said once the nurse had fitted his hand with an IV, checked the line, and then started pumping poison into his veins.

There were no angels in cancer. Only horrible, terrifying monsters. The doctors brought in second, bigger monsters to fight the first, somehow hoping the two would cancel each other out. There had to be a better way. Why had no one discovered a better way?

She pulled her chair even closer to his bedside and tried so hard not to cry as she said, "Things, they're just things. You're what matters."

He sighed as if it were Hazel wearing him down and not the invasive medical treatment. "What about work? What about money? Money is a very important thing."

"My clients understand. Besides I have the rest of the team to cover for me as long as needed." They rarely fought and she wanted to keep it that way, but she wouldn't back down on this. She needed her dad for however long the doctors could keep him around. She'd give up everything—even her hard-earned success—if it meant she could deliver him from the inevitable.

"Careful they don't steal your business right out from under your nose while it's turned away," he warned with a dry chuckle.

Hazel had often heard the story of how her father's earliest business partner, Frank Hutchins, had absconded with their full client list in an unseen power move that led to a couple of very difficult years right before Hazel had been born. Although he spoke from experience, she still couldn't bring herself to listen to his advice. Not now. Not in these circumstances.

She leaned forward and grabbed his free hand, squeezing it gently. "Even if they do, I don't care. All I care about is you."

"Well, that's a horrible way to go about things. You'll still be here after I'm gone. Money may be just *a thing,* but it buys all the other things, chicky girl."

Ugh. She hated when he called her that. He used "chicky girl" the way other parents whipped out the first and middle name combo. That nickname meant she was being unreasonable and often that she'd fallen into trouble to boot.

"You're not going to convince me to stay away while you're going through this," she told him. "But I'll make sure to check in at work at least once per day so that you don't have to worry about my team pulling a Frank Hutchins. Deal?"

He offered her a weak smile, then closed his eyes. "If that's what it takes."

Hazel looked up just as a hospital staff member glided into the room.

"How are we doing in here, Mr. Long?" he asked with a slight tilt of his head that reminded Hazel a bit of the golden retriever she'd had growing up. Oh, how she'd loved that dog. Thinking of him, she wished he would come back at least for one night so she could hug him and cry soft tears into his fur.

She sniffed and turned her full attention to the man wearing aqua-green scrubs. Even his hair was sandy blond like that of her late pet. All of this put together made her like him instantly. "How much longer will this session last, Doctor?"

He wagged a finger at her. "Nope. Not a doctor, but I am a nurse on this ward and I'm here to help make you and your father more comfortable in whatever way I can."

"Oh, okay," Hazel answered pathetically. Had she just committed a sexist faux pas? In her defense, she still envisioned nurses as the old-fashioned candy stripers with paper hats and white Keds, the kind who'd treated sick patients long before she'd ever even been born. Whatever the case, this blond-haired male nurse, with his strong, sharp jaw and features that suggested a Scandinavian lineage, did not seem to mind her assumption.

"I'm Keith," he added, directing his words toward Hazel but his eyes toward her father. "And it will be about another three hours before we can remove the intravenous drip. You're looking kind of tired, Mr. Long. Would you like me to close the curtains and dim the lights so you can get some rest?"

Her father took a deep breath. "That would be nice, although I doubt I'll be able to sleep through this. Perhaps Hazel can use it as an opportunity to go get some work done."

"Dad . . ."

"We had a deal, remember?"

Keith looked to her with raised eyebrows as she gathered her bag and coat from the corner of the room. A moment later, as if remembering himself all of a sudden, he shook his head and went to check on her father's IV. After assuring himself that all was in order with the treatment, he collapsed the blinds and headed toward the light switch just beside the doorway where Hazel stood waiting.

"Call me if anything   *anything*—happens," she pleaded

with the nurse, widening her eyes as he passed to show just how seriously this request was meant to be taken.

He gave her a quick nod and a broad smile she found to be quite charming, then disappeared from the room.

"Now you go, too, chicky girl," her father croaked. Why did his voice suddenly sound so hoarse? Could so much really change in only a matter of days?

She took a step toward him to investigate, but he coughed and demanded in a clear, somewhat exasperated voice, "I'll still be here when you get back. Now get gone before I ask them to add you to the 'do not visit' list."

She forced a laugh, but the stubborn old man didn't back down.

"You think I'm kidding? I'll do it."

"Fine, Daddy." She raised her palm and pressed her lips to the fleshy part by her thumb, then tossed the kiss to her father like a wild softball pitch—the same way she'd always said good night to him as a little girl. It felt right to revert to their old habits, those precious shared memories.

"I'll be back soon. Love you."

Chapter 3

Hazel didn't like lying to her father, but she'd like it even less if she was too far away to get to his side in the event of an emergency. Figuring a little white lie was a small price to pay in this scenario, she headed to the hospital cafeteria to grab a cup of coffee and spend some time alone with her thoughts.

The huge, open eating space proved to be a strange mix of life's best moments and its worst. Patients, loved ones, and staff filled up the bulk of available tables. People celebrating births and long-awaited surgeries sat shoulder to shoulder with those mourning losses and waiting for news in uncertain situations. Hazel belonged to neither of these groups, and yet she belonged here in this place, where just four floors above, her father's body was being filled with a poison that was also meant to be an antidote.

Such a strange thing modern medicine was, but then again, she'd take today's poison over yesteryear's treatment by leech in a heartbeat. Especially if it worked.

She drained her first cup of coffee, then grabbed another shortly after. If she returned to her father's room too quickly, he'd suss out her dishonesty and let her know his disappointment in her.

The last thing she wanted to do was make him believe his opinions didn't matter to her, to disrespect him when he was already feeling so physically vulnerable.

The warm coffee gave her something external to focus on, which she appreciated in that moment. Would the next several weeks—several months—be like this?

No, she realized. It would only grow more difficult as her father's health deteriorated further. God help them both.

"Hey! Hey, lady with the purple sweater!" a high, lilting voice called from across the way.

Hazel glanced down just to make sure she remembered correctly—the morning seemed to have been ages ago at this point—and, yes, she was, in fact, wearing a purple sweater. She glanced up and searched until she found the source of the voice.

Two tables in front of her and one row over, she saw a group of three women sitting together with coffees of their own. They appeared to be more or less her age, although she couldn't be certain. The weirdest thing was that two were smiling brightly at her, and the third was wiping at tears with the edge of her hand.

It was the one who was crying who'd spoken to her, and she spoke again now. "I recognize you from the oncology ward, I think. First timer?"

Hazel nodded. Should she go over to join them at their table, politely look away, or continue to speak loudly over the other tables?

The woman answered that question for her in short order. "Come sit with us. We have a free spot."

One of the woman's friends pulled out the empty chair and motioned to it to further strengthen this invitation.

Well, she still had at least an hour to kill if she didn't

want to raise her father's suspicions, and the three women seemed normal enough. . . .

She gathered her beverage, phone, and purse, then went to join them.

"It was you I saw this morning, wasn't it?" the woman said with a confident smile. Her bright teeth shone against her tanned skin, leaving Hazel to wonder whether she artificially tanned it during the winter months or if she might have a bit of Inuit blood in her. The woman's prominent cheeks and dark hair seemed to further indicate a native lineage.

"Yes, it's my father's first day of chemo," she confided, dropping her voice low as if adding volume would add strength to the statement she very much wished were untrue.

The three friends nodded in unison.

"We're all here for the same thing," one of them explained. "By the way, I'm Amy. My mom has a stage four glioblastoma. Surgery helped for a little while, but it's back and bigger than ever."

"I'm so sorry," Hazel said with a frown of solidarity.

Amy just shook her head, making her unkempt blond hair fall forward like a curtain. "The worst part is she's so scared and confused. She doesn't even know who I am most days anymore."

Cancer alone was an overwhelming foe, but at least Hazel still had this time with her father. Poor Amy's torment was at a new, painful level that no one deserved to bear.

"I'm Bridget," said the first woman, the one with the tan and the cheeks. "My mom has breast cancer. We were in remission for a few years, but now it's gone metastatic. It's in her lungs and bones and who knows where else."

"I'm sorry," Hazel said again, wishing there was something more she could do or say for all of them.

Finally, the last woman spoke up. Her long dark hair had been swept back in a single braid that fell halfway down her back. She appeared to be the most dainty of the group, though her voice came out the deepest—husky, sultry like an old-time singer. "Nichole. Dad. Prostate," she said simply.

"Nichole's new, too," Bridget explained. She seemed to be the unofficial group leader. "With time it gets easier to talk about. You'll see."

"But it never gets easier to go through," Amy added with a sigh before taking another quick sip of her drink. "That's why we've formed our little support group."

"The Cancer Cafeteria Club," Nichole said with a sarcastic, bitter laugh.

"Okay, so the name needs work," Bridget conceded. "But we've found it's better to go through this together than apart."

Hazel nodded. "That's nice of you. Good friends can make a huge difference." Well, at least that's what she assumed. Hazel had been too busy growing her business to worry much about friends. Besides, she'd always had her father when she needed someone to listen to her troubles or attend events with her. Maybe it really was time for her to branch out socially. She'd need someone who was on her side when her father could no longer be there.

"Yup," Bridget said with a pucker of her lips. "Now tell us about you."

"Oh, right." Hazel looked toward Nichole for support, but her focus seemed to be elsewhere. "I'm Hazel, and my dad has, um, unresectable pancreatic cancer. We just found out last week."

"Ouch," Amy said while Bridget sucked air in through her teeth.

"That sucks," Nichole offered with an even deeper frown than she'd had before.

"Yeah, it really does," Hazel agreed. Despite the strange circumstances, a smile crept across her face. She hadn't made friends this easily since grade school. It seemed someone up there just might be looking out for her, after all.

"Well, welcome to the club, I guess," Nichole said.

Bridget picked up on that line and seconded, "Yes! Welcome to the Cancer Cafeteria Club." The earlier tears had all but vanished, and Hazel liked to believe that she had somehow helped to make that happen.

"We have got to work on that name," Amy said with a smile.

Chapter 4

Although Hazel had only wanted to focus on her father during his final months, it did feel nice to have a network of new friends who understood what she was going through. At the same time, it felt selfish to even worry about herself when he was fighting for his life. Still, this was the hardest thing she'd ever experienced *in her life* as well.

"Do you have any tips for getting through all this?" she asked the other women as they all took long, contemplative sips of their coffees.

"Just keep swimming," Bridget answered right away. "That's my mantra."

"No, that's a line you stole from Disney," Nichole grumbled, then channeled her full attention toward Hazel. Her green eyes bored into Hazel's brown ones. "You want my advice? Just when you think it can't get any worse, it always does."

"That's not advice," Bridget corrected with a frown. Her entire face looked different without her ubiquitous grin. "And it's not very encouraging, either."

"Fine," Nichole grumbled as she picked her coffee back up and squeezed it between both hands. "Here's the advice part. Never assume you've reached rock bottom. The bottom can always fall out again and send you crashing down farther than you ever imagined."

"That's really grim, Nic," Amy said with a sigh. She glanced toward Hazel with an apologetic shake of her head before continuing. "I think our new friend was looking for advice to make things less depressing. Not more."

"No," Hazel insisted. As much as she appreciated kindness, there was definitely something to be said for mental preparedness. "That helps. She's the first person who's been willing to tell me like it is. What else do I need to know?"

Nichole smirked as if she'd won some type of horrible prize that none of the others wanted. "Be prepared to change your dad's diapers. Yes, there will be diapers."

"C'mon, Nic. Enough. Stop," Amy warned. Her petite features pinched in irritation. "Not everyone gets to diapers, and they have a great staff here, so . . ."

"Yes, she's right. Sometimes they die much quicker," Nichole explained with a toss of her braid. "Honestly, I don't know which is better. It's like a lesser of two evils situation, except there is no lesser. Everything sucks equally."

Bridget rolled her eyes, but Hazel caught fresh tears welling in the corners of her already red-rimmed eyes. Still, the poor thing smiled.

"You know," said Amy, who had apparently been assigned as peacekeeper for the group. "Speaking of the great staff here, have you met Keith yet?"

Hazel hummed, immediately conjuring up the picture of the good-looking nurse she'd met not even an hour ago. It was impossible to stop the smile that formed on her face as she thought of the kind and handsome man who was helping to care for her father.

"I recognize that smile!" Bridget teased. "That's the Keith smile. Amy gets it, too."

"I don't get it," Nichole added, but now she was smiling, too. "That blond, All-American thing is so not my type."

Amy rolled her eyes. "I'm beginning to think that maybe you don't have a type."

"Well, if he's out there, this mythic *guy of my type*, I sure haven't met him yet," Nichole agreed. "But really, romance is the last thing on my mind these days. As it should be for all of us."

"I get where you're coming from." Amy swept her messy hair back into an even messier ponytail. "But when you're starving and someone shoves a giant piece of chocolate cake at you, you've gotta pick up a fork."

Bridget guffawed, eliciting glances from the folks at the next table over. "I'm glad you said cake, and not meat!"

Hazel and Amy joined in the laughter, and even Nichole let out a soft chuckle of her own. It felt nice to laugh, to have something to think about other than the doom and gloom that clung to the dark edges of her mind. Being with this group of women felt like riding a roller coaster in the dark. You didn't know when the next twist, turn, or drop would be coming, only that it inevitably would. And soon.

Bridget fingered the silver-and-amethyst bracelet Hazel wore on her right wrist. It had been her mother's, and she only took it off to shower. "This is pretty. Everything you're wearing is pretty. It's how I could tell you were new."

Hazel had dressed in one of her dowdier outfits that day—straight-leg jeans, ballet flats, and a scoop-neck blouse in her favorite shade of burgundy—but she wasn't about to insult Bridget when the woman had just paid her a compliment. "Thanks," she said simply.

"Do you work in fashion? Because maybe when this is all over, you could give me a makeover or something. What do you say?" Bridget leaned over the table and turned her head to either side to show her profile.

All four women fell silent, knowing that "when this is over" meant "when all of our parents have died."

"Bridget's the youngest of us," Amy explained. "Kind of like our kid sister, and she has a way of saying whatever's on her mind."

Hazel shrugged off the excuse. "It's fine, really. I don't work in fashion. I own an interior design firm." She didn't mind discussing trivial things right now, not if it would help to keep her light and happy while she was with her father. He didn't need to worry about his daughter's hurt feelings when he was already facing the end of life.

"See," Bridget clucked proudly, sitting taller now in her chair. "I knew it was something like that. And I'm not *that* much younger than everyone else. I'm twenty-two. Luckily, I was able to finish my bachelor's degree before Mom got sick, so I could take some time off before going back for veterinary school. Right now, I'm working as a vet tech, usually the night shift at this emergency place. Yeah, I hate seeing the worst of the worst cases, but at this point, I'm almost numb to it, given . . . yeah. Anyway, my dad or brothers often stay with Mom through the night when she's checked in for a while, but I still always feel guilty leaving her. Like it's me and me alone who understands what she's going through, just because we both have boobs."

Wow, that was an earful. Hazel was beginning to see that this particular new friend never found herself without something to say. She herself was closing in on her thirtieth birthday, which made twenty-two seem impossibly young. She'd been a whole different person at that age and wondered now what kind of person Bridget would become as she completed school and learned more about what she wanted from life. No doubt, losing a parent would change her permanently. It would change all of them.

"I'm a teacher," Amy said. "Second grade, but currently on sabbatical. Nichole's a social worker."

"It's why she's such a Debbie Downer all the time," Bridget explained. "When she's not here at the hospital with us, she still has to deal with the most awful stuff that can happen to people."

Nichole shrugged. "She's not wrong, but I do love my job. If anything, it helped prepare me for what's going on with my dad now. I can be more realistic about the outcomes. No false hope here."

And on that pleasant note, Hazel really needed to get back to check on her father. She pushed back her chair and grabbed her belongings, including the empty coffee cup. "Thank you so much for introducing yourselves. I'm sure I'll be seeing all of you around the ward."

Amy stood and pressed her phone into Hazel's hand. "Not so fast. Give us the digits, babe. We're going to be seeing a lot more of each other. Just you wait."

Hazel had no doubts about Amy's prediction. Seeing them more would mean being here more. Being here more would mean that her father was still with her.

Welcome to the Cancer Cafeteria Club, indeed.

Chapter 5

Hazel sent a quick email to her assistant while riding the elevator back up to the oncology ward. That way, if her father asked, she wouldn't need to tell a complete lie. She had officially checked in at work, and so far everything was fine.

When she returned to the tiny hospital room, she found it dark, with the curtains drawn. She hesitated in the doorway, not wanting to disturb him but also not wanting to turn away.

A familiar voice from the hall informed her, "He's awake if you want to go back in."

She whipped around at the sound of the voice, and—sure enough—Keith stood at the nurses' station, staring at her with a smile that seemed so at odds with the situation and the place that it gave her pause.

Only she realized now that she wore a smile, too. No wonder Amy found him so alluring. Hazel would be willing to bet that many of the younger patients and family members harbored similar secret crushes on Nurse Keith.

She, however, could not be one of them.

"Thanks," she muttered, disappearing into the room

and out of his view before she accidentally did something crazy like smile at him some more—or, God forbid, flirt.

"You're back," her father said with such forced animation it made her want to start crying all over again.

"Well, I only left because you made me," Hazel reminded him. "Want me to turn on the lights?"

He adjusted himself on the thin hospital mattress. "Leave the lights, but get the blinds, chicky girl."

Uh-oh, there was "chicky girl" again. She decided to breeze past it and hope the obnoxious nickname didn't mean he'd somehow become unhappy with her in the short time they'd been separated.

After pulling the squeaky blinds back open and letting in a blast of harsh sunshine, she reclaimed her seat at his bedside. "Did you get some good rest while I was gone?"

"Not rest." He licked his lips and straightened the blanket on his lap. "But I did manage to do some thinking."

Hazel raised a suspicious eyebrow at the man she loved more than anything in the world. "Oh?"

"Remember that time when you were six or seven, and you came home from school telling me you had life all figured out? You were going to be a rock star, and you wanted me to play the drums. You said we could see the whole world together, and that it would be so much fun. Only later did I find out it was because you figured rock stars didn't need to learn math and thought the sudden shift in career choice would be a good way to explain away a bad grade." He laughed so heartily it brought on a coughing fit.

Hazel handed him the Styrofoam cup from the bedside tray and held it in place so he could sip water through the bent straw. "I'm not sure I remember it happening, but I do remember you telling me about it again and again growing up."

Her father sucked a long drink in through the straw and then waved the cup away and got a far-off look in his eyes. "I was thinking of that and all my other favorite memories, and I'll be honest, I was feeling rather sorry for myself that I have to die early and miss out on making more memories, on ever having grandchildren."

Hazel was about to soothe him with the usual platitudes when he continued with the speech that seemed to have been written and rehearsed while she'd bided her time in the cafeteria.

"Then I thought, actually, I'm so lucky that I got the chance to make all the memories we already have. I've been very blessed to have almost thirty years with you, my chicky girl."

She bent forward and gave him a kiss on the cheek. "I'm the lucky one. I got the best father in the world." Tears threatened at the corner of each eye.

"But your mom died when you were so small. You never got the chance to make memories with her, the way you and I did together. She missed out on seeing you grow into this strong, smart woman—of whom I'm incredibly proud."

"I know, Daddy." If he was going to call her chicky girl, then she'd use her long-ago nickname for him as well. "We've made some great memories over the years and we'll keep making them as long as we can. There could still be a miracle. We could still have years—decades even—left."

A miracle. Did she believe that? Did he?

Her father shook his head subtly as if to answer her unspoken question, but he also smiled as he said, "Whatever the case may be, I'm going to be okay. You see, I'm the lucky one, because I got time with you both."

Lucky? Nothing about this situation was lucky, not for

either of them. Hazel wanted to scream until he understood just how unfair it all really was. He'd lost his first business, his wife, and was now in the process of losing his life. How on earth could that be lucky?

The gleam of unshed tears reflected in his eyes, but still her father smiled. He swallowed before speaking again. "That's why before I go, I want to tell you about your mom. Not just the usual facts about how we met and how she died, but everything. I want you to know her as best you can before I go."

Hazel nodded. She'd agree to anything he wanted these days just to keep him smiling. She'd always been curious about her mother, wondered about the hidden stories that her father hadn't chosen to share with her. Would these new stories change anything? Would they be a comfort to her father as he looked back at his favorite memories instead of looking forward into his dark future?

"I'd like that," she said when she realized he was waiting for a response.

His smile widened as he closed his eyes contentedly. "Perfect. And then, when I get to Heaven, I'll tell her all about you."

Chapter 6

*H*eaven.

Hazel and her father had dutifully gone to church each Sunday while she was growing up, a tradition she'd failed to carry into adulthood. But suddenly the teachings of all those years came crashing back.

Streets of gold, mansions in paradise, the right hand of the Father . . . It didn't feel so far away now. Would this really be the scene of her parents' grand reunion? And was it just like the Sunday school teachers had taught, or was the concept so far beyond their grasp that she could never understand it no matter how hard she tried?

Here on earth, her father had poison flowing through his veins as his body attacked itself—killed itself. But in Heaven, he'd be free to run again, to love, to exist without pain, heartbreak, or limitations of any kind.

"Every time I think I'm all cried out," she told her father, "you get me going again."

She sniffed and rooted through her purse for a tissue. She could contemplate the mechanics of Heaven later, maybe ask her new friends what they thought happened to the soul after the body died. "I'd love to hear more about Mom. Whatever you're willing to tell me."

He nodded and dropped his hands to either side. His body looked so small lying in the center of that plain, white bed. How had he managed to become so tiny in such a short span of time? Or was it that he'd been small all along, but she'd never paused long enough to notice?

"I'm going to tell you everything," her father said with a slight dip of his chin. "That's how you get the full picture of a person, by learning the good and the bad. And your mother, angel that she was, had plenty of bad in her, too."

With that, Hazel's mind floated back toward Heaven. What might her father say about Hazel when he met her mother again in Heaven? What did he consider the bad parts of his only daughter?

"I want to hear it all." She took his hand in hers and fixed her gaze on his eyes, the soft hazels she'd been named for. "I'm ready."

He let go of her hand and moved his fingers to the thin gemstone bracelet she'd inherited from her mother. When she moved her wrist closer so he could get a better look, the diamonds caught the light streaming in from the window and shimmered vibrantly.

He chuckled to himself as he continued to stroke the bracelet. "Did I ever tell you about how your mother got this?"

Hazel thought back to the story she had heard many times before. "When you proposed, you didn't have enough money to buy a ring so you gave her this bracelet instead, along with a promise to buy her the world's most magnificent diamond ring just as soon as you could afford it."

He nodded thoughtfully. "That's the story we told everyone, but it was only partially true."

The story of her parents' engagement was a family

legend. She'd grown up picturing that romantic moment time and time again, while wondering if one day a man might propose to her in the same fashion. Only to find out it had been manufactured . . . but why?

"I'm intrigued," she said at last, not knowing what else she could say until she heard the true course of events. "Go on."

"Well, Frank and I were just getting started with our architecture firm, and I couldn't afford a decent ring even though I wanted to marry your mother more than anything. So I proposed without a ring, but with the promise of my eternal love and devotion and the best ring money could buy down the road."

"And the bracelet," Hazel finished for him, still longing to hold on to the story she knew so well.

Her father winked at her. "Nope, that's where the real version of events is a little different. Your mother already had the bracelet when we met. Her ex-boyfriend had given it to her for Valentine's Day. When we got together, she offered to get rid of it, but it always suited her so perfectly, and she deserved to have beautiful things, so the bracelet stayed. Besides, it was her ex that introduced us on one of those 'you set me up and I'll set you up' deals."

She knew that her parents had been fixed up on a blind date, but not that the matchmaker was her mother's ex-boyfriend. "That's a little weird," she said, twisting her features in dismay as she thought of letting one of the few girlfriends she had fix her up with someone they'd deemed unworthy of dating themselves.

Her father laughed in earnest now. "Yes, but it all worked out in the end. And Frank always was a bit weird, if you ask me."

"Wait, Frank?" Hazel asked in disbelief, eyeing her

mother's once beautiful bracelet with feelings of shock and revulsion. "The Frank who screwed you over Frank?"

"None other." He folded his hands in his lap, looking pleased with Hazel's reaction—or perhaps pleased that the truth had finally come to light.

"No wonder you kept that a secret all these years." She sighed, a new thought occurring to her now. "When he stole the business out from under you, why didn't you get rid of the bracelet then?"

His eyes glistened once more, all the lightness of the moment evaporated from the air. "Because your mother had already fallen sick, and she planned to leave it to you. To remember her by."

This was a memory she was glad she couldn't recall on her own. From the worn expression on her father's face, she knew he remembered it clearly enough for both of them. She had to keep him talking, had to move past this.

"Did she die without getting the ring you promised her?" Hazel had often contemplated this question but had never had the courage to ask it aloud before.

Her father closed his eyes and smiled. Hazel wondered if he was recalling his late wife's face, if he was more eager to be reunited with her or saddened to be separated from Hazel. "She got her ring. It's buried with her now."

"*How?* You were even more broke when she died than when you'd first met, what with the medical bills and Frank's betrayal."

"We redefined what made a ring the best. In the end it wasn't carats or clarity ratings, but rather what it represented."

"Your love," Hazel murmured reverently.

He pointed at her and made a small clicking noise. "Bingo."

Someday she hoped a man could love her like that,

although it seemed like such a silly thing to wish for while she was losing one parent and finally learning all the secrets that had been kept about the other.

Besides her dear, sweet father, Hazel's greatest love in life had been her work. She'd relished every moment of building her business, watching it grow, and she loved delighting clients with the beautiful home interiors they'd craved but hadn't known how to request.

She created a special joy that few others could by taking a person's home and turning it into the perfect sanctuary.

And now her father was doing her a similar favor by handing his memories over to her so they could stay with Hazel all through her life. She realized then just how much she needed this, but the burden of confessions already made seemed to weigh heavily on his weakened body.

The rest would have to wait.

Chapter 7

Following six grueling hours of chemotherapy with a brief rest period afterward, the oncologist cleared Hazel's father to return home for the evening. The team had originally requested to keep him at the hospital overnight, but he'd already fought hard to achieve day patient status and intended to keep the arrangement that way as long as possible.

Despite the long, emotional day, Hazel didn't feel the least bit sleepy. Her father, on the other hand, fell asleep in his favorite recliner almost as soon as they'd gotten back home.

And yet the treatment team eventually wanted to add radiation to his plan, too. Did that mean the rest of his days would be just like this . . . or worse?

She drifted through the halls of her childhood home, taking in the familiar fragrances and vivid memories that lived within these four walls. At the bottom of the big staircase lay a deep indent accented by a flurry of scratches from the time Hazel had tried to ride her bike down the stairs but wound up crashing into the hardwood landing instead. She'd been lucky not to break any bones during that stunt.

Even though she'd always loved pretty things, Hazel had been the very worst kind of tomboy. The more dangerous the stunt, the better as far as she'd been concerned. It was almost as if she'd been taunting the grim reaper for taking her mother away, daring him to take her as well. Of course, she hadn't consciously realized that as a child.

Instead she grew up and left that phase far behind as she became increasingly mild-mannered with the passage of each year. But she liked to think that audacious little daredevil lived within her still, ready to jump to attention the moment Hazel needed her.

And, as she already knew, that moment would be coming soon. For what was more courageous than living on when you no longer had the will to keep going? She had no idea how her father had survived losing his wife so young. He'd been younger than she was now, which she found almost impossible to imagine.

Would a life snuffed short by illness be Hazel's fate one day, too?

She tried to imagine her mother as a young woman falling in love, starting a family, saying good-bye. What dreams had she needed to leave uncaptured?

Whenever her father shared memories with Hazel, he tended to focus on how much her mother had wanted her, loved her. Was her greatest aspiration really to be a mom as he'd always insisted, or was her father leaving out a much larger chunk of the story?

Even as a young child, Hazel had known she wanted to design homes for a living. What had her twenty-six-year-old mother wanted to do before she'd closed her eyes for the very last time?

And why hadn't Hazel ever thought to ask before now?

In her mind, her mother lived on as the perfect fifties housewife—always looking beautiful, smiling for her family, serving dinner, keeping house. And that vision had helped her growing up when her father burned yet another pot of spaghetti or sent little Hazel to school in a wrinkly dress. She'd once had someone to look after her and take care of these things, but that person had been taken from her too soon.

They all had love in spades, though. That was what united the three of them. With her mother's domestic thread broken, Hazel had become industrious and ambitious like her father. She'd devoted her career to making homes more special, just as she believed her mother had done before her.

But what if that wasn't true?

She'd never have pictured her late mother on the arm of that snake, Frank Hutchins, and yet . . . The truth her father had shared earlier that afternoon still troubled her. What other memories had he changed in order for them to appear more perfect?

What if her parents' marriage hadn't even been a happy one?

What if she'd harbored some other aspiration that Hazel knew nothing about? And why hide the truth for so long?

She wanted to be angry with her father, but she understood why he'd done it. Little Hazel had needed that pedestal for the memory of her mother, even if it had been constructed on misdirection and half-truths. But big Hazel, the one staring now at her parents' framed wedding portrait that stood atop her father's otherwise bare nightstand, she needed to know the real person behind the idol, to find out who her mother had really been.

Entering now into her childhood bedroom, she paused in the doorway. Her mother had never known her here. Hazel and her father had moved to this new house a couple

years after her mother's death. He said they needed to
build something new instead of living in the ruins of
something that had already been destroyed.

He'd been so sad back then. Much sadder than he
appeared even now, face-to-face with his own pending
demise.

Hazel sank down onto the old mattress that had been
dressed neatly with one of her aunt's homemade quilts.
She'd been happy here. Her father had always taken care
of her, taken care of them.

But now that she knew some of her memories had been
fabricated, she had to wonder if he might have deprived
Hazel of something important as a way of protecting himself. She also wondered what would have happened if
he hadn't fallen ill. Would he have ever chosen to share
this undoctored history with his daughter?

The truth was already coming out, and she desperately
hoped it wouldn't change things between them.

Chapter 8

Hazel didn't sleep well that night or any of the many that followed. Not only did she have a seemingly unlimited stream of worries coursing through her mind, but she also mistook every little sound for her father calling out to request help.

A full two weeks had passed since he'd begun chemotherapy, and with each passing day, he seemed to grow weaker—not stronger as they'd all so desperately hoped. Hazel, too, became increasingly weak as the weight of her fatigue combined with the enormity of her anxiety.

Nothing helped, not even the new friendships she'd forged in the hospital cafeteria or her secret crush on the ward's most charming male nurse. As the treatments continued, day by brutal day, her father had begun to lose his smile. He'd spoken less, shared fewer stories of Hazel's mother, and just generally seemed to be calling it quits.

How could she encourage him to fight harder, when the fight itself had become part of what was killing him?

She didn't have the answer to such a hugely daunting question, but she could start by preparing breakfast. They'd get through this one day at a time, one more meal, one extra moment spent triumphing over death.

They didn't have forever, but at least they had right now.

Her father woke and joined her not long after she'd cracked the eggs over the frying pan. The man loved a hearty meal. Some things never changed, while others switched direction so fast they gave Hazel mental whiplash.

"Do you want two eggs or three?" she asked him with the brightest smile she could manage in her exhausted state.

"Better make it one," he answered, hobbling over to the table and pulling out a chair. "My stomach isn't too happy with me today, I'm afraid."

"But you slept great," she pointed out, deciding to compromise and prepare two eggs for his breakfast.

"That I did." He grabbed his tablet from the center of the table and opened his favorite news app. Hazel had bought the gadget for him as a birthday present when the new technology had first come out, but he'd never used it for anything more than an electronic newspaper.

He groaned and shook his head while reading over the latest headlines. Even with so much going on in his own life, he still worried about the wider world, still wanted to be informed. She herself found the news so distressing, she tended to avoid it as much as she could. Her father refused to accept this apathy and did his best to ensure she heard about any major local or national developments, whether or not she wanted to.

Hazel finished preparing both their plates and brought them over. "Dad? Do you want to keep reading, or is it okay for me to ask you some questions while we eat?"

In lieu of sleeping, she'd ended up thinking long and hard about how to push him gently for more information about her mother. While he had been eager to share earlier, he had chosen to hide some truths from Hazel for her entire life. There had to be a very good reason for that. But now that she knew her family's history had been altered, she couldn't back down until she found answers to the myriad questions crowding her mind.

Her father pushed the iPad aside and picked up the fork that Hazel had lain beside his plate. "You can always ask me anything, chicky girl. Is this about Mom?"

Her eyes widened with surprise. Maybe this wouldn't be so difficult, after all. "How did you know?"

"I'm imagining the story I told you about the bracelet came as quite a shock. Probably kept you up all night wondering what else you don't know about your mother's and my past. And whether I'd be willing to tell you about it."

She shook her head and took a giant gulp of juice from the crystal tumbler she'd always favored growing up. "You know me so well."

"That's my job as a father," he answered, setting his fork back down without taking even a single bite. "For years, I also thought it was my job to remove the bitter spots when I talked about your mother, so that you'd only be left with the sweet. Now I'm not so sure that was the right call."

Hazel remained silent, craving more, whether it be bitter, sweet, or some other flavor altogether. It had been more than a week since he'd last shared, and there was still so much more she needed to know.

He cracked his knuckles before continuing, a bad habit that came out whenever her father was feeling distressed. Hazel had to know why.

"I loved her more than anything. Well, besides you, chicky girl. To me, she was perfect, but she also made some less than perfect choices. We all do. The more I think about it now, the more I wonder if I've kept you from truly knowing her by leaving out certain aspects of the truth."

Oh, gosh. She would soon learn something terrible. She just knew it. *This is what you want*, she reminded herself as she fought against the rising surge of panic. *The truth.*

She nodded in an attempt to encourage herself just as much as her father. "I want to know everything, all of the parts you haven't told me."

He licked his lips and placed a hand on the table. "I will try my best to do just that. Although I worry a bit that I've been altering the truth so long that even I may have forgotten exactly how it goes."

That is the danger, Hazel thought. *Lying to yourself so much that the lies become the truth.* What would her mother think, knowing she'd been remembered this way?

Seeing that he was waiting for her to speak next, Hazel decided to ask the most pressing question first. "You always said that the only thing Mom ever wanted in life was to have me, but she was so young when she died. Was that really true? Did she never want anything else besides a baby?"

Her father sighed and picked up his fork again, slowly, methodically cutting off a piece of fried egg white and lifting it to his mouth. He chewed intentionally, biding his time, presumably searching for the perfect words to offer his daughter.

Which meant the answer wouldn't be one either of them liked.

"She was a dancer," he said at last, studying his daughter to gauge her reaction before saying anything more. "The best dancer I'd ever seen. She wanted to go on tour with this pop group that had become very popular at the time, talked about it constantly."

This seemed a tame enough confession, so why hide it? And why had her larger family been complicit in keeping this a secret?

Hazel wrapped both hands around her glass to steady them. "How come no one in the family ever told me about her dancing? How come there are no pictures of her dressed for recitals? No videos?"

He licked his lips again. "I don't think anyone knew how special dance had become to her. She kept a lot of things private over the years. Or maybe they thought it was just a phase. Something she'd done growing up but quit after going off to college."

"But she never quit," Hazel prompted, needing more, so much more.

Her father smiled for a beat, then wiped his face clean of all expression. "No. In fact, she auditioned for that tour, hoping to be one of the backup dancers."

"But she didn't get it?" Hazel wondered aloud. Her heart ached for her mother, a woman brave enough to reach for her dreams but not lucky enough to grasp hold.

"No, she did." He fixed his eyes on his plate rather than his daughter as he mumbled, "But a week later she found out she was pregnant with you."

Hazel's heart thumped heavily in her chest. "Oh," she said simply. "I see."

Her father cleared his throat several times. Even though it seemed he had something to say, the words didn't make it past his lips.

She waited, unwilling to be the one to speak first after this revelation. She'd always thought she'd been the one to fulfill her mother's lifelong wish for a baby, but instead she'd been the one to take her true wish away, to make it impossible due to poor timing. Had her mother planned to take up dance again once Hazel was a little older, not knowing her second chance would never come?

They each twiddled their forks anxiously as they picked silently at their breakfasts.

"Hazel, I . . ." he at last began, but before her father could say whatever he thought might make this moment sting less, his cheeks puffed, and a hand shot in front of his face. A second later, he jumped up from his chair, raced to the kitchen trash, and retched violently.

"Dad?" she asked, unsure, shaky. "Are you okay?"

Am I?

Chapter 9

Hazel couldn't believe the two of them turned up at the hospital in one piece. Even on their short journey, she'd needed to pull over to the side of the road several times so her father could work on expelling whatever little remained in his stomach.

His chemotherapy treatment for the day wasn't scheduled to start for another couple hours, but the staff welcomed them in all the same, especially upon spotting the absolutely miserable condition of Hazel's father.

"Just couldn't stay away, eh?" Keith asked with a smile as he took her father's vitals.

Despite his severe nausea, her father chuckled and answered, "Something like that."

Keith jotted down a note on his chart, then helped his patient to lie back on the exam table. "I'm sorry we don't have a room cleared for you just yet, but we will soon. The doctor will probably be in to talk to you first, though."

"Thank you," Hazel said, catching his eye just as the nurse was about to leave the room.

"My pleasure." He winked at her before disappearing down the busy hallway.

What was that about? she wondered. *Relax. He probably treats all his patients and their families that way.* Surely, Keith's heartthrob status in the ward hadn't escaped his attention, and now he was hamming it up to put her at ease. Yes, that had to be it.

A quarter of an hour later, the chief oncologist entered. He was the same one who had given her father his initial diagnosis and had stopped in briefly to check on him during his first couple of treatments. "Good morning, Mr. Long," the doctor said with a practiced smile. "Although I hear it hasn't been quite so good for you."

Her father nodded glumly.

Hazel noticed then that the doctor had to be a good decade older than her father, yet he appeared fit, trim, and full of good health. How was that fair—that one man could stride happily into old age and another would never get the chance to achieve it?

The doctor pulled out a wheeled stool and sat hunched forward with his fingers steepled in front of him. "If you'll recall, Mr. Long, when we first met to discuss your treatment plan, I recommended in-patient care. Then it was a choice, but now I'm afraid it's a necessity. Your body is having a hard time handling the chemo. I'd feel a lot better if you'd stay here round the clock so we can help to ease your discomfort as much as possible."

Her father pulled at his fingers, cracking each in turn. "You're saying I don't have a choice?"

"It will be difficult for us to effectively pursue treatment with you as an outpatient, yes."

"Difficult, but not impossible?" her father pressed. His brows furrowed in frustration; clearly, this was not news he had wanted to hear.

The doctor sighed and made a face before quickly regaining his composure. "Nothing's impossible, I suppose, but you'll have a very rough time of things at home."

"Good thing I'm tough then, because I refuse to check in overnight. I know I haven't got much longer before this thing claims me, but I'm not living out my final months here. I need to be at home."

Hazel admired his willpower but wished her father would just do what the doctor suggested. After all, it was their best chance at getting all the time owed to them.

The doctor shook his head as if delivering this decree truly pained him. Hazel couldn't help but wonder whether it actually did or if it was all an act. "I'm sorry, Mr. Long. We just don't have that option anymore."

"Because of my reaction to the chemo?"

"Yes."

Her father crossed his arms over his chest, and it made him seem like a toddler throwing a fit, not a man putting his foot down. "Then I guess I'd like to decline further treatment."

The doctor took a deep breath. Apparently, he wasn't used to patients outright refusing his orders. "You guess? This is not something you should guess about. It's literally a matter of life and death."

"Fine. Have it your way." Her father paused for effect. "I'm absolutely one hundred percent sure I'd like to decline further treatment."

"Dad!" Hazel cried, unable to remain quiet for even a second longer. "You need to do what the doctor says. It's his job to help make you better."

The doctor turned to her as if noticing her for the first time since he'd entered the room. His eyes locked with hers, and they shared a subtle nod. "I'll just leave you two to discuss things privately. I'll be back in a little while to see if you have more questions and if you plan to go ahead with today's treatment."

"I don't," her father called as the oncologist strode out of the room.

Hazel sank onto the stool the doctor had vacated and wheeled herself close to her father. "Daddy, why did you say those things?"

"I said them because I meant them." He uncrossed his arms and placed both hands on his knees. "It's up to me how I'm treated. Not him."

"But what about me?" she asked, doing her best not to start crying all over again. "Doesn't my opinion matter?"

Her father reached forward to grasp her hands, his vision lingering on the thin gemstone bracelet she always wore on her right wrist. "Of course, it matters. I just . . . I need some time to be alone with my thoughts for a bit before we talk more. Okay?"

Hazel gasped. This was not how she'd thought this day would go, and yet here they were right in the thick of this living nightmare. "Dad! We need to discuss this."

"And we will, once we've both had a little bit of time to gather our thoughts. Please, chicky girl. Please understand." He squeezed her hands and let go, a sad smile on his face.

Hazel shook with rage, fear, sorrow—every negative emotion she'd ever had—all bottled into one horrible moment. "Fifteen minutes. I'll be back in fifteen minutes, and I hope you're ready to talk to me then."

If they'd been at home, she'd have slammed the door on her way out. Instead she stomped away as noisily as she could. So what if she was acting like a petulant child; so what if she was making a scene?

Her father's life was on the line, and he wanted to jump off and into oblivion. She wasn't ready to lose her father, so why did he seem so ready to leave her behind?

Chapter 10

Hazel sat in the small waiting room at the end of the hall, her knees bouncing nervously as she stared at the old analog clock on the wall above. She'd gone to the bathroom to splash some water on her face and grabbed a drink from the vending machine before coming here to pass the remainder of the period.

Still, twelve more minutes of the original fifteen remained.

Time had never moved so slowly in all her life.

"Hey," a male voice said from the spot where the bright linoleum hallway met the worn carpet of the waiting room.

She looked up to find Keith studying her with gentle eyes, his lips pressed into a firm line. "Hey," she croaked back.

He stepped farther into the room, his voice a little quieter as he approached. "Dr. Jefferson told me what happened, and I wanted to come see if you were doing okay."

Hazel shook her head and turned away from him just in time to conceal the fresh tears that spilled from her red-rimmed eyes. "I'm not sure," she admitted with a sniff. "He won't talk to me."

Keith grabbed a tissue box from the nearby end table

and passed it to her. "He's probably just as scared and confused as you are," he offered, squatting before her on the balls of his feet.

"He seemed pretty sure about ending treatment. All because he doesn't want to sleep at the hospital, when he already has to be here pretty much all day." Hazel twisted the tissue in her hands, but the motion did nothing to lessen her frustration.

Keith hadn't given up on trying to find a solution, though. "What about in-home care?" he suggested.

"His insurance won't cover it. I already checked when he first told me about the diagnosis."

"Hmm."

She sighed and reached for another tissue. "I just wish he would tell me what's going through his head."

"All the same things that are running through yours, I'd imagine. In a way, it's harder for you because you have to watch from the outside."

Hazel let out a sarcastic laugh, but it didn't seem to faze Keith.

His expression remained kind as he said, "We all want to do whatever we can to help our loved ones, and sometimes that means supporting their choices, no matter how much they hurt us in the process."

This all sounded correct in theory, but there was one very important point that Hazel just couldn't get past.

"How can I support his choosing to die, though?" she murmured.

Keith shook his head, and a wisp of sandy blond hair fell onto his forehead. "He's not choosing to die. The cancer made that choice for him. What he is choosing is to die with dignity, on his own terms. It takes an incredibly brave person to do that."

No matter how much she liked Keith, Hazel just

couldn't agree with that. Her father had chosen to run away from his problems rather than facing them head-on and dealing with the consequences. He'd chosen to leave Hazel sooner, knowing that he was her whole world.

"No," she said firmly. "It takes a brave person to fight, to keep going when you're not sure whether you'll succeed. That's what strength is to me."

Keith appeared to think about this for a moment before a slight smile crept across his face. "Can I tell you a story to help pass the time?"

Hazel glanced around the empty waiting room and back up at the clock. She still had at least nine minutes before she could go back to her father. Looking up at Keith, she nodded instead of voicing her consent aloud.

He rose from his haunches and took a seat two chairs over from Hazel, so she could turn and watch him comfortably as he spoke. "A lot of people seem to think that I became a nurse because I wasn't smart enough, or didn't have enough money, to be a doctor."

"But that isn't why," she stated for him. Every moment with the male nurse these past two weeks had screamed just how much he loved his job.

Keith bobbed his head. "I chose *this* profession. Ever since I was a little boy, a nurse is the only thing I ever wanted to be. You know why?"

She shook her head and waited for him to continue.

"To others, being a doctor may seem better. More money, more power, more respect. But when I was eight and my grandmother was battling a terminal diagnosis of her own, it was the nurses who helped me and my family more than anyone else. They were the ones who were with us day to day. They were the ones who took time to talk to us and listen to what we said in response. As hard as it was losing my grandma, I will forever be grateful to those nurses for easing the heartache."

"And now you do the same for others." She liked that. Keith's job felt so important, making her own career choice feel frivolous by comparison.

"Now I do the same for others."

"I'm sorry about your grandma."

"I'm sorry about your father."

Hazel hesitated before asking, "Do you still miss her?"

He chuckled softly. "Every day, but I don't feel sad anymore."

"How long did that take?"

"I don't know. It wasn't a sudden thing. It happened gradually, over time. Sometimes I still miss her so much I can't stand it, but most of the time when I think of her, I smile." He closed his eyes and when they blinked back open, they seemed even bluer than before.

Hazel took this opportunity to ask a question that had stayed with her ever since her father had mentioned seeing her mother again. "Do you think she's in Heaven?"

"I don't know what I think," Keith answered with a determined look. "But I know what I believe."

Hazel had once thought she knew, too. But being faced with the reality of losing someone close to her now, she questioned everything she had once happily taken for granted. "And what do you believe?"

"Whether there's proof, whether it makes any sense at all, I believe in my heart that she's with God and that she's happy now."

Chapter 11

A blond head popped up behind the large window that divided the waiting room from the rest of the ward. Hazel instantly recognized Amy, one of the three new friends she'd made in the cafeteria the same day her father had first begun chemo. Had that really only been a couple weeks ago? It felt as if a lifetime had passed since then.

"Knock, knock," Amy sang, floating into the room. As it turned out, she was much shorter than Hazel had realized when everyone had been sitting together at the table. "Hope I'm not interrupting anything."

"I've got to get back to work," Keith said, rising to his feet and offering Amy a friendly nod. "Looks like you're in good hands here."

Amy gave Hazel a thumbs-up and a broad grin the moment their shared crush left the room. "You're so lucky," she cooed. "Getting him all to yourself like that."

"Yeah, *lucky*. That's me." Hazel couldn't help bursting into tears for the second time in the span of just a few minutes.

Amy moved instantly to her side and gave her an awkward hug over the arm of the chair. "Oh, I'm sorry. I didn't know something had happened. Is your father not taking the chemo well?"

Hazel glanced up at her new friend through watery eyes. "How did you know?"

Amy grabbed a tissue from the box Hazel still held on top of her lap and dabbed at her friend's eyes. "The first round is brutal. It gets easier, or at least your dad will get used to the side effects."

Hazel shook off Amy's assistance, needing personal space more than physical comfort just then. "He wants to stop treatment," she said flatly.

"Oh, he needs a break? Well, I guess, that's not totally unheard of." Bless her, Amy still remained optimistic. Hazel would have preferred that the more cynical Nichole had found her at this moment. Now she had to explain her grief to the perky elementary school teacher, and she didn't look forward to the moment her new friend's spirits would fall on her behalf.

Hazel took a deep breath, but it did nothing to center her. "No, he wants to stop altogether and just . . ."

The next words stung her throat as she struggled to push them out. "Wait to die. At home."

"Oh," Amy said, falling silent.

"Yeah."

They sat for a few moments of companionable silence, each understanding the other better than she would like.

Finally, Amy said, "Everyone struggles in the start. I'm sure he'll change his mind in no time." However, her pinched features suggested otherwise.

"That's the thing," Hazel answered glumly. "*No time* is exactly what we have. The doctors gave him a year at best with treatment. Without, though?" She shook her head and laughed bitterly. "Well, your guess is as good as mine."

Amy hugged her again. "Look, I know we haven't known each other long, but the other girls and I were serious about being your friends. If you're not going to be here, then we'll come to you. We could all use a break and someone who understands. Otherwise, this is just impossible to get through alone."

She needed her father, not a new friend group. But then again, talking to Amy, Keith, and the others was definitely better than trying to make sense of all this on her own.

"Do you really mean it?" she asked, her voice shaky and suddenly desperate. She'd enjoyed her visits with them in the cafeteria, but they'd banded together because they were all stuck here. It looked like Hazel would no longer be stuck. She'd be forced to suffer alone, unable to do anything to slow her father's demise. It would be so nice to have someone to lean on, but each of the other women had huge problems of their own to manage. Why would they want to take on the weight of a near-stranger's despair?

Hazel had a hard time meeting Amy's eyes as she said, "You already have each other, and you hardly even know me. I could be the worst kind of person for all you know."

Amy bumped Hazel with her shoulder. Her smile had returned. "Yeah, but you're not. Your kind heart shines through, whether or not you like it."

"Thanks," was all Hazel could think to say.

"Tell you what." Amy dug into her pocket and pulled out her phone, then began flipping through the calendar app. "Today's Tuesday and I bet your weeks are just as jam-packed as the rest of ours. So how about . . ."

Amy pressed a few more buttons on her phone and then looked up at Hazel triumphantly. "How about Saturday the girls and I come over with some food for you and your dad and we can exchange our war stories from the week. Sound good?"

"Better make it Sunday," Hazel said with a sigh. "My dad has some kind of date with his girlfriend, Meryl, and I'm not sure how long he's planning to stay out."

"A date? Well, good for him." Amy's smile widened; obviously, she didn't understand just how horrible Meryl was or she'd be reacting quite differently.

"It'll probably be their last one. He hasn't told her he's sick yet, and I don't expect her to take the news well."

"*Ahh.*" Amy tapped their weekend get-together into her phone, then slid it back into her pocket. "I'd say that's awful, but honestly, why stick around when you don't have to?"

She paused for a moment before popping back onto her feet. "Well, I need to get back to my mom, but I'll let the other girls know about our thing on Sunday. Take care, Hazel."

As she watched Amy disappear from view, Hazel wondered about the other woman's strange reaction to the news of her father's date with Meryl. Unlike Amy, Hazel wouldn't give the woman a free pass just because she wasn't family.

Fair-weather friends were bad enough, but fair-weather lovers? Her father deserved far better. She just hoped Meryl would let him down gently. The poor man had already suffered more than his fair share this week—this life, for that matter.

Glancing up at the wall clock once again, she saw that her predetermined waiting period had ended, which meant the time had come for her to go confront her father, and pray he'd changed his mind.

Chapter 12

Back in the exam room, Hazel found her father shrugging into his coat and patting his rump to make sure he hadn't misplaced his wallet.

"Let's go," he told her, pushing past his daughter into the hallway and striding quickly toward the bank of elevators.

She chased after him, even more upset than she'd been before. "Wait, aren't we going to talk about this like you promised?"

"We can talk in the car," came his grumbled reply.

"What about chemo?" she shouted, not caring whether they made a scene, only about whether her father would finally listen.

He continued forward without so much as an apologetic glance back at his daughter. "I canceled it."

"For today, right? We're coming back tomorrow." Even as she said the words, she knew they wouldn't be coming back— not unless she resorted to some next-level trickery to get him here, and she just didn't have it in her to do so.

Her father pressed the button beside the elevators and immediately one dinged open. He wiggled his eyebrows at this good luck, then stepped inside. This sudden lightness wasn't enough to make her back down, though.

"Dad?" Hazel murmured. She placed a hand on the wall to steady herself as the elevator jolted to life. "What's going on?"

Her father stared straight ahead with his hands clasped in front of him. "We're going home, Hazel. That's what's going on."

"But won't you tell me why you suddenly changed your mind?" She closed her eyes and willed her voice to stay calm, but if her father was upset, he didn't show it. In fact, he didn't show much of anything. That's what she found so frustrating.

"The circumstances changed, so I changed with them," he said in a voice that was eerily devoid of emotion. "It's that simple."

This infuriated her. "No, it's *not* that simple. You're choosing to die."

He sighed and shifted so the two of them now stood facing each other. "I was already dying, chicky girl. Now I'm choosing to die at home. To me, it just makes good sense to end my life in the same place I lived it. Don't you think?"

The elevator ground to a halt, and they both stepped out onto the main level of the hospital.

"What about me?" Hazel asked as they strode quickly toward the parking garage. "What about our time together?"

Her father stopped walking suddenly and put a hand on each of her shoulders once she stopped, too. "We may have less time together this way, but it will be better. Part of the reason I'm doing this is for us. I know you don't want to watch me die while attached to some machine, just like I don't want to take my last breath in a bed that will be turned over and assigned to a new patient the moment I'm gone."

How could she argue with that? It felt selfish even to try.

He squeezed her shoulders and leaned forward to give her a kiss on the cheek. "Let's go home and raid our old movie collection. Are you in the mood for some *Princess Bride*?"

They hadn't watched that one in ages, but to this day it remained one of Hazel's all-time favorites. "As you wish," she said, offering him a weak smile as they resumed their journey toward the exit.

While they watched, she'd surreptitiously do some research on her phone. First, to see if there was anything she could—or should— say to help push him toward treatment, and then to decide if she even wanted to fight his dying wish.

Or rather his wish on how he would die.

She also needed to figure out how long the chemo would stay in his system and when he'd start feeling better. Would he change his mind once he could keep a meal down? Or would that only cement his decision to die naturally and at home?

If only she knew what was right in this situation.

Until then, she would love him as best she could and with everything she had.

Back in the car, her father rolled down all four windows despite the chilliness of the season. "The fresh air will do us both good," he explained with a tilt of his head as a breeze swept through the car.

"What did Mom do when she found out she was dying?" Hazel asked. He'd told her this story before, but now she wasn't so sure he'd been completely honest about it. Besides, if he was going to act as if nothing upset him, she might as well take advantage and ask the hard questions while she could.

Her mother had died at the age of twenty-six from complications following a car accident. Luckily, neither Hazel nor her father had been in that car. Unluckily, the accident had punctured one of her mother's lungs, which led to a respiratory disease. Later that year when she'd contracted the flu, it proved too much for her already weakened system to handle. After just two days in the hospital, she was gone.

"She didn't have much time to think things over. We were all hoping she'd get better," he explained, stretching an arm out the window so his hand could surf on the rushing currents of air. "It seemed so silly for her to die of the flu after she'd survived that terrible car crash."

Hazel nodded thoughtfully. "Where was she going when she got into the accident?"

Her father swallowed hard and rolled up the windows. "To a hotel," he answered plainly. His emotion had returned. Even though he couldn't mourn his own death, losing his wife more than two decades earlier still destroyed him.

She'd definitely never heard this tidbit before. Hazel tried to remain collected as she asked the next question. "Was she having an affair?"

"No, no, no. Your mother wasn't like that, not one bit."

They shared a smile, and both took deep breaths.

But her father hadn't revealed everything yet. He then said, "She was taking a break from us, deciding if she still wanted to be a part of our family."

Hazel jerked the car hard and rolled to a stop on the shoulder. She turned to her father, who looked overburdened by the weight of this particular truth.

"She left us," Hazel shouted. "She left us, and you let me put her on some pedestal! You let me believe she wanted me, that she loved me!" She hated to yell at her father when this obviously hurt him, too, but now it felt as if she was losing both of her parents. It was just too much for any one person to handle.

"*No.*" Her father's voice shook, but he didn't back down. "No, she came back."

"Because she had an accident," Hazel spat, shaking with the very worst kind of betrayal.

"No," he corrected her again. "That accident showed her a lot of things, like how much she needed both of us to be happy. She came back and she stayed until the good Lord took her home."

Hazel let out a sarcastic laugh. "The good Lord? He doesn't seem so good these days."

If her old Sunday school teacher, Mrs. Timmons, could hear her now, she'd surely wash Hazel's mouth out with soap. Still, it was easy to believe in a benevolent creator when life zoomed along with purpose and without an overabundance of pain. Lately though?

She shook her head sadly. "All you went through then. All we're going through now. Why, Dad? If God loves us so much . . . If He's so good, then why torture us like this?"

"You know the answer to that, chicky girl."

Hazel shook her head to clear her thoughts before something hurtful escaped her mouth. The truth was she didn't know the answer. Lately, it felt like she didn't know anything at all.

Chapter 13

The days passed slowly, but still too fast given how few her father had left. Hazel worked mornings from her pop-up office at the kitchen table while her father either slept late or poured over the news on his tablet.

They spent their afternoons walking through the park, eating at all their favorite restaurants, or rewatching their favorite movies from long ago. It all seemed rather mundane to Hazel, but when she brought up the idea of a bucket list–style adventure, her father shook his head and laughed.

"I already told you, I want to die as I lived. I don't need to become some daredevil in my final days just to prove a point."

While Hazel might have liked to form some new memories with him while they still had the chance, she stayed mum on the issue.

After a few days, she at last gave up on the possibility of her father returning to the hospital for treatment. He seemed quite happy with their new arrangement, especially once Hazel officially moved back home.

"It reminds me of when your mother and I first moved in together," he said wistfully. "We'd closed on that little house on Eagle Banks Drive just days before the wedding and could hardly believe it was all ours."

Hazel smiled and nodded. Lately she didn't enjoy stories of her mother so much. Ever since her father had revealed that she'd been planning on breaking apart their family, Hazel found it hard to find an emotional connection to the woman who would probably have walked away from her if the car accident hadn't changed the course of her life.

Still, he continued to share as if his memories were ones they both should treasure. "Did you know that whenever your mother was thinking real hard, she'd scrunch her nose up all cute-like? She always insisted she didn't, but every single time she got thinking hard, the wrinkles would appear over her nose along with that determined set of her jaw. You do the same thing, you know."

Hazel bristled at the comparison. "I do not."

He just laughed. "Exactly the same. You are so much her daughter, chicky girl. Sometimes it's like she's still here."

Hazel tried her best to keep her features neutral, light. She knew it made her father feel good to talk about her mother, but she herself was having a hard time forgiving. Apparently, Hazel's attempts to hide her discontent failed miserably.

"You're doing it now!" her father pointed out with glee.

"Am not," she shot back.

"Why so prickly today? Did something happen at work? It's okay if you need to head in for a bit. I can manage here on my own just fine." The hopeful glint in his eyes seemed to imply that he almost wanted her to leave him alone for a bit, but why?

"Work is fine. I'm planning to go in for our team meeting next week, and I had a conference call with everyone earlier today. Everything is moving along as it should."

His previous joy deflated. "Then?"

"Then what? *I'm fine*," she insisted. "Just worried about you is all."

"That's moose pucky, and you know it. You're still mad at your mom. Aren't you?" Her father cracked his knuckles as he waited for her to reply.

She couldn't hide her anger any longer. He'd already sussed it out, so she might as well come clean. "She was going to walk out on us, Dad! That's not something you can just forgive overnight."

"I was worried I hadn't explained right and for good reason, too." He hung his head and pinched the bridge of his nose. "She wouldn't have left *you*. You were her world."

Hazel turned away to avoid looking her father in the face. She couldn't stand to watch him as he lied to her or as he told another truth that would shatter all she knew about her past. "I'm not sure I believe you. You kept a couple very big things hidden from me all these years. How do I know you're telling the truth now?"

His voice came out pinched, pained. "I had an affair."

"What?" She spun around to glare at him. Her voice shook, too. "How could you?"

"It only happened one time, and I immediately told your mom, groveled, begged her to forgive me." He cried in earnest now, but she couldn't bring herself to feel sorry for him. She almost wished he'd continued to lie to her, that she never had to know.

"But she needed space to think. . . ." Hazel puzzled out.

"So she went to the hotel and all our lives changed. I made one stupid mistake. Maybe because I was overly exhausted from work. I don't know, but I have never forgiven myself for hurting your mother. If I hadn't been weak and stupid, she wouldn't have been in that car. She wouldn't have died. She'd probably still be with us now, helping you through all this."

What could she possibly say to that? *You're right. You did an awful thing. I wouldn't have forgiven you, either.* "I . . . I need some time to process this."

"I'm so sorry for what I did then and that I hid it from you until now. I needed you to idolize me, just as much as you did your mother. And my guilt was already tearing me apart. I couldn't stand to see it reflected on your face, too. L-l-like it is now."

Hazel's breaths quickened as she tried to figure out what she should do or say next. Ultimately, she threw her hands up and charged toward the door. "I can't do this right now."

Pacing toward her car, which was parked at the curb, she changed her mind at the last minute and veered off down the sidewalk.

Distance. That's what she needed. From her father. From the past. From all of it. Was he trying to ensure she'd miss him less once he was gone by admitting his culpability in her mother's death? Or had he invented this lie to make her look better and him worse?

She sensed this latest version of events was the truth, which made it sting that much more. She needed time to work her way through what this revelation meant, but time was the one thing she didn't have, couldn't have. . . .

Chapter 14

Hazel power-walked around the neighborhood in an attempt to burn off her anger. It didn't work. She didn't know what to feel or whom to be upset with anymore—and she doubted she had the full picture, even now.

Her father hardly seemed the type to engage in an affair, but why would he lie about something so awful? Growing up, he'd made sure they were both in church every Sunday. He taught Hazel manners and morals, how to be kind.

Was that his penance?

And was it enough to compensate for the sin that had cost her mother's life?

She didn't want to be upset with him now, not when he'd chosen to be honest with her, not when they had so little time left together.

All of life's most difficult questions swirled about her head. Do we make our own fate, or is it preordained? Would her mother have died regardless of her father's actions? Or was her father's cancer some sort of karmic retribution for the events that had unfolded more than twenty years before? Did Heaven really exist, and would both of her parents earn a spot? Would she?

Charging around in the brittle autumn air did nothing to relax her anxious mind. With each step, more questions appeared. Every new realization etched itself over something she'd previously thought she understood.

Her father loved her. That was a fact. Perhaps, it was the only one of which she could be certain.

She needed to get back to him. As much as learning of his affair had hurt her, she knew it must have cut a thousand times deeper into his already battered heart. Her father didn't deserve to die with a guilty conscience, and since her mother wasn't around to forgive him, the task fell to Hazel.

Quickening her pace, she zipped around the block, back toward her father's home—*her* home. She called out for him while pushing the door open and attempting to block the cold wind with her body. "I'm back!"

He didn't answer.

Fear twisted in Hazel's gut. "Dad!"

Nothing.

A hurried search of the downstairs level revealed a series of achingly empty rooms. She raced up the stairs, taking two at a time as she frantically called out to him. "Dad! Where are you? Are you okay?"

A pained moan sounded from his bedroom.

Hazel charged through the door and found him lying sprawled on his back, right in front of the open closet. She couldn't spot any blood or other visible wounds, but still he seemed to be having a hard time getting up again after his fall.

"What happened?" she cried, rushing to his side and helping him to sit up.

He seemed dazed. His eyes refused to focus as he leaned in to her.

"Did you hit your head? Should I call an ambulance?"

"N-n-n-no," he sputtered. "I just need a moment to . . ."

Hazel glanced around the room, searching for an explanation of what had happened. The closet hung open, a mess of clothes and hangers scattered about the floor. A stepstool lay on its side in the midst of the mess.

"Were you trying to find something?" she asked, turning back to him again.

He licked his lips and nodded. "Not trying. I know where it is. I was trying to bring it down from the attic when I fell."

Now that her father seemed to be okay, she let him sit back against the bed and went to peek into the closet. Sure enough, a ceiling panel had been pushed aside to reveal a crawl space above. She hadn't even known it was there, but then again, she'd never spent time digging around her father's closet before, either.

"What's up there?" she asked, almost afraid to find out.

"Old photos, keepsakes, things of your mother's that I wanted you to see." Her father lost his balance and struggled to remain sitting.

"That's it. I'm taking you to the hospital."

"I don't need to . . ." His words trailed off, replaced by a drawn-out sigh. "Fine."

Hazel braced herself to make sure she wouldn't lose her balance too, then helped him to his feet and very slowly guided him down the stairs.

The attic and whatever secrets it held would have to wait.

Chapter 15

Hazel perked up when the doctor entered their curtained-off section of the emergency room. Even though he'd agreed to the visit, her father had complained the entire drive over. Still, she'd rather be safe than sorry when it came to health—which was another reason why his refusing chemo had been such a tough pill to swallow.

"Good news! It's not a concussion," the doctor informed them both with a dashing grin Hazel was sure charmed many of his patients. "But since you're a patient on the oncology ward, they're sending someone over to check you out before we discharge you."

Her father groaned and shifted uncomfortably on the thin, wheeled bed. "Those jerks are just bound and determined to suck me back in," he grumbled.

Hazel rolled her eyes. "They're jerks for wanting to help you get better? *They're* the ones who made you go on some wild goose chase in the attic? Oh, and they're probably the ones who knocked you over, too. Right?"

"All right, chicky girl," he groaned, and lay back on the bed. "You win!"

They waited in silence for their oncology consult to arrive. Although Hazel couldn't see past the curtain the staff had used to create a private area for her and her father, the ER sounded nothing like it did on the television. Mostly the floor was quiet with occasional hushed voices, metallic pings, and digital beeps to offset the whir of the heating system.

Now that the fear aroused by his fall had begun to subside, Hazel's earlier anger started to return. *An affair!* Her sweet, clueless father had cheated on her mother. She still couldn't believe it even after his confession. Would the items he'd tried to recover from the attic have helped to dissipate her anger, or would they only reveal more shocking truths she wasn't yet ready to hear?

No matter what, her father was her best friend. They'd always looked out for each other, enjoyed spending time together, made a whole family despite its tiny size. She'd always assumed she knew him inside out, but in just the past week, she'd learned that he was a liar and a cheat.

But he was trying to make things right now, and he'd spent years comforting Hazel when she felt sad, showing up to all her most important events to cheer her on from the sidelines, loving her the best he knew how. Did these two new wrongs erase the many good things he'd done right over the years?

She wished she knew how to make that call. Then again, maybe it wasn't up to her to decide. . . .

About twenty minutes later, the curtain opened to reveal a doctor in aqua-green scrubs. He had his face turned away to greet one of the emergency room nurses, so it took Hazel a second before she recognized Keith.

"Sorry about the wait." He nodded to her father and flashed Hazel an arresting smile. No doubt, he had known she'd be here, thanks to the chart he carried clutched beneath his arm. "It's nice to see you both again, though I do wish it was under better circumstances."

"The doctor said it's not a concussion," Hazel explained, hoping Keith hadn't brought them bad news from the oncologist.

He shook his head, and the sandy-blond hair Hazel had somehow already grown to love fell against his forehead. "It's not, but I think the fall is definitely cause for concern. I've talked with Dr. Jefferson, and we're going to recommend in-home care going forward."

No. Her father was supposed to stay healthy for as long as possible, maybe even make a miracle recovery. Besides, while she could have helped her father with a few odd bills here and there, the cost of hiring a live-in nurse was not something she could afford.

"But our insurance doesn't cover it," she mumbled with a quick glance toward her father. His expression gave nothing away.

Keith's smile came back. It seemed so out of place, given the nature of the news he'd just shared. "I believe they will now in light of today's events. Besides, now that he's refused further treatment from us here, they're more likely to agree. At the end of the day, a home aide costs less than hospitalization or chemo, which is the main thing they care about. Tell you what. I'll put a call into them as soon as they open on Monday to personally check on the status of our request."

Was he suggesting this aide because her father needed one, or was he using the situation to push for something that, while not strictly required, would make Hazel's life easier? And if he were truly trying to help, was this how he treated all his patients and their families . . . or was Hazel somehow special?

She tucked a loose strand of hair behind her ear and tried not to blush. "Thank you for your help, but what should we do now?"

"Go home and get some rest. I'll call with an update on Monday just as soon as I have one." He looked at her father and nodded before returning his full attention to Hazel.

"Thank you, Keith." Heat rushed to her cheeks as they shared an awkward smile.

Somehow he had become even more handsome in the few days since she'd seen him last. Was it because he had found a way to help her and her father? Was he just a crush? Or something more?

She cleared her throat and averted her gaze.

He adjusted his chart in his hands. "Um, okay then. I'll just go update the ER team, so they can begin to process your discharge. Good-bye, Mr. Long. Hazel." Keith lingered a moment before disappearing through the curtain.

"What was that all about?" her father asked with one eyebrow raised.

Hazel looked away just as her father's curious glance became a full-on smirk. "He's calling the insurance, so we can—"

"Not that." He waved a hand, batting away Hazel's explanation. "The shameless flirting."

Hazel felt the air whoosh out of her lungs as if her father had just sucker-punched her with this unneeded observation. "Shameless, Daddy? Really?"

"Well, don't just stand there gawking at me." He widened his eyes and made shooing motions with both hands. "Go ask him out."

"Dad, no. This is hardly the time to—"

"It's the perfect time! Gives me less to worry about when I go. Besides, it's not like you denied the flirting."

Hazel crossed her arms over her chest and stared her father down.

And he did the exact same. "Hurry before he gets away!"

She threw her hands up in the air. "Don't say I never do anything for you," she hissed as she pulled the curtain aside.

Her father's laugher followed her out into the open floor area.

"Thinks this is the last scene in a romantic comedy," she mumbled under her breath while sweeping the area in search of Keith. With any luck, he'd have already returned to the oncology ward and she'd be cleared of this insane mission.

As it turned out, though, luck was not on her side. Not that she should have been surprised.

Keith spotted her from across the floor and waved her over. "Did you forget something?" he asked, barely concealing a smile.

Hazel glanced over her shoulder but decided that making a run for it would be even more embarrassing than just asking the nice man for a date. "Not me. My dad."

His smile faltered and concern overtook his features. "Sure, what does he need?"

"He . . . I . . ."

"Yes?"

She decided to just spit it out, so that she could finish this awkward exchange as quickly as possible. "He won't leave until I ask you out on a date."

Keith's grin widened, showing off two clean rows of perfect sparkling teeth. "I knew I liked that guy."

Chapter 16

Hazel returned to her father with her phone clasped tightly in her hand. Keith had just added his number so the two of them could plan a night out sometime next week. Much as she didn't need another distraction, she couldn't help but feel excited about the idea of going out with Keith—maybe even getting the chance to kiss him before the night was through.

"Well?" her father asked the very moment she pulled aside his curtain, stretching out the single syllable to an irritating degree.

She shook her phone back and forth. "He's going to text me later to work out the details."

His eyebrows furrowed at this. "Bah, technology takes all the romance out of everything these days. You're going to get together in person for your actual date, right?"

"*Daddy*," she warned, narrowing her gaze on him and placing a hand on her hip.

He blushed before breaking out into a huge smile. "I'm just teasing. I'm happy you'll have something fun to do. You needed a break from me, and now you've got one."

"I'm still not sure right now is the best time to be starting a new relationship." Hazel shifted her weight from foot to foot. Despite all the new tension between them, it was so easy to fall back into their old patterns. Was it wrong to start something new when something else was ending?

"It's the perfect time, and you know it. Besides, it makes me feel good, knowing that if I had to die, at least I could do it in such a way that helped you find someone who might turn out to be your soulmate."

She gasped at how easily he discussed his own death, but her father seemed bright and cheerful now. She'd missed this side of him.

"No pressure, right?" she teased right back.

"Absolutely none."

On the drive home, her father mostly remained quiet, seeming lost in thought. Though their trip to the hospital had pushed his confession to the back of her mind, Hazel knew she wouldn't feel better until they talked it out. They'd always talked things out, although nothing had ever been as huge as this.

She cleared her throat before asking, "Do you think Mom was your soulmate?"

He turned to her but didn't answer.

Adjusting her hands on the steering wheel, she continued, "You know, since you said that Keith was mine even though it's way too soon to even start thinking about that. So I wondered if you thought Mom was yours?"

She caught him shaking his head in her peripheral vision as she attempted to keep her focus on the road.

He fiddled with his seat belt for a moment, then rested both hands in his lap. "I don't think," he said. *"I know."*

This reminded her of her earlier talk that week with Keith. She'd asked about Heaven, and he'd said he didn't know but he chose to believe.

"But . . ." she started, unsure of how she wanted to

finish. Anything she said now would come out cruel and judgmental.

Luckily, her father knew just what she wanted to ask. "But how could I if I cheated on her?"

"Well, yeah." She risked a glance his way and found him with his head back and his eyes closed. She wished she had waited to have this conversation at home, so as not to miss the visual cues that came with conversation.

"Just because your mother was my soulmate, it doesn't mean I was ever deserving of her." His voice sounded weak, far away. "I think the pressure got to me."

This baffled Hazel to no end. "You thought she was too good for you, so you had an affair? That doesn't make any sense."

"No, I don't suppose it does, but it is how I felt. Keep in mind, I was younger then than you are now. But much, much dumber." He chuckled here, but Hazel didn't join him.

After a few moments of awkward silence, he continued. "It was almost like I was so afraid of losing the best thing that ever happened to me, a part of me wanted to hurry the losing along. Once it happened, I wouldn't have to fear it anymore."

"That makes a little bit more sense, but it doesn't make what you did any less awful." She squeezed the steering wheel so tightly, her knuckles turned white. She didn't want to understand, didn't want him to think what he'd done was okay.

Her father sighed. "Oh, don't I know it. I've never forgiven myself for it, either."

She turned toward him and took in his drawn expression. "Did Mom forgive you?"

"Not in so many words, but she stayed. And for that

little bit of time we had left together, things were the best they'd ever been between us."

She couldn't fit these two pieces of information together in a way that satisfied her. How could such a terrible betrayal actually work to improve a marriage? She shook her head. "Okay, you're losing me again."

"I'm not sure how to explain it exactly. I guess since we'd hit rock bottom and still wanted to be together, we knew our love was something worth fighting for." The smile returned to his face, the same one he wore whenever he thought of his late wife. Hazel loved that smile more than anything. "That's when I got her the ring and we renewed our vows to each other."

"Is that the ring that was buried with her? I wish I could see it." Hazel glanced at her own naked fingers and then at her mother's bracelet, which she still wore proudly even after learning of its origin.

"I do, too, but I have something even better to show you. It's what I was trying to find when I fell." Her father rolled down his window and propped his arm on the edge. They'd be home soon.

"Well, I'm not letting you up there by yourself again, but if you tell me what I'm looking for and where, maybe I'll be able to find it for you." Already her hands were itching with the desire to hold this mysterious item from her mother's past.

"I'm actually not so sure it's going to be easy to find. A part of me never wanted to share it with you, but I realize now that was selfish."

Hazel's voice quavered. "What is it?"

"After the accident, your mother wrote you a letter. I never read it myself, but since I assumed it talked about my affair and her almost leaving, I didn't want you to have it."

"A letter from Mom?" Her voice cracked on that last word.

"Yes, it's somewhere in the crawl space with all the rest of her things. I never got rid of any of it. It felt too much like getting rid of her. I'm so sorry I didn't share it with you before now. If I could go back, there are so many things I would change."

"It's okay, Dad." She smiled over at him. "*We're* okay."

"Just know that even my mistakes, I made out of love."

"I know, Dad. I love you, too."

Since his diagnosis, Hazel had learned many things she never knew, but none of it changed the beautiful life she and her father had lived together. None of it changed how she felt about him now.

And none of it lessened how much she would miss him once he was gone.

Chapter 17

Later that day, Hazel brought everything down from the attic and stacked it all in the living room. She almost took a tumble a few times herself but managed to finish the job without requiring a second visit to the emergency room.

The number of boxes, bins, and baubles overwhelmed her, though she'd do whatever it took to find that letter. Somehow it felt as if only her mother's words could provide guidance for Hazel and freedom for her father.

The clock ticked on.

When they didn't find the letter on Friday, Hazel searched again Saturday. Her father disappeared briefly for his date with Meryl and returned less than an hour later.

"I'm disappointed but not surprised," he admitted with a heavy sigh. "Besides, I'd much rather spend whatever time I've got left with you, chicky girl."

Hazel produced all the normal platitudes one offers after a breakup, but her father didn't want to discuss his failed relationship beyond letting her know that it had ended, and he was fine. Instead, they both threw themselves into the task of sorting and chronicling the boxes they'd pulled from the attic. They worked slowly. Each item brought with it a story, and each story made Hazel's mother seem more real than she'd ever been.

Still, she craved that letter—needed to know what words of wisdom or solace her mother had left behind. Unfortunately, neither of them had managed to find it yet.

"We've been through every single one of these boxes at least half a dozen times, and the only letters I could find were ones you'd written to Mom while away on business trips," Hazel said, angrily shoving the nearest cardboard box aside. "Are you sure she even wrote a letter to me?"

Her father struggled to rise from his chair and came over to crouch beside Hazel on the floor. "I'm positive, but remember, I wasn't sure I ever wanted that letter to be read. I must have taken extra care hiding it."

"Or you threw it out." Hazel knew she was pouting, but she didn't care. They'd both worked so hard, only to come up empty-handed in the end.

"No," he said sternly. "I know I saved it. I just don't know where."

"Well, it's definitely not here, so . . ." She sat back on her heels and worried her lip.

"I'll find it," he promised with a reassuring nod.

A knock sounded on the front door.

"Shoot!" Hazel cried, jumping to her feet and taking in the enormous mess that had exploded right in the middle of their main sitting room. "I totally lost track of the time. The girls I met at the cafeteria are coming by today."

This time the doorbell rang.

"Make that right now," she corrected, frowning at the disaster zone that had taken over their living room.

Her father waved her off. "You go greet your guests, and I'll see about pushing all this stuff to a corner or into a closet somewhere."

She hesitated for a moment. Her father wasn't at his best these days, but he had regained a good deal of his strength as the chemo left his system. She gave him a quick peck on the cheek and then bounded toward the door.

"Surprise!" Bridget shouted, holding a giant, steaming Crock-Pot in both hands. "I made fondue."

"She melted some cheese," Nichole said with a light-hearted eye roll.

"And bought a fantastic selection of pretzels and breads," Bridget added with a Cheshire grin as she squeezed past Hazel into the house.

"I made cookies," Amy squeaked, holding up a Tupperware box with pride.

"And Nichole ordered pizza," Nichole added. "Believe me, you don't want me anywhere near a kitchen. Not if it can be helped."

"C'mon in," Hazel told them, accepting the baked goods and a quick hug from Amy. "It's so good to see you all."

The women all followed Bridget toward the kitchen. Somehow the younger woman seemed to instinctively know her way around the house even though she'd never been there before.

"None of us brought anything to drink," Amy said with a frown. "Do you have something, or should I make a quick stop by the store?"

"Oh, yeah. Don't worry, I've got us covered," Hazel answered, accepting hugs from Bridget and Nichole now, too. "Thank you again for coming by. It's been quite the week."

Amy dropped her voice to a whisper and leaned in close to Hazel. "Did your dad change his mind about treatment?"

"No, but that wasn't even the worst part about this week." Hazel pulled out a bar stool and sat, bringing her feet up onto the kick bar and folding her hands in front of her on the counter.

"It's tough in the beginning." Bridget grabbed a serving platter from above the stove and began arranging bread and crackers in an artful display. "You're not equipped for it yet."

Nichole sighed and sat down heavily beside Hazel. "Yeah, and that's when all the family secrets start to come out, too."

"S-s-secrets?" Hazel sputtered, shocked that Nichole's mind would instantly go to the right place.

"Yeah, who'll stab who in the back for a shot at the inheritance, what everyone really thinks about each other after all these years, which past mistakes have been forgiven and which have turned into grudges. My dad isn't even dead, and already my sisters are squabbling over who *deserves* what. Can you believe that? I'd rather keep my dad than get my hands on his stuff."

"I'm so sorry to hear that." Hazel patted her new friend on the shoulder, wishing that inheritance claims were the worst of her family "secrets."

Still, Nichole's cynicism made more and more sense the better Hazel got to know her. As much as it might help to have siblings to share the burden of care, that clearly wasn't the case for Nichole. Hazel couldn't wrap her head around why family would want to make a tough situation worse by fighting at a time like this.

"Okay, Nic. Enough of that!" Bridget said with a giggle that didn't seem to fit the situation. "We're here to cheer Hazel up, not bring her down with us."

"Does that mean you had a hard week, too?" Hazel asked, raising both of her eyebrows.

"Every week is hard," Amy answered for them all. "But still we keep going."

"Haven't got much other choice," Bridget added.

Movement near the doorway caught Hazel's eye. When she glanced up, she saw her father lingering at the threshold. His skin had reddened with embarrassment. Even after all his years as an entrepreneur, he was still very much an introvert, and new people had a way of unnerving him.

"C'mon in, Daddy. Meet the girls." She gave him an encouraging smile and moved to the table so he wouldn't be forced to sit alone.

"Are you sure you have room for an old man in this party?" he asked, looking at each of them in turn.

"It's not a party," Nichole answered helpfully. "More like a 'yay, we survived' get-together."

He chuckled and gave Nichole a huge smile. "Well, seeing as I'm not dead yet, I guess I can drink to that."

"Absolutely not," Hazel scolded. "Water only."

"Oh, c'mon, chicky girl," he said, still looking at Nichole for solidarity. "You only live once."

"Hazel's right," Amy said, stepping into her role as schoolmarm effortlessly. "It's not good for you. But, tell you what, we can all stick to water in solidarity. Good?"

Her father shrugged and wrapped his knuckles on the table. "You ladies sure know how to throw a party," he said with a chuckle. "Hazel's mother, though. Now that was a woman who knew how to celebrate life."

Bridget brought her platter of bread over to the table and set it in the center. "We'd love to hear about her. Maybe over some fondue?"

His eyes widened with mirth. "Fondue? Well, there's a

blast from the past. Your mother and I had it on one of our first dates, Hazel. Can you believe that?"

"Seeing as that happened in the eighties, yes, I can." She helped Bridget set the table and brought bottles of water for everyone.

"Do you have any pictures of you two back then?" Amy asked, taking a seat on the other side of Hazel's dad. "I just love the fashions from that era, and I bet your wife was beautiful."

"*Era?* Am I so old that my youth is now an era?" He chuckled again. "You know, as a matter of fact, we were just going through some of her things this weekend. I believe I have a photo album or two within easy reach, if you'll excuse me for just a second."

The women watched as he moved slowly out of the room and back toward the space he'd just tidied.

"Your father is so nice!" Bridget exclaimed, loud enough for him to hear, no doubt.

"And I can tell he loves you a lot," Amy said with a sweet smile.

Everyone looked at Nichole.

"I can't believe you called the eighties an era, Amy," she said with an exaggerated roll of her eyes.

They all laughed at that. When her father returned with the photo album, they all arranged their chairs in a tight semicircle so they could see each snapshot. Hazel had already heard the stories that went with each picture earlier that weekend, but she loved listening to them a second time and watching how each of her new friends reacted to the funny bits.

A short while later, the pizza arrived, and they all took giant slices with glee. Her father quickly relaxed into his role of entertainer and even shared some embarrassing stories from Hazel's childhood.

It was a small price to pay for friends who understood, who wanted to make things better for her even though they were struggling themselves.

By the time the evening came to a close, they'd all agreed that this type of get-together should become a weekly affair—and that it might be time for a new name since their cancer club was no longer meeting at the hospital cafeteria.

"I don't want to have cancer in our club name anymore," Bridget said with a scowl. "The whole point is to take a break from it for a little while, right?"

"How about Hazel's House something?" Amy suggested rather unhelpfully.

"Or maybe we don't need a name," Nichole said. "Seeing as we're all adults and this isn't some afterschool thing."

"How about the Sunday Potluck Club?" Hazel suggested. "That way we can rotate houses, and no one is ever under pressure to play hostess. We can share our food, just like we share our burdens."

"Okay, yeah, that's kind of perfect," Bridget said with a fist pump.

Even Nichole had to agree the name suited them.

And so, the Sunday Potluck Club was officially born.

Chapter 18

Hazel hesitated over her email. Her newest junior designer had forwarded her plan for a high-profile client's home office, and it was just awful. Part of her wanted to be gentle, while another part wondered how she'd managed to hire someone with so little insight into their clients' needs. She might have to go in and fix this one herself.

Her cell phone buzzed beside her, skittering across the table from the force of the vibration.

"Got you," she cried, grasping it in her hand and hitting the ACCEPT CALL button.

"Hazel?" a familiar voice asked.

Oops, she'd been talking to her phone aloud when she should have been greeting the caller. She hoped someone from her office waited on the other end. Maybe the terrible proposal was nothing more than a practical joke. *Ha-ha*.

"Yeah, it's me," she answered suspiciously. That's what she got for never saving anyone's number in her phone. "What's up?"

"It's Keith," came the cheerful reply. "Remember I said I'd call you first thing Monday morning?"

She nodded dumbly before finding her voice. "Yes, sure. Thanks for calling." Had it really only been a couple days since her father's spill, their emergency room visit, the secrets about her parents, and the *shameless* flirting with the hunky male nurse?

He could hardly contain the glee in his voice. "Insurance approved a part-time home aide for your father. I wanted to be the one to tell you."

"Keith, that's fantastic!" Elation rippled through her along with an equally refreshing wave of gratitude. "Thank you so much. How did you get them to change their minds?"

He rushed through his response, stumbling over a couple of the words on their way out. "They were pretty amenable once I told them he had declined chemotherapy. This new arrangement actually saves them quite a bit of money, and that's what they really care about, so yeah."

She smiled to herself. "Thank you again. This means a lot to both of us."

"It will probably be a few days or even a couple weeks before someone gets assigned, but, rest assured, that person is coming . . . Um, are you?"

The line remained quiet as Hazel tried to decipher his question.

Keith inhaled sharply before clarifying, "Coming, I mean, for our date?"

She had to fight back a laugh. He felt nervous, and it was adorable. Somehow that made her even more excited about the chance to go out with him. "Of course I'm coming. Just as soon as you tell me when it is."

Another several days passed before Hazel's big date with Keith. They decided to go out together on Wednesday afternoon since it was his day off work. He insisted on picking her up rather than letting her meet him at the restaurant they'd chosen.

Her father delighted in every moment of watching her put the finishing touches on her look. He even learned how to take pictures with his tablet for posterity.

"Daddy!" she protested. "I'm an adult going on a date. This is not high school prom."

He laughed but continued snapping pictures at the same furious rate. "Of course it isn't. I like your date tonight *much* better."

She rolled her eyes at him in the mirror, then snapped the cap back on her lip gloss and turned to him with a look of poorly concealed enthusiasm. "I should hope you do, seeing as you're the one who played matchmaker."

He stood a little taller in that moment, pride obvious in his posture. "*Nah*, I just pushed you along a little faster. You would have eventually gotten there yourselves."

The doorbell chimed its greeting song, and Hazel shot daggers at her father, praying he wouldn't embarrass her as she hurried to greet Keith at the door.

"You look beautiful," he said with a sigh that flustered both of them. He held up a shiny blue gift bag. "I brought a little something for your dad. I hope you don't mind."

She worried her lip. Well, so much for her fresh coat of lip gloss. She could already taste it on her teeth as she responded, "I was kind of hoping to escape without your having to see him, but since you brought a present . . ." She guided him into the living room, where her father sat pleased as punch.

"It's just something small that I've found helps patients relax and get some of their frustrations out." Keith handed him the bag rather unceremoniously, then rocked on his heels as he waited for the gift to be opened.

"Thank you," Hazel said for the both of them as her dad riffled through the gift paper like a kid at Christmas.

He pulled out a pair of large books and a box of pencils, then shot Keith a quizzical glance. "*F Cancer*," he read from the first cover and then let out a boisterous laugh.

"I love it!" Shifting the second book to the front of the stack, he studied its cover a moment longer. "*Beautiful Patterns for Scrapbooking*."

"They're both adult coloring books," Keith explained with a nervous smile. "I figured you could use the first when you're angry and need to let off some steam. The second is meant for you to color and then use in a scrapbook. I don't know if you and Hazel are working on one yet, but it's a great way to revisit your favorite memories and build something special together."

Her father pulled himself to his feet and offered the other man a hug. "Thank you so much. These are perfect."

Hazel struggled to hide the tears pricking at her eyes. "Thank you, Keith. You keep spoiling us." She tried to laugh, but her breath caught in a sob.

"Well, you both deserve a little spoiling." He put an arm around her shoulders and gave her a side hug. It was the first time they'd touched, and a bolt of warmth shot through her straight to the heart.

"Ready to go?" Keith asked gently, and Hazel nodded.

"I'll have her home by ten, sir," he said with a salute.

"Try to stay out of trouble while we're gone," she called back over her shoulder, and laughed. Oh, it felt so good to laugh!

Once they were buckled into Keith's modest SUV, she

turned to him and placed one of her hands on his. "That was a really sweet thing you did for my dad."

He shrugged and jabbed his key in the ignition. "It was nothing."

She moved her hand to his upper arm and widened her eyes. "No, it was everything. I wasn't sure this was a good time for me to be dating, but seeing you there with Dad . . . Well, I don't feel that way anymore. Thanks for giving me some peace of mind."

"I know how hard it is," he answered, his voice quiet but strong. "And I don't want you to have to go through it without support."

Support. All her life Hazel had done fine with just her and her dad. Now it seemed as if her circle had widened overnight. The new home aide who was coming to help, the girls of the Sunday Potluck Club, and the kindhearted man sitting before her . . . It was amazing how quickly people could move from strangers to indispensable figures in one's life.

"It's funny you should say that," she told him. "I still can't believe how much support I've found through the hospital even though we spent so little time there."

Keith's cheeks reddened as he placed his hand on top of hers. "I'm very glad I was at work that day, that I got the chance to meet you."

"Me too," Hazel said. "I'm also glad that you're not working today."

"Hold off on that statement until you see how the date goes," he said with a self-deprecating laugh.

She squeezed his hand in hers. "Honestly, we haven't even left the driveway yet, and already this is one of the best dates of my life."

"That's kind of weird," Keith said with a laugh. "But I like it."

"Haven't you ever heard?" Hazel asked, giving his hand one more gentle squeeze before letting go. "The way to a girl's heart is through her family."

Chapter 19

After that first date, many more followed in rapid succession. But as Hazel and Keith's relationship grew stronger, her father's body continued to weaken. Most of their recent dates had been at home, spent in the company of her dad. Thankfully, Keith didn't seem to mind as long as they still got their time together.

The home aide became indispensable in offering both company and palliative care for her father while Hazel snuck off to the office or to meet with clients. By the time his bed needed to be relocated to the ground floor, however, they all knew the end was upon them. He spent day and night in that bed, unable to leave unless he had a great deal of assistance—and even then, it was only to take the occasional sponge bath and allow the aide to change his bedclothes.

"Do you want to watch something on TV?" she asked him now from her perch on the couch. His bed sat across the room, and he barely left it these days.

His voice came out hoarse and dry. "I don't want to do much of anything other than to spend time with you, chicky girl."

She felt the same, but he'd also fought with her countless

times to make sure she didn't fall behind at work while she spent extra time taking care of him. "I have to answer some emails from the office, and I don't want you to be bored. Maybe you can read the news on your tablet?"

"Sure, that sounds nice," he answered, but when Hazel brought him the device, he set it facedown in his lap and closed his eyes.

"Are you feeling okay? Should I call the doctor?"

He coughed and shook his head. "Enough with the doctor. What can he do for me now? Besides, I like spending time in my thoughts, remembering."

She smiled brightly at him, hoping it didn't come across as fake, then returned her attention to the computer she'd set up on the coffee table. Every few minutes she checked to make sure his breathing seemed normal, that he was still with her.

When she glanced over at him the next time, she found him staring at her.

"Yes?" She closed her laptop and folded her hands on top of it.

"I don't want to distract you from your work, and I don't want to get your hopes up . . ." He paused and took several deep breaths. "I think I remember where I hid your mother's letter."

"You do?" This news had not been what she'd expected. Did she dare hope? She'd all but given up on the letter in the months that had passed since she'd learned of its existence, but apparently, her father had not forgotten his promise to find it for her.

He licked his lips and smiled as best he could. "The garage. There's an old box of books that we brought over with us when we first moved into this house. I believe you'll find the letter tucked into your mother's old copy of *The Bonfire of the Vanities*."

She still couldn't believe this. For months, they'd searched, and now suddenly he plucked the location perfectly out of his memory? It didn't make any sense. "How on earth did you remember that just now?"

He turned slightly in the bed, so it was easier for him to look at Hazel while they spoke. "I was picturing her in bed beside me. She always had a book with her. I didn't much care for reading, so I liked to grumble about the light being left on all hours of the night. When she died, I was torn apart. I could hardly focus on anything." He took several breaks to catch his breath while revealing his story, but always came right back to it.

"Then one day, I came across that letter still waiting in its envelope as it sat on the top shelf of our closet. I hated that letter, because I was sure it told about what I'd done and her description of how much I'd hurt her. I wanted it somewhere that no one would accidentally stumble across it again and so I shoved it in the first hardcover book I could find and forgot about—" He broke off in a coughing fit.

She jumped up to grab his water bottle and offer him a sip. "I think maybe that's enough talking for now," she told him with a frown.

"I'm fine," he insisted, widening his eyes to emphasize the fact that he was no longer coughing.

Hazel bit her lower lip before asking, "Should I go see if it's there?"

"Yes, it's past time you knew the full truth and that you heard it directly from your mother."

"I'll be back as fast as I can. Please call if you need anything."

"Don't worry. I promise not to die before you get back," he said with a chuckle.

She glowered at him. "You know I don't appreciate jokes like that."

"And you know a smile makes sad news easier to bear." For a moment, it seemed as if he were going to cough again, but somehow he managed to hold it back. "Now go. I'm just as curious as you are."

Hazel studied her father for a moment, but he simply closed his eyes without saying another word. They were so close to the end now. What if her mother's letter made her angry with him all over again? What if reading it caused her father to die with a guilty conscience and a broken heart?

Maybe once she found it, she could privately read it by herself. If it was awful, she'd tell him she hadn't managed to locate the letter. Yes, that seemed the best course of action.

Thankfully, the garage was mostly tidy. Her father had always been a bit of a neat freak and labeled everything. Before long, she found a couple large boxes labeled *books* sitting together in the far back corner of the garage. A neat line of packing tape sealed each box, but it ripped apart easily with a gentle tug from Hazel. She guessed that neither had been opened since the move. Relics, that's what they were.

Inside, Hazel found a varied assortment of classic novels and bestsellers from the eighties. After unpacking almost all of the books from the first box, she found *The Bonfire of the Vanities* at the very bottom of the old cardboard container. Its shiny cover looked far less worn than its companions, leading Hazel to wonder if perhaps it had been the book her mother was reading when she died.

She flipped through the pages but didn't find a letter.

However, when she removed the dust jacket, a small envelope dropped onto her lap.

Hazel, it read in a large, loopy script she'd seen only a few times before.

"*Mom*," she whispered, caressing the letter with her fingertips. "I can't believe this is really from you."

With shaking hands and teary eyes, she tore open the envelope and unfolded the paper waiting inside. The ink had faded over the years, but not so much as to make the words illegible.

Hazel took a deep breath, tucked her legs up underneath her, and began to read:

Dear Hazel,

I know it will be years before you can read this letter and understand, but I wanted to get these words down while they were still clear in my mind.

I almost died this week, and just as you can probably guess, it was so scary. The most frightening part, though, wasn't what would happen to me. It was what would happen to you. It was how much I didn't want to leave, knowing that you would be too little to even remember me.

Life is fragile. I learned that the hard way.

Relationships are fragile, too. Another hard lesson.

I know your father thinks it's all his fault, but we both share the blame. It was I who chose to run away instead of talking through our issues. It was just so much easier to pretend our problems weren't there, that our fairy tale continued and would always continue.

But that's not how life is.

My daughter, never be afraid to have the difficult conversations, to ask the hard questions. It is exactly those things that define who we become. It's how we overcome challenges rather than how we celebrate wins that reveal our hearts.

I almost died, but instead God gave me a second chance. So here I am, grabbing hold of it with both hands.

Sometimes life doesn't go as planned, but that's what makes it so exciting.

I didn't know how much I wanted to be a mom until I held you in my arms for that first time. I didn't know how much I loved your father until I almost walked out on him, until we almost lost each other for good.

So I guess what I'm trying to say is that the best things aren't always what you expect. Keep an open mind and an open heart as you go through life.

That's what I learned this week and it's how I'm going to live from now on.

That way, when I finally do die, it will be with no regrets and only a legacy of love.

You, my sweet Hazel, are that legacy, and I love you more than you can possibly imagine.

Mom

Chapter 20

Keith arrived less than twenty minutes later. He'd been scheduled to work for several more hours that day but had found someone to cover the rest of his shift so that he could be there to support Hazel when she shared her mother's letter with her father.

He met her outside the house and instantly wrapped her in his arms. "So you finally found it, huh?"

She nodded as a warm summer breeze blew past. "And just in time, too. I have to keep checking on him every few minutes to make sure he's still breathing. I don't know what reading the letter will do to him."

Keith's head tilted with a question. "But you said the letter was good, that your mother didn't blame him for what happened."

"Yes, but I'm worried it also gives him permission to let go, and I'm not ready to lose my dad yet."

He kissed the tears trailing down her cheeks, then laced his fingers through hers. "No matter what happens, I'm here for you. I love you."

They'd exchanged those three little words before, but on this day she felt they meant so much more, that they weren't just a confession but also a promise. Soon Keith would be her only family, and she was so grateful for him even if she wished they'd met under different circumstances.

"Let's go," she said bravely, feeling anything but.

"Dad," she called, entering again through the garage. "Keith's here."

They removed their shoes and padded quietly into the living room.

Her father opened his eyes and breathed heavily before speaking. "Did you find the letter?"

"Yes, it was right where you said it would be." She handed the unfolded letter over to him, and Keith followed up by offering the old man his reading glasses.

His hands shook as he attempted to hold the letter out before him.

"Do you want me to read it to you?" Hazel asked gently.

He shook his head decisively. "No. I need to see it for myself."

Keith and Hazel stood quietly nearby as her father struggled to read the letter. What would he think of her mother's words? Would he be relieved? Sad? Ready to go?

By the time he had finished, a smile filled his face. "I'm so glad we found it."

"You found it," Hazel corrected. "And, see, Mom wasn't mad at you. She didn't blame you."

He choked on a laugh but didn't seem to mind. "I told you I never deserved her. I never deserved you, either, chicky girl."

"Dad . . ." She didn't know what she needed to say, only that she didn't want to stop talking.

"I trust you'll take good care of my girl once I'm gone," he said to Keith with a slight nod.

"You can count on it, sir."

"Then I'm ready." Whether he was telling his daughter or God, she couldn't be sure.

Still, those words tore a terrible sob from Hazel. "Dad, you can't just give up."

"I'm ready to see your mother again," he rasped as he closed his eyes again. "It's been such a long time."

Hazel came forward and held on to his hand. Her amethyst bracelet caught a ray of sun from outside and created a gorgeous pattern of light on the wall.

Her father opened his eyes and smiled again. "Remember the story about that bracelet? The real one?"

She returned his smile, even though inside her heart was breaking. "Yes, it was the first one you told me back at the hospital. That was also the day we met Keith."

"It was a good day." He glanced toward Keith and raised his other hand in a weak thumbs-up, which Keith happily returned.

Then he asked, "Do you know what that bracelet reminds me of every time I see it?"

Hazel shook her head. A tear fell on their clasped hands.

"It reminds me of how one of the very worst things in my life gave way to one of the very best. Frank Hutchins may have been a rat, but he introduced me to your mother. He's the reason I got you."

She squeezed his hand, hoping somehow the simple gesture could communicate just how much she loved him, how she'd always loved him. "You still have me, Dad. Just hold on."

He coughed but refused to accept the drink Hazel

offered. "You two remind me of us, your mother and I. You met the same way. Something horrible giving way to something beautiful."

Keith wrapped an arm around Hazel's waist, and she leaned in to him.

"I'm so happy I got to be a part of it." Her father licked his lips, then fell silent. He closed his eyes.

A moment later, his breathing slowed.

Hazel's voice trembled with fear. *"Dad?"*

He continued to take slow, shallow breaths, all the while wearing that same peaceful smile.

"Dad?" she asked again, squeezing his hand, trying to discern a heartbeat.

The breaths stopped. His pulse stopped. Her father was gone.

Hazel turned to Keith and cried into his chest. "I wasn't ready," she sobbed.

"I don't think we're ever ready to lose the ones we love."

"Do you think he's in Heaven with Mom?"

He pushed her hair away from her face with both hands and kissed her forehead. "I do, Hazel. I really, really do. Isn't it great they get to be together again? That neither of them have to feel any more pain?"

She knew Keith was right, that her father had been ready to go. But still she just couldn't accept it. Not yet.

"I wish they were both still here," she said. "That none of us had to say good-bye."

"What did the letter say? It seemed to really help him. Maybe it can help you, too."

"Go ahead," she said, and watched in tears as Keith removed the letter from her father's lap.

He read it quickly, then turned back to her. *"A legacy*

of love," he murmured, echoing her mother's words. "That's beautiful."

She nodded and nuzzled into his chest.

They stood together quietly for several minutes—Hazel crying, Keith comforting—until finally he asked, "Are you ready for me to call someone or do you need more time with your father first?"

She shook her head and bit her lip to help stave off the pain in her heart. "I've been preparing for this moment a long time, but it still hurts worse than I could have ever imagined. I'm never going to be ready, but maybe that's okay."

She broke away from Keith and tiptoed toward her father's bed. Taking his hand in hers, she said, "I love you so much, Daddy."

Then unclasping her bracelet with her free hand, she told him, "But you got one thing wrong. You said this bracelet represented how something terrible turned into something wonderful, but that's not what it means to me. I like the first story better. You proposed to mom before you could even afford a ring. You told her to keep this bracelet, because she deserved to have something beautiful."

Hazel laughed sadly and swiped at her tears. "But it was just a silly bracelet, Dad. The real beauty was in the short but happy life she got to live with you—her one, true soulmate. You both made mistakes, but you never gave up on each other. And you never gave up on me."

She placed the thin gemstone bracelet in his palm and folded his fingers over. "I want you to take this back to her. It's already given me everything I need."

She stepped back, and Keith pressed a kiss to her

temple. Together they stood in silence to remember the life that had changed both of theirs for the better.

Now it was up to Hazel to continue not only her mother's legacy, but her father's as well.

And she was ready for the challenge.

Connect with Us

Visit us online at
KensingtonBooks.com
to read more from your favorite authors, see books
by series, view reading group guides, and more.

Join us on social media

for sneak peeks, chances to win books and prize packs,
and to share your thoughts with other readers.

facebook.com/kensingtonpublishing
twitter.com/kensingtonbooks

Tell us what you think!

To share your thoughts, submit a review,
or sign up for our eNewsletters, please visit:
KensingtonBooks.com/TellUs.